BLACK WIDOW

A Special Agent Dylan Kane Thriller

By J. Robert Kennedy

James Acton Thrillers

The Protocol
Brass Monkey
Broken Dove
The Templar's Relic
Flags of Sin
The Arab Fall
The Circle of Eight
The Venice Code
Pompeii's Ghosts
Amazon Burning
The Riddle
Blood Relics
Sins of the Titanic
Saint Peter's Soldiers

Special Agent Dylan Kane Thrillers

Rogue Operator
Containment Failure
Cold Warriors
Death to America
Black Widow

Delta Force Unleashed Thrillers

Payback
Infidels
The Lazarus Moment

Detective Shakespeare Mysteries

Depraved Difference
Tick Tock
The Redeemer

Zander Varga, Vampire Detective

The Turned

BLACK WIDOW

A Special Agent Dylan Kane Thriller

J. ROBERT KENNEDY

Copyright © 2015 J. Robert Kennedy

CreateSpace

All rights reserved. No part of this publication may be reproduced, stored in or introduced into a retrieval system, or transmitted in any form, or by any means (electronic, mechanical, photocopying, recording or otherwise) without the prior written permission of the publisher.

This is a work of fiction. Names, characters, places, and incidents are products of the author's imagination. Any resemblance to actual persons, living or dead, is entirely coincidental.

ISBN-10: 1519197128

ISBN-13: 978-1519197122

First Edition

10 9 8 7 6 5 4 3 2 1

For Master Sergeant Joshua L. Wheeler, the first known Delta operator to die fighting ISIL.

BLACK WIDOW

A Special Agent Dylan Kane Thriller

“The Hour (of Resurrection) will not come until the Romans land in Al-A'maq (valleys in Antioch, southern Turkey) or in Dabiq (a plain near Aleppo, Syria). An army consisting of the best of the people of the Earth (an international Muslim army) at that time will come out of Medina (in Saudi Arabia) to face them.

“When they will arrange themselves in ranks, the Romans will say: ‘Do not stand between us and those (Christian Converts to Islam) who were taken away from amongst us. Let us fight with them’; and the Muslims will say: ‘No! by Allah, we will not stand aside and let you fight our brothers.’”

Abu Huraira quoting the Prophet Mohammad

PREFACE

This novel was written during the height of the Syrian refugee crisis. Much has been reported and said about the situation, and this novel uses many of those opinions and theories, with the experiences of those involved mirroring actual events reported on the news, though often not on the mainstream outlets.

It is important to remember when reading this novel that it is just that—a novel. And though it shows the horrors and hardships many of these people have endured, it also shows how easily the generosity our Western societies have been raised to believe in, can be abused. To our own detriment.

And as time passes, and this crisis abates, as all do, it may be easy to dismiss the warnings that follow as the overactive imagination of a fiction author, and that would be fair.

Yet it may also simply mean that the security apparatus that we so often criticize, worked.

And we just never knew it.

Like the 69 terrorist attacks prevented on American soil since 9/11 as of this writing.

If we had let our guard down because nothing had happened for several years after that horrible attack, would we be as safe today? Would we *feel* as safe today?

Like the real life heroes those within this novel are modeled after, they never let their guard down.

And we are all safer for it.

Vedeno Gorge, Chechnya

Colonel Kolya Chernov kept any of the emotions he was feeling off his face, though inside he was fuming. As the commander of Alfa Group Six, part of Russia's elite Special Forces unit, Spetsnaz, he knew everything in their arsenal, and everything in pretty much anyone else's, at least those that mattered.

Though here he didn't have to go far from home.

What he had caught a glimpse of were type BGE 75-T containers.

Russian.

Or more accurately, Soviet.

A remnant of the Cold War—soon to be replaced with a new one, if their illustrious leader in Moscow had his way. Chernov loved his country, the Russian Armed Forces, and certainly his unit. Getting into Spetsnaz was one of the proudest days of his life, being promoted to colonel one of the more disappointing ones. He didn't want to command a desk, he wanted to be out in the field, but as the general had told him, "You're the boss, you can do what you want".

So he did.

And when the Foreign Intelligence Service of the Russian Federation, the SVR RF, had contacted his unit requiring a four-man team to provide additional security in Chechnya, he had decided the request was suspicious enough to pique his interest, and the assignment possibly dangerous enough to satisfy his craving for action.

And now his suspicions were proven well founded.

The SVR were merely the renamed First Chief Directorate of the former KGB, and the new reality in Russia was that they and the remainder of the former agency, the FSB, were more like their old namesakes with each passing day. He didn't trust the SVR as far as he could throw one of them, their motivations completely different from a soldier's. He trusted his men, would die for his men, yet he'd have to seriously consider whether he'd hit the brakes if one of these SVR bastards were to step in front of his vehicle.

The six canisters contained Cesium-137, extremely dangerous, and more than enough to build multiple dirty bombs. This was a substance terrorists the world over were desperate to get their hands on, and here he was, standing guard while two SVR agents sold a batch to what were clearly Chechen rebels, he recognizing the leader.

Each group had a computer hooked to satellite links, and money transferred.

Smiles.

Handshakes.

And the deal was done, the Chechens climbing in their Toyota and leaving, the SVR agents heading toward the Mi-24 Hind helicopter now powering up.

He could hold his tongue no longer.

"I assume we're now going to stop them?"

The lead SVR agent—his name never provided—looked at him, a bemused expression on his face. "Why would we want to do that?"

"Because we just sold terrorists nuclear materials."

Any humor disappeared, the man's eyes boring into Chernov's as he stepped closer. "You are mistaken as to what you saw. Do you understand me?"

The attempt at intimidation probably worked on most, but not on Chernov, though he valued his life enough to know to drop the subject. "Understood."

"Good. Now let's go. There's vodka to celebrate!"

Chernov was the last to board, his men, his friends, all giving him a look that told him they too knew what had just happened and were none too happy about it.

But this was the new Russia.

The same as the old Russia.

And those that questioned the KGB—or the SVR—might just live long enough to regret it.

Al-Raqqah, Syria
ISIL controlled territory

Maloof stood, hands clasped behind his back, keffiyeh covering his face, his eyes squinting against the harsh sun of the Syrian midday. Safar stood on the other side of the door, a devout Sunni Muslim and longtime member of ISIL, he one of the originals before it had even become known by that ever-changing moniker.

Some would call him a fanatic.

And a moron.

He wasn't very intelligent, which was why he continued to be a foot soldier, though now given the honor of guarding the Caliph himself, the leader of ISIL, a man few even knew existed, the Western press for some reason content to let people believe this was some ragtag group of loosely associated cells. Instead, it was a well-organized group with a clear organizational structure, which made it far more formidable than anything preceding it.

It had taken him six months to gain his position, distinguishing himself in battle, using his brains and training to get himself noticed. And when offered a promotion, he had declined.

"Rank means nothing to me. I serve Allah, and I can think of no better way than to protect the Caliph."

His commander had smiled. "So you want to be on his personal guard?"

He nodded.

His commander's eyes narrowed. "You wouldn't be trying to get yourself away from the front, would you?" Maloof laughed, his commander joining in. "No, I don't think anyone could accuse *you* of that."

And arrangements had been made.

He had met the man, their supreme leader. He wasn't what he had expected. Rather unassuming, fairly quiet, considering the amount of blood that had been spilled under his orders. But that was neither here nor there. The man had a mission, one handed down to him since the Archangel Gabriel delivered the words of the Koran to Mohammad so many centuries before.

The Global Caliphate.

The Caliphate had now been reestablished after collapsing post-World War One. The previous had been massive at one point, extending from Spain to North Africa to the Philippines. What existed today was a pale imitation.

Yet it was a start.

What many didn't understand was that the goal of many in Islam wasn't world domination or intentional death and mayhem, it was the end-times—not something to be feared, but to be embraced. Many Muslims felt their duty was to spread the influence of Islam until the return of the Mahdi and Isa—the Prophet Jesus—who would defeat evil and rule those who survived until the Day of Judgement.

And unlike most people of faith, Twelvers believed it their duty to do anything they could to bring upon Armageddon, so that they might achieve paradise sooner.

Twelvers led Iran.

And they would have the bomb within ten years should the new nuclear deal stand.

His comrades-in-arms had chuckled at the naiveté of the West when the deal was announced, the jokes quick, the wit sharp concerning its main proponent. It was gallows humor, everyone in the room knowing full well this could mean the end of their nation, a fiery death of nuclear hell now almost inevitable.

For he was Israeli.

Mossad.

Not a Jew, but an Arab, one who liked to think Islam had been hijacked by madness, and had worked hard to get to where he was today.

Undercover at the doorway of the orchestrator of so much mayhem.

The meeting taking place on the other side of the door he guarded had been routine—at least that's what he had thought initially. A simple meeting of regional commanders to discuss the progress of the war.

Yet it had turned into much more, the open window over his right shoulder allowing him to hear every word said. The arrogance of these men was supreme, it never occurring to them that the enemy might overhear their discussion.

"We have managed to identify a source and arrange a purchase," said one, he doing most of the talking, the Caliph alone responding.

"Excellent. When will we have it?"

"Very soon. It will be expensive, however."

The Caliph laughed. "Money is no problem. Thanks to our generous benefactors and a healthy black market for our oil, our coffers are as rich as anyone's. Just tell us what you need and we'll see it transferred."

"Very good, sir, I will let you know as soon as the final figure has been negotiated."

"The source?"

"Chechens."

"How did they get it?"

"Russians, apparently."

"Soon they will pay the price for their arrogance, but first, the West." The Caliph coughed then there was a pause, the clinking of a glass suggesting a parched throat quenched. "And the infiltration plan?"

"Going perfectly. We're already moving men and equipment into place. The Americans and Europeans won't know what hit them."

"Excellent. Their political correctness and misguided compassion will be their undoing. They falsely attribute their ways to all others, naively believing in the basic good of people because they believe *they* are basically good. Little do they realize that theirs is ours for the taking, as they are the kafir, the infidel, and it is our sacred right to do whatever it takes to further our cause. Allah is on our side, brothers, and with us as his sword, we will strike a blow that will once and for all rid us of the American presence here in our homeland. Now and forever."

Shouts of Allahu Akbar erupted and Maloof glanced over at Safar, who he could tell was dying to join in, though his doing so would betray the fact they had both been listening.

Maloof shook his head slightly, Safar nodding, his cheeks sucking in slightly as he clamped down with his teeth, resisting the urge.

As the cheers continued, Maloof surveyed the barren landscape surrounding the compound, wondering what this plan could possibly be. Clearly they intended to strike America and Europe with a blow painful enough to rid them of the American bombing campaign. He personally thought that a foolish assumption, since after 9/11 the American beast had been awoken, unleashing its fury on Afghanistan and Iraq, and pursuing the perpetrators across the globe. To think that Americans would retreat, with their tails between their legs due to a terrorist attack, was foolish.

Even for these people.

So it had to be something more.

But what could possibly hurt the Americans enough to want to give up?

What could the Chechens be providing, sourced from the Russians, that would cause enough devastation to make the Americans pull out?

9/11 had pissed America off. It hadn't scared them. If it had, then perhaps a terrified public would have demanded their government stand down from its policy of active engagement. If they expected anything different this time, then the threat must be something so horrifying it would strike fear into the hearts of its victims.

He sucked in a breath as he realized what it might be.

And knew he had to get this intel to his handlers as quickly as possible.

Or millions could die.

Arbat, Moscow

Colonel Kolya Chernov tipped the bottle of vodka, draining the last few ounces into his glass, the fresh ice crackling in protest. It wasn't tradition for a Russian to drink his vodka over ice, but he had acquired a taste for ice cold drinks while serving in too many hot and dusty shitholes where ice and refrigeration were rare commodities.

Even in the dead of a Russian winter, he preferred his drinks cold.

He loved the freezing, harsh wind on his face, the crisp air filling his lungs.

Embracing the winter—it was what made one Russian.

He closed his eyes, leaning back in his chair, his feet up on a ratty ottoman, and sighed. He loved his country, hated his government, and hoped he'd die before he saw it completely go to shit. And he had a sneaking suspicion that might be sooner rather than later.

He'd been benched.

Three weeks ago they had returned from the mission in Chechnya and the general had sent him home. "Take some time for yourself. Courtesy Moscow." The last two words had been delivered with a look that implied it was a warning, the general's embrace suggesting he didn't expect to see him again.

If he was going to die, then so be it, but why the hell did it have to take so long? The waiting was worse than the deed. It left him thinking that perhaps they had changed their mind, that the phone might ring telling him to report to base.

Yet the fact it was just he and the others from that mission sent home told him this was SVR related, and they rarely changed their mind.

He sipped his now ice cold drink, letting it sit on his tongue for a moment before tilting his head back and letting gravity do its job, the delicious concoction created from boring ingredients something he had been enjoying since he was a boy.

A knock at the door had him putting his glass down and frowning.

This is it.

Nobody visited him. Not without calling first or using a coded knock a few trusted souls knew. He glanced at his PSS Silent Pistol sitting on the table beside him then stood, leaving the weapon where it was.

Where's the fun in that?

It would be a four man team, two below, two sent in to do the job, their arrogance at being the best—which they weren't—enough to think they didn't need greater numbers. In fact, they were probably foolish enough to think he'd just stand there and die honorably.

Sorry, comrades, you'll have to work for it.

He opened the door and his eyebrows jumped.

It was the quintessential little old lady.

"What can I do—"

The back of a fist swung at him from just out of sight, cutting him off. Expecting it, both hands shot up, blocking the blow, as a second man came into sight, weapon drawn. He grabbed the forearm of the first man with his right hand, bracing it at the elbow with his left, then jerked back, the arm snapping, his still unseen assailant screaming in agony as Chernov pulled him inside by the now broken arm, using him as a human shield as the other man advanced, weapon aimed directly at him.

Chernov shoved the screaming man at his still advancing partner, the man tossing him aside with his gun hand. Chernov darted forward, smacking the man's hand as it swung around, hitting him on the wrist and forearm, the gun clattering to the worn linoleum floor with a thud. His hand clamped around the man's now tender wrist and twisted, hauling him forward while he stepped to the side, knocking the man off balance. Controlling his fall, he swung him around, his arm hooking under the man's chin and pressing against his neck.

A moment later it snapped.

His partner was still on the floor, gripping his dangling forearm, pushing himself toward the door when the little old lady stepped inside, brandishing a gun. Chernov stepped forward, snapping a foot directly at her chest, her surprised expression almost comical if she didn't remind him so much of his own grandmother as she sailed out of the apartment and crashed against the neighbor's door, her head slamming against the cheap wood, leaving her dazed.

He picked up the now dead agent's gun and placed two rounds into the back of the crawling man then two more into granny before stepping into the hallway and listening.

Nothing.

He pulled the old lady's body inside, closing the door, then stepped over to the window and peered at the street below. There was a black Lada Priora below, idling, the exhaust from the tailpipe a dead giveaway, the make and model, and the fact it was illegally parked, almost acting like a large SVR sign on the roof.

He stuffed his feet into a pair of boots, grabbed his jacket, hat, and gloves, then the go bag sitting inside his closet, ready for just such an event. He had money, passports, weapons, ammo, and a couple of untraceable cellphones.

Just for the day his country might betray him.

He stepped out into the hall, closing the door as his neighbor stepped out, a bitter widow who had yet to say a kind word to him in the ten years he had lived there.

"Did you hear that?"

"Hear what?"

"Somebody hit my door." She spotted the dent the old lady's head had made. "Oh my God, what's this!"

"Probably some drunk."

"Drink will be the death of this country!" cursed the woman, shaking her fist at the world. "The death of it! It took my husband, and it will take my country!"

Chernov took the stairs two at a time, leaving the still ranting woman alone, her shouts good cover for his footfalls, though they were light, he putting as much weight as he could on the handrail in anticipation of a third SVR operative at the ground level.

Second floor.

He paused, peering down, and smiled. It was the third man, standing at the mailboxes, checking his watch, probably wondering what was taking so long.

Chernov began to whistle, taking the remaining steps at a leisurely, calm pace, his hands in his pockets, one gripping his gun, the other balled into a fist. He stepped onto the marble floor, it cheap and cracked from years of neglect—as was most of Russia—and nodded at the man. "Beautiful day, isn't it?"

The man avoided eye contact, instead grunting, SVR notorious for not wanting to be looked at.

It would be his downfall.

The man glanced up as Chernov approached and his jaw dropped as he recognized the man his partners had failed to terminate.

He reached for his gun.

But Chernov had his out and pressed against the man's chest before he could get a grip on it.

"ID."

The man glared at him then reached inside his jacket.

"Slowly."

A wallet inched into view.

Chernov took it, flipping it open and chuckled. "SVR. What a surprise."

"You're a dead man."

Chernov smiled. "You first." He put two rounds into the man's chest, pocketed his ID, then exited out the rear door, leaving the fourth agent to wait in his warm car to finally get concerned enough to check on his tardy comrades.

As he headed out into the brisk fall day, he dialed Yenin, a trusted comrade and friend, and his second-in-command on the mission.

It went to voicemail.

He frowned.

"It's me. If you hear this get to safety, immediately."

He dialed the other two members of his team and both went to voicemail.

He left similar messages.

But it was too late.

This would have been a coordinated op, all four hit at once. Either his men were still alive, going into hiding just as he was, or they were dead, not so lucky as to have as suspicious a nature as he had, a little old lady known immediately to simply be a diversion.

Yenin didn't live far, only a few blocks away, and he kept a swift though not too attention drawing pace, cursing as he rounded the corner, the distinctive flash of emergency lights greeting him along with a throng of onlookers, all staring up.

He looked.

And his chest tightened.

He couldn't tell from the distance and the rapidly failing light who it was that hung by his neck from a balcony three stories up, yet he knew exactly who it was.

Yenin.

I'm sorry my friend.

He wanted to defend the man's honor and shout down those gathered who disparaged the man's memory by criticizing his committing suicide. It wasn't suicide; there was no way. Yenin was one of the happiest men he knew, and this was a cover up. Suicides were far too frequent in Russia, especially among men, and this wouldn't even be investigated.

The SVR would see to that.

I wonder what they had planned for me.

A quick cab ride had him at Lieutenant Vasnev's apartment, there no commotion outside, no obvious SVR presence.

He decided to risk it. If there was even the slimmest chance of saving one of his men, he had to take it.

What he found had him cursing.

Vasnev, dead in his bed, an empty bottle of pills at his side, a note resting on his chest.

I'm sorry for what I did.

Vague, meaningless. Enough to know he had committed suicide, not enough to know what he was talking about.

Unchallengeable.

Vasnev's cellphone vibrated on his nightstand.

He ignored it.

It stopped, then a text appeared. He looked.

And frowned.

Answer the phone, Colonel.

He cursed.

Another text.

Or Lieutenant Ishutin dies.

He grabbed the phone and hurried from the apartment, it clear he was under surveillance.

The phone vibrated in his hand and he took the call.

"Surrender yourself, Colonel, or he dies."

"Go to hell, we're dead already."

"You still have one way out of this, Colonel."

He stepped out into the street, checking both ways, seeing no one obvious that might be tracking him. He returned to his brisk pace, dodging into an alleyway and sprinting. "Put him on."

"Very well."

There were some shuffling sounds then the young lieutenant's voice.

"Colonel?"

"Yes."

"Don't do anything these bastards say! Save yourself, I'm already dead!"

A gunshot rang out and he ended the call, grabbing a young boy by the back of his jacket as he rode by on a bicycle.

"Hey, what are you doing?"

"Want an iPhone?"

The boy eyed him suspiciously. "What do you mean?"

Chernov handed over the phone. "It's yours. Just pedal as fast as you can to Gorky Park then back. Got it?"

The boy grabbed the phone, his eyes wide, a greedy grin on his face.

And he was around the corner in seconds.

Chernov tucked himself between a couple of garbage bins and waited, the cold slowly eating into him as he plotted his revenge.

Maggie Harris Residence, Lake in the Pines Apartments, Fayetteville, North Carolina

"I think I'd like to wait until my hair grows back."

Command Sergeant Major Burt "Big Dog" Dawson raised his eyebrows, glancing at his fiancée, Maggie Harris. "That could take a while."

She grinned at him and jumped on the couch beside him, resting on her knees and leaning forward, giving him a cleavage shot that his comrade in arms Niner would have had a hard time resisting commenting on, and he couldn't help but glance at, she the most beautiful woman in the world as far as he was concerned.

Regardless of her very short hair, a result of surgery after a gunshot wound to the head in Paris months ago.

"You in a hurry?"

He smiled, looking up at her. "There's no right answer to that."

She squeezed her arms together, glancing down. "See something you like, soldier boy?"

"You know it." He grabbed her, flipping her on her back, a delighted squeal escaping as he climbed on top of her, their bodies intertwining as passion replaced wedding planning. As they tore each other's clothes off, he reveled in the fact that this woman he loved had bounced back so quickly from her near death experience and seemed to have lost none of her zest for life. Her recovery had been slow and painful at first, though the men and women of the Unit had been a huge help, she never left alone to dwell on her situation.

And her beautiful hair growing back enough to hide the vicious scar on her head had triggered a breakthrough.

An outing.

Repeated many times since, the barrier broken.

"You like my hair, don't you."

He bit her earlobe. "Yes."

She returned the favor. "I mean my long hair."

"Yes." He kissed her hard, gripping the back of her head, careful not to put any pressure on the scar, it no longer a pain issue, simply a comfort issue for her.

She pulled her lips away. "Are you even listening?"

"Kind of busy, babe."

He got to second base.

She moaned.

"Screw the hair," she groaned, grabbing his head with both hands and shoving him down her chest. "Remind me why I put up with you."

He looked up and grinned. "I love it when you talk dirty."

"Oh no!"

"Huh?"

"I'm on your phone and it's vibrating."

He winked. "Umm, is that a bad thing?"

She laughed, reaching under and pulling his pants out from under her. "How the hell did they get there?"

"Who cares?" She tossed the phone on the table and stared down at him. "Weren't you on a mission?"

He laughed, then rocked her world.

And she his.

Gasping for breath from the other side of the room, they somehow having left the couch, clearing the table and chairs, Dawson stared up at the ceiling, Maggie draped across him, a finger circling his nipple. "That was fun."

He kissed the top of her head. "Yeah, we should talk about your hair more often."

She rolled on top of him, her hands pressed into his chest, her chin resting on top as she stared at him. "I never did get a straight answer."

She loved her long hair, and its now short length was a constant reminder to her of what she had been through.

And wedding photos were a once in a lifetime thing.

He hoped.

"I'll tell you what," he began, carefully. "I want to marry you. Whether that's two weeks from now or two years from now, I don't care. As long as I know you feel the same way about me as I do about you, then I'm not worried about trying to seal the deal. We'll get married whenever you want. If you want to wait for your hair to grow back out for the wedding photos, then we'll wait."

She stared at him, the love in her eyes crystal clear. "How did I get so lucky?" She slid up and gave him a kiss, her legs trapping the little sergeant major between them. "Ooh, I think someone's looking for seconds."

The phone vibrated again for the fourth time.

"You better get that first."

He sighed. "Yeah, I guess." He was off duty and if it were Unit related, a coded message would have been left. None was, the caller always hanging up before his generic greeting played.

He was always on-call, it simply a fact of life as a member of America's elite 1st Special Forces Operational Detachment—Delta, more commonly known to the public and Hollywood as the Delta Force. They were the elite of the elite, sent on their country's most dangerous missions, and the only military unit authorized to operate on American soil, the President having authority to suspend Posse Comitatus for this unit only.

Maggie rolled over and Dawson stood. She gave the little sergeant major a smack. "Hurry back."

He winked, grabbing the phone and swiping his thumb before it went to voicemail. "Hello?"

"Do you recognize my voice?"

Dawson recognized the accent. Russian. Though not the voice.

"No."

"We've met."

"That narrows it down." It actually did. The number of Russians he had met that might actually call him, he could count on one hand. "Give me a hint."

"We enjoyed some boating on the Black Sea once."

Dawson immediately knew who he was speaking to, and context gave him the voice recognition he needed. It still didn't explain why this man, a Russian Spetsnaz Colonel, would be calling. "I know who you are."

"Good. I need your help."

Dawson sat on the couch, Maggie wrapping herself in a blanket, she already sensing the fun was over. "Our countries aren't exactly on the best of terms."

There was a chuckle. "Indeed. But this has nothing to do with my country. This is one soldier talking to another soldier."

Dawson's eyes narrowed. "Why me?"

"You're the only person I trust right now."

His eyes opened slightly wider. *Interesting.* "What's happened?"

Colonel Chernov quickly filled him in, Dawson beginning to get dressed within the first thirty seconds. This was huge. Horrifyingly huge. Nuclear materials delivered into the hands of Chechens, by the SVR, was almost inconceivable.

If it hadn't happened several times before.

"What do you want from me?"

"I need you to get this intel into the right hands. There's nothing I can do with it at this point."

"Do you need help getting out?"

"No. I have a few loose ends to, shall we say, tie up? Then I doubt you'll be seeing me again, my friend."

Dawson knew what that meant. Chernov was going to eliminate the SVR agents involved, then disappear to some island somewhere under a new identity.

"They'll want proof."

"As soon as I hang up I'll text you a link. User ID is *your* first name, password is *my* first name. The cloud site has everything I know. It's all verbal, that's the best I can do, but I've given enough details that you should be able to verify at least some of my story." There was a pause. "Listen, friend, I have no reason to lie about this, but I need to know if you believe me."

Dawson had to admit he did, there no conceivable reason for this to be a lie. The question was whether what the man was telling him was accurate, not truthful. "Yes. I believe *you* believe you're telling me the truth."

Chernov laughed. "You should go into politics, my friend."

Dawson chuckled. "As I told our President once, I'd probably kill too many of my opponents for them to ask me to stay."

Chernov roared. "I like you, comrade. You and I will drink some vodka together one day perhaps, when we are both old men, hiding from our governments." The joviality suddenly disappeared. "Listen. This is legitimate. I saw it myself. If you do not stop them, I don't know how many will die, but it will make 9/11 look like a training exercise."

Philadelphia, Pennsylvania

"Raptor One, Sierra Four! Abort! Abort! Abort!"

Dylan Kane bolted upright, his body dripping in sweat, his head throbbing in protest at the sudden movement. He looked around the dimly lit room, trying to gain his bearings. He was in an unfamiliar bed—not that that was unusual—and it was daytime, the sun mostly blocked out by heavy curtains, but from what he could see the room was immaculate, a print depicting the Chinese zodiac over the bed.

Fang!

He lifted the sheets, found his underwear still on, and breathed a sigh of relief. Lee Fang was a beautiful woman—gorgeous—but if they were going to sleep together, he'd definitely have wanted to remember it, and his throbbing headache suggested there had been a hell of a lot of alcohol enjoyed the night before.

Yet it wasn't that.

If he were to sleep with her, he wanted it to be special.

Which was totally out of character for him.

His life was a string of short-term relationships based on the three most important things to him. Sex, sex and sex. Perhaps that was being unfair to himself. Good food, good drink and good company would probably be more accurate, though he often found that the good food and good drink led to the good company hopping in his bed for a good romp.

And he had been quite happy with that for years, his job taking him into harm's way more than it didn't, his free time short and unpredictable.

Hardly something to build a relationship around.

Especially when you couldn't tell a prospective mate why you might only see them half a dozen times a year, and not to bother making any plans since you might be called away at any minute.

Which was why he was so confused about his feelings for Fang.

His fetish was Asian women, though he found all women beautiful in their own way. It was probably because he spent most of his time in that part of the world, so that was what was available to him. And when you were in the Third World, it was easy to find a beautiful woman who was willing to have some fun for a few days or a week, if it meant living the dream.

He wasn't a pig. He treated with respect every woman he had relations with, and made them feel like a princess when they would go out for dinner. And everything they did for him, or to him, he liked to think was because they were appreciative.

Though he knew deep down he was kidding himself.

When off duty he was a self-destructive drunk who slept with as many women as he could, all in an attempt to forget what he did when sober.

Kill people.

A lot of people.

The Central Intelligence Agency was a cruel taskmaster at times, and if he were FBI or regular forces, he'd probably have been pulled off the frontlines long ago for failing a psych eval. But being a Special Agent in the CIA meant training to beat any such evaluation, so they rarely bothered with them, at least not for the deep cover operatives like himself, who lived a cover day in and day out.

He was Dylan Kane, Insurance Investigator for Shaw's of London. A jetsetter who travelled the world to investigate large insurance claims and potential fraud for the large, well-known company that insured the rich and powerful for things State Farm wouldn't touch.

Like half-billion dollar yachts and gold trimmed 747s.

The reality was much less glamorous, the shitholes he usually found himself embedded in fine examples of human progress like Yemen and Pakistan.

He had lost count of how many people he had killed over the years.

Though he knew exactly how many innocent people he had killed.

Happy humming from the kitchen and the smell of something wonderful had him swinging his legs from the bed, eager to see the woman who had him completely confused, questioning his entire way of life.

At least the downtime.

Lee Fang was a Chinese national—a traitor, if you believed her government. Caught up in a scandal involving supporting an attempted coup here in the United States, she had been forced to kill a Chinese general and flee to America. Kane had been her contact.

She was a member of the Beijing Military Region Special Forces Unit, an elite group of soldiers in the People's Liberation Army, and exceptionally good at her job.

Yet now she was an exile, living under an assumed identity, with no friends or family and no prospects, her agreement with the American government—who were providing a generous pension for life in thanks for her service—not allowing her to use any of her skills she had acquired over years of training.

The last time he had seen her, recruiting her to help him on a mission here at home, he had made a promise to her that he would be that friend she needed. Hell, he only had one friend that he could think of, and that was Chris Leroux, an old high school buddy that now happened to work at the CIA as an analyst.

And one more friend would do him good.

She had happily, though shyly, agreed.

He had stopped in yesterday, determined to show her a good time.

With their clothes on.

They had hit a nice restaurant, Fang clearly enjoying dressing up and getting out. She had been breathtaking, the line of her dress plunging down her back revealing a physique that had mini-Dylan demanding a peek. It had been everything he could do not to stare, then when he realized she actually seemed to enjoy his attentions, he simply gave up and admired her all evening. Dinner had been fantastic, then dancing at a club turned crazy with Kane impressed at how the tiny woman could hold her liquor.

He had a feeling he had been conned though, he pretty sure she was tossing some of her shots.

It had been the best time he could recall ever having.

And I just wish I remembered it all.

He looked about for his clothes and found none.

Uh oh.

He glanced down and just prayed she was clothed or his desires might be revealed.

Pointedly.

He stepped into the hallway and walked toward the kitchen and the singing, which had replaced the humming, a beautiful Chinese lullaby about a girl and her forbidden love.

He smiled.

I wonder if she realizes what she's singing.

And that I speak Chinese.

"Good morning!" he called before rounding the corner, giving her a chance to prepare should she not be decent.

You must really *like this girl.*

He rounded the corner and found Fang standing at the stove, a smile on her face, something white on her forehead, standing out against her brown skin. "Good morning!" she beamed, clearly in better condition than he was. "Traditional American breakfast?"

He glanced about. "Umm, what do the Chinese consider a traditional American breakfast?"

"Gluttony with a side of greed is the official line, but this is from your famous Denny's commercials." She pointed at various stations around the kitchen. "Scrambled eggs, bacon and toast." She pointed at a stack of black—objects. "I tried pancakes. Much harder than it looks."

He laughed, stepping forward and wiping some of the mix off her forehead. "I'm sure everything is terrific." He paused, looking at her then away. "Umm, awkward question, but, umm, did we, you know…"

"Sleep together?"

"Yeah."

"No. You were a perfect gentleman until you passed out in the stairwell."

He flushed. "Sorry."

She shrugged. "I carried you in, put you to bed then slept on the couch."

A sudden revelation had him staring at his underwear. "Wait a minute, these weren't what I was wearing when we went out."

It was her turn to blush, her eyes quickly darting away. "Well, I had spilled my drink on you and you were soaked." She glanced up at him. "And you were in no condition to change!"

"Uh huh. And I'm sure you didn't look."

She flushed again, turning away. "Of course not."

"Liar."

She glanced tentatively over her shoulder at him. "Are you saying that you'd look at me?"

His cheeks burned. "Well, that's different. I'm a guy and you're gorgeous."

He heard her take a sharp breath. "You really think so?" she asked, her voice barely a whisper.

"Don't you?"

"Th-that wasn't the question."

He took her by the shoulders and turned her back around, facing him. He tilted her head up and gazed into her eyes. "Trust me, you're *gorgeous.* Any guy would be lucky to have you."

Gloom spread across her face as her chin dropped to her chest, her shoulders slumping. "No guy can have me. I'm damaged goods."

Kane squeezed her shoulders, chuckling. "You're watching too much TV." He tilted her head back up and smiled at her tear-filled eyes. "You're perfect."

She closed her eyes and leaned toward him. He bent down, angling his head, his lips quivering in anticipation, his heart pounding harder than he could ever remember any other woman causing.

This was special.

This was different.

This could be a big mistake.

He closed his eyes, their noses bumped.

And the smoke alarm went off.

Fang darted away, grabbing the now smoking pan of bacon and tossed it into the sink. Turning the tap on, she threw a dishtowel to Kane and pointed up at the smoke alarm as she yanked open the window. Kane fanned the alarm as he felt his watch give him a slight electrical shock.

Shit!

The alarm stopped its wail and Fang held up the soaked bacon. "Umm, scrambled egg sandwich?"

The toast popped.

Burnt.

Her shoulders slumped. "Scrambled eggs?"

Kane laughed and pulled her toward him, giving her a hug. She returned it, holding him tightly, it the most comforted he had felt in years. There was something about someone who genuinely cared holding you, and he was pretty sure this woman did.

There was something there.

Something that would have to wait.

He pushed her back gently, smiling down at her. "Let's agree that *I* do the cooking in this relationship."

She stared up at him, her eyes dancing with happiness, bright and wide. "Relationship?"

His cheeks burned and his jaw dropped slightly. "Umm, I mean, well—" He tapped his watch. "I gotta get this."

Fang's eyes narrowed, clearly puzzled.

He shook his head. "I'll explain later. Just give me a minute."

She let him break the embrace and turned her attention to cleaning up the breakfast disaster as he headed for the bathroom. His CIA issue watch looked like any other luxury watch, but it had a few features most didn't. Including a discrete messaging system that, when activated, would send a small electric pulse into his skin, a silent notification that he had a message waiting. It was completely undetectable.

Unlike a vibration.

Closing the door, he pressed the buttons in a coded sequence and a message scrolled on the special display, the glass face anything but. His eyebrows popped.

Now what could he *want?*

1st Special Forces Operational Detachment - Delta HQ, Fort Bragg, North Carolina A.k.a. "The Unit"

“Secure call for you, Sergeant Major.”

Dawson nodded, jogging to the secure communications room, he deciding to hang around after he sent his message to Kane. Sometimes he had to wait a while to hear back from the CIA operative, though sometimes he heard back within minutes.

It all depended where in the world Kane happened to be.

Or what he was doing.

Kane had been a member of his Bravo Team before recruitment by the CIA. Dawson had been disappointed to see him go, but the guy had mad skills and was always a bit of a lone wolf. Dawson was too much of a team player to want to go CIA—not that they hadn’t asked. He had refused the offer, in no uncertain terms, and told the colonel about it, telling him to let CIA know not to bother ever asking again.

They hadn’t, though the option was always out there if he wanted it.

And he never would.

He loved his team.

Eleven of the best guys a soldier could ask to serve with.

There wasn’t a man on his team that he wouldn’t trust with his life, even the new guys. If you could make it through Delta training, you were good.

Damned good.

Over one thousand people worked at the Unit, and he was but a small part of a much larger machine, everyone here the best of the best.

And it was the only place he really thought of as home.

He fit the headset on then hit the button.

"Go ahead."

"You rang?"

Dawson chuckled at the not-too-bad Lurch imitation. "I did. You busy?"

"I have a few minutes. What's up?"

"I've got some intel I can't act on, but someone has to. The colonel has tried to raise it to the Pentagon but his CO is dismissing it because of the source."

"Who's the source?"

"Colonel Kolya Chernov, Spetsnaz."

"You'd think he'd be reliable. What's the problem?"

"He's made the top ten of Interpol's most wanted."

"Really? Moving up in the world."

"Yeah, apparently he killed three of his men and some SVR agents who tried to arrest him."

"Bullshit."

Dawson's head bobbed in agreement. "That's exactly what I said. They're claiming he's involved in the theft of some Cesium."

Kane whistled, a burst of static in Dawson's ear. "But he's saying the opposite."

"Exactly."

"Who do you believe?"

"Do I believe a man I've dealt with honorably on several occasions, or the Russian government? Hmm, let me think about that."

"Haw haw," replied Kane. "Okay funny guy, what are we doing about it?"

Dawson shook his head. "Nothing I can do here, but the colonel greenlighted me contacting you."

"Uh huh. So this is now my mess."

Dawson grinned. "Yup. Have fun with it."

"What the hell did I ever do to you?"

Dawson leaned back in his chair. "Give me a minute, I'm sure I can come up with a list."

"Okay, okay, I'm hanging up now before you truly hurt my feelings."

"Good idea. I've sent everything I've got to the usual place. Good luck."

"Thanks buddy. If you don't hear from me, count the stars at Langley. Then blame yourself."

Dawson chuckled. "Hey, you chose a career path where no one has your six."

"Yeah yeah. Maybe I was just tired of Niner commenting on it."

"It is a nice six."

"Good bye."

The line went dead and Dawson pulled off the headset, laughing.

And praying he hadn't just set a friend up to die.

CIA Headquarters, Langley, Virginia

"What have you got?"

CIA Analyst Supervisor Chris Leroux looked up from his desk as his boss, National Clandestine Service Chief Leif Morrison, poked his head inside his office. Two of his analysts, Sonya Tong and Marc Therrien, jumped to their feet before Morrison could wave them off.

Leroux motioned toward a spare chair. "It's looking like the colonel's story is true, as far as we can tell."

Morrison dropped into the chair, crossing his legs then reaching back to swing the door shut. "So he isn't a mass murderer?"

Therrien shrugged. "I wouldn't say that. He is Spetsnaz after all."

Morrison grunted. "They can be brutal. But usually only to their enemies. Career jackets aside, let's focus on recent events. What can you tell me?"

Leroux handed him a tablet computer. "The first three are from his unit. All found dead. Official reports show them all as murdered, but eyewitness reports and Internet postings suggest the first one was found hanging from his apartment balcony, the second one swallowed a bottle of pills, and only the third one was murdered. Shot in the head."

"And we don't believe any of it."

"No, in the files the colonel sent he said they were all murdered by the SVR. He killed the team sent to terminate him but couldn't save his own men. The only thing all four of them had done together recently was provide security for an SVR op in Chechnya."

Morrison shifted in his chair. "That's the part of the story that piqued my curiosity. What have you been able to find out?"

"Well, this is where it was a little more difficult to check. If SVR agents did indeed sell Cesium-137 to the Chechens like the colonel claims, they're not exactly going to file a report on it. My guess is they were rogue agents and this was a retirement plan, not something sanctioned by Moscow."

"Agreed. There's no way the Russian government would sell anything to the Chechens if they thought it might be used against them."

"That's what I was thinking," said Therrien. "I mean, you'd have to either really hate your country or be blinded by greed to risk that. My guess is they had some sort of assurances beforehand."

Morrison smiled. "Guessing is all well and good, but we need facts if we're going to act. Do we have anything to actually show this happened?"

Sonya Tong raised a finger. "We did pick up some chatter that a Chechen cell had something for sale at a huge price on one of the dark web arms trading networks, but the listing went down. We didn't pay it too much mind until we had this bit of intel to match it against."

Leroux tapped his desk as he chewed his cheek. "Sir, if the listing went down, either it was BS in the first place—"

"Or it's been sold."

Leroux nodded at his boss. "Or a sale has been arranged."

"What do we know about these Chechens?"

Leroux motioned to Sonya. "Go ahead."

She smiled at him and Leroux resisted the urge to look away. He was in a committed, long term relationship with the most incredible woman he had ever known, and young Sonya Tong had a bit of a crush on him. He had always considered himself a geek, socially awkward, few if any friends his entire life that weren't cyber, chronically single with no prospects, but when Sherrie White had come into his life, all that had changed.

He was no longer single.

He was still socially awkward and all that nonsense, but he no longer cared. He had a girlfriend that he felt was way out of his league though truly did seem to love him, and now the attentions of this other woman.

It was too much for his fragile ego to know how to handle.

So he ignored it.

Almost thirty years with no girls interested, and now two at once.

He smiled. Inwardly.

You da man! Self-five!

He tuned back into what Sonya was saying. "—Alambek Vok even running for office now, though we think that's a cover. He has numerous offshore accounts where he seems to be funneling money."

"Retirement fund?"

"That was the prevailing wisdom. He lost the war against Russia so he's looking to set himself up somewhere comfortable."

"Exactly how much money does he have?"

Sonya waved her tablet. "None."

Morrison's eyes narrowed. "Excuse me?"

"Mr. Vok's bank accounts were completely drained over the week leading up to Colonel Chernov's alleged meeting."

Morrison sucked in a breath, pursing his lips. "The SVR payoff."

Leroux nodded. "That's a good assumption."

Morrison looked at him. "What does your legendary gut tell you?"

Leroux flushed a bit.

His "gut" was well known at the CIA, it how he got his job as a supervisor, something he had *not* wanted. He had a hard enough time dealing with people as it was, so to become the supervisor of a team of almost ten, many of who were much older than him, had been unbelievably stressful.

He had turned it down.

But he wasn't given a choice.

Forcing him had been the right decision, and he was now excelling at it, though at times he still felt awkward. But his team had been great, and after running a few successful ops, they were solidly behind him, everyone benefiting from his uncanny ability to take seemingly unrelated data and find how they were related.

And today was no different.

He looked at Morrison, the man who had given him no choice. "I think Colonel Chernov is telling us the truth and that Chechen separatists, with known ties to Islamic fundamentalists, now have their hands on enough nuclear material to create a dirty bomb that could render much of Manhattan uninhabitable for decades."

Al-Raqqah, Syria
ISIL controlled territory

Maloof glanced over his shoulder, seeing no one. He casually walked farther out of the town, puffing on a cigarette, it a nasty habit he had acquired while here. The cigarettes were plentiful, and there was nothing else to do, the joke here that if anyone ever lived long enough to get lung cancer, they weren't trying hard enough.

But he had no intentions of being here much longer.

He had his intel.

A conversation today referred to a meeting that would take place in two weeks with a group of Chechens to make the final purchase necessary for the largest ISIL operation in history, and he knew immediately what it was for.

The missing nuclear material.

His latest briefing from Mossad suggested a not insignificant amount of Cesium-137 had been sold to the Chechens and that they were looking to flip it. The Americans were desperate to find it, and Mossad sources within the CIA had caught wind of it, passing the intel on. Since he was one of only a few agents embedded in the area, he had received a burst communique a few days ago.

And now it appeared the group he had infiltrated were directly involved.

He had to get that intel to Mossad so somebody could act upon it. Who, it didn't matter. No one with half a brain wanted Islamic fundamentalists with anything nuclear. He always returned to the example of Pakistan. When they finally had the bomb, what happened? Their nuclear scientist, a national hero, immediately sold it to the Libyans, Iranians and North

Koreans. And God knew who else. It reminded him of what an old lecturer of his from university said.

The Mutually Assured Destruction doctrine only works when the other side doesn't want to die any more than you do. With Islamic fundamentalists, you can't be that sure.

Which was why any Islamic state with the bomb was a terrifying prospect.

Especially Iran.

When a government and its leaders call for Israel to be wiped from the map, its citizens forced into the sea should they survive, when Hitler's Final Solution is described as a good start in one breath and a hoax in another, one could forgive the Jews he worked with for being a little nervous.

He cleared the rise to the south of town then dropped down the other side and out of anyone's line of sight who might be watching. Sprinting to the east several hundred feet, he dropped behind a rock outcropping and quickly began scooping sand away, a plastic bag a foot down soon revealed. With a glance over each shoulder, he unzipped the bag and removed the phone and satellite transmitter.

Firing up the transmitter, he waited for the phone to boot up as he gathered the sand around in a pile next to the hole he had just dug.

There wasn't a second to waste.

The phone was up and he quickly typed in his message, letting them know about the meeting he had overheard and the meeting to purchase possible nuclear material from the Chechens in two weeks.

A foot scraped behind him.

He spun toward the sound and saw a sneering Safar standing with his gun pointed at him.

"I told them you couldn't be trusted."

Maloof rose slowly, his hands up at his shoulders. "What are you talking about?" He motioned toward the phone. "It's how I keep in touch with back home."

"I could smell the Jew on you the moment you arrived."

Interesting. Having lived among them all my life, I didn't realize they had a smell.

"I'm not a Jew, of that I can assure you."

"You're not one of us. And when I show the Caliph your equipment there, he'll agree with me having killed you."

Not planning to take me prisoner, are you?

"He might not be too pleased, since I'm doing *his* work."

Safar's smile disappeared, replaced with confusion. "Umm, what do you mean?"

Maloof took the opportunity to take a step forward, a smile on his face. "Listen, brother, how do you think we update social media? We need computers and satellite uplinks. But we have to hide them from the infidel." Another step. "We can't be sending these signals from within the towns, they'll be able to track them then bomb us." Another step. "We hide them outside in the middle of nowhere so that if they do bomb the source of the signal, no one gets hurt, and they waste a million dollar missile destroying a cellphone." He laughed, taking the final step. "You see, it's all explained, no need to be concerned."

Safar stared at him. "Then why did the Caliph himself send me after you." Safar squeezed the trigger, a single shot erupting from the barrel of the AK-47, the searing hot round tearing through Maloof's stomach before he could stop him. Agony ripped through him as he reached behind his back, pulling his knife while swatting the barrel of the gun away, the next several shots firing harmlessly into the sand. His knife surged forward, into Safar's own stomach, plunging deep into the fleshy mass, all the way to the hilt. Safar cried out in shock and pain as Maloof twisted the blade, scrambling the organs, the two of them dropping to the ground.

Maloof let go of the knife and grasped at his stomach. Blood poured over his fingers and he knew he was going to die, the life sustaining fluid quickly draining from him.

He had only seconds.

He turned, crawling on his knees, back toward the phone, its bright display beckoning, as Safar moaned behind him, his prayers getting weaker. A jolt of pain surged through Maloof's body, taking his breath away, and he fell forward, onto his hands, the last few feet covered on all fours. He reached out for the phone, falling onto his side.

And hit Send.

Then rolled over onto his back, staring up at the stars, more brilliant than he had ever noticed before.

And hoped that his service to Allah had made him worthy of the same paradise Safar seemed to think he was destined for.

Khirbet Awwad, Syrian-Jordanian Border

"Allahu Akbar!"

Kane smiled and returned the salute, he soon exchanging pounding hugs with several men he had just met. Yet today he wasn't Dylan Kane, he was Bryce Clearwater, a naïve young man who had converted to Islam and wanted to join the cause, his profile, built up over a couple of years online by the CIA, now given a face.

His.

And here he was, the latest misguided foreigner yearning for a life of violence and sex, denied to him by his oppressive Christian regime back home.

"How was your trip?" asked his contact, Aziz Kanaan, as his duffel bag was taken and tossed into the back of a waiting pickup truck.

"Fine. A little surprised at how easy it was to get here."

Kanaan laughed, nodding toward Kane's pocket. "It's that American passport you carry and that smooth white face. It's like a key that unlocks any door."

The others laughed, all clearly Middle Eastern men with thick beards. Kane ran his hand over his face. "I cut it off before I left. I thought it would help."

Kanaan slapped him on the back. "My friend, you definitely did the right thing. Whenever one of us goes somewhere the infidel controls, we shave, otherwise our devotion gives us away."

Kane smiled, climbing into the back of the truck with Kanaan, the other two taking the cab. As they pulled away from the border, he couldn't help but marvel at how easy it indeed had been. He was deep undercover so he hadn't used his CIA contacts to smooth the way, just in case there was a weak point along the journey. He was going into the lion's den, and someone knowing who he was would mean certain death.

He had bought his own ticket to Jordan, met up with a Médecins Sans Frontières team, made it to the frontlines, then walked away.

All too easy.

New York City to the Islamic State in less than forty-eight hours.

Now he just hoped he could confirm the intel provided by Mossad and get it back to his handlers so they could call in a team to recover the black market nuclear materials.

"What are you thinking?" asked Kanaan, staring at him.

Kane smiled and shrugged. "I don't know, I'm just so excited. I can't believe I actually had the guts to come, you know. It's like, the craziest thing I've ever done."

Kanaan roared with laughter. "You think this is crazy, wait until tomorrow! You're going to be so busy you won't know what hit you!"

Kane smiled. "Your English, it's very good."

Kanaan nodded. "Thank you. I've had a good teacher. And now you will teach others as well. We need converts like you, not only to help recruit others to the cause, but to teach us English and the ways of the infidel. You grew up as one and only recently came to Allah. There's much we can learn from you."

"I look forward to serving Allah in spreading his word as told to the Prophet, peace be upon him."

Kanaan leaned forward and slapped him on his leg as the truck bounced along what some might call a road, though most wouldn't. "I think you will fit in here very well, my friend. Now let us rest. It is a long journey." With that, Kanaan lay down in the bed of the truck and closed his eyes, his head resting on a rolled up jacket. Kane propped his duffel bag against the cab then leaned back on it, turning to his side so he faced outward.

And with one eye closed, he watched the terrain whip by, using the stars overhead to guide him, allowing him to know pretty much exactly where they were when they arrived several hours later.

The truck skidded to a halt, a cloud of dust flowing over them causing Kane to cough. Kanaan laughed, slapping him on the back before jumping to the ground and stretching. Kane followed, aping the movements, not to fit in, but because he truly was tight, the accommodations of the past few hours sadly lacking.

Kanaan motioned to him. "Come, come, let's get inside and out of sight of the infidel." Kanaan pointed up and Kane glanced at the sky. He had no doubt there was a satellite overhead, watching him, though there'd be no drones.

It could raise suspicions.

He stepped inside a rather modest building and two men raised their weapons, aiming them at his chest. "Hey, what's this? I thought we were all friends here!"

Kanaan stepped in front of him, removing Kane's duffel bag from his shoulder and tossing it to another who quickly began to empty it on a nearby table. "We are, my friend, we are. But you are leaving your old life behind and committing yourself to Allah. Lose the clothing of the infidel and all his trappings."

"Really?"

Kanaan nodded. "Please."

Kane frowned but knew he had no choice, the two men, AKs aimed at him, didn't appear to have been properly trained, their fingers actually on the triggers instead of resting against the guard. Any surprise, any twitch, and lead would be belching at him.

With that in mind, he carefully undressed, down to his underwear.

Kanaan pointed at them. "Please."

Kane sighed, dropping his underwear to the dusty floor, naked for the world to see. Or at least his new friends, all of whom seemed a little too interested in his junk. He eyeballed one of the men who couldn't seem to tear his eyes away, his trigger finger twitching. "Never seen a white one before?"

The man looked at him, startled, then flushed, raising his weapon slightly higher.

Kanaan roared with laughter, slapping Kane on the back before coming between the embarrassed man and Kane. "You're lucky he doesn't speak English, my friend, or he may have killed you." Kanaan pointed at the only thing that remained on Kane's person. "The watch. Give it to me."

Kane felt his heart slam a little harder as he removed his only lifeline to the outside world. As the man searching his bag would find, there was absolutely nothing there *to* find. He had brought no weapons, no comm gear, nothing that could raise suspicions.

Except his watch.

An ordinary looking watch with extraordinary capabilities.

He handed it over.

It would appear to anyone to be a regular watch, it deactivating the moment he removed it. If he was lucky, Kanaan would take to wearing it, which would give him a chance to retrieve it later.

Kanaan tossed it to the floor and crushed it with the heel of his boot.

Well that makes things a little more interesting.

Operations Center 3, CIA Headquarters, Langley, Virginia

"How late is he?"

Leroux frowned, glancing at his boss then at one of the displays on the massive, curved wall of plasma in front of them. "Two days."

Morrison shook his head, dropping into a spare chair, the operations center currently manned by Leroux's staff plus several support personnel. "Two days."

"Yes, sir. He hasn't responded to our communication attempts, and we're getting no indication that the messages have actually been received by his watch."

"What's the log show?"

Leroux motioned toward Sonya Tong, she responding. "Last signal was an indicator that it had been removed from his wrist, then nothing."

"You're sure it was removed?"

Sonya nodded. "Yes, sir. It transmits a distinct signal when that happens unless the agent presses down on the face first."

"In case they're monitoring for signals."

"Exactly. And since he didn't do that, we believe he wanted that signal sent."

Morrison pursed his lips, looking at Sonya then at Leroux. "Or it was taken off without his consent."

Leroux nodded. "Definitely a possibility. Either way it suggests he's in trouble."

"And with it being two days, we wouldn't even know where to go." Morrison sighed, clasping his hands behind his head as he leaned back in the chair. "I wouldn't be concerned if he was at least wearing the watch. It wouldn't be the first time an operative was under constant surveillance. Hell, days or weeks isn't out of the question." He tilted forward, unclasping his hands and resting his elbows on his knees, his voice lowering slightly. "Right now, for all we know, he's dead."

Leroux felt weak, his chest tightening, blood rushing, pounding in his ears at his boss' words.

Kane. Dead.

It was too much. Kane was his only friend besides Sherrie, someone he rarely saw yet always knew was out there, somewhere, ready and willing to help if ever needed.

He looked at Morrison. "Can we at least assume he's alive for now?"

Morrison smiled slightly, the concerned father figure returning for a moment. He put a hand on Leroux's shoulder and squeezed. "Absolutely. Until I see a body, Dylan Kane is alive and well and fulfilling his mission."

Leroux smiled weakly. "Thank you, sir."

Morrison motioned to one of the screens, satellite footage on a loop. "Now, is this what you called me down here for?"

Leroux drew in a quick breath, pushing his emotions aside for the moment and rose, walking down the steps of the operations center and into the pit, pointing toward the screen with a laser pointer. "Sir, we were able to pull some satellite footage that caught the tail end of the exchange." He glanced at Randy Child, the newest and youngest addition to his team. "Bring up Isolation Zero-One."

Child hit a few keys and one of the displays showed an image with about a dozen men, a helicopter and a pickup truck. He pointed at the helicopter. "This is a Russian Mi-24 Hind helicopter. The tail number"—he snapped his fingers and an isolation of the tail number appeared—"shows it's Russian Army, and still in service." He pointed at four men spread out at the top of the photo, closest to the helicopter. "By their uniforms, we believe these to be Colonel Chernov and his men." He pointed to the men on the north side of the SUV. "We believe the men in the suits are the SVR agents identified by the colonel." He motioned toward the other men occupying the bottom of the image. "And these are the Chechens they met." He aimed the pointer at one of them. "And this is Alambek Vok, the man we think is at the center of this."

"And we're sure this is it, this is the meeting?"

"It matches the date, time and location precisely."

Morrison rose, walking toward the displays. He pointed at a table that had been set up between the helicopter and SUV. "Did they open the case?"

Leroux smiled. "Bring up Isolation Zero-Three." An image of an opened case appeared, six distinct shapes inside. "Exactly as the colonel described. Six canisters."

"Can we know what they are?"

Leroux shook his head as he motioned for Child to zoom in, the image pixelating then resolving. "We can't be certain." He motioned at Child. "Split screen with a known Cesium-137 canister." A second image appeared. "You can see they definitely appear the same."

Morrison nodded, stepping closer. "And how much does a canister carry?"

"This size, if full, contains a little over a kilo of material."

"And how much is that?" Morrison looked at Leroux. "From a dirty bomb perspective?"

Leroux sucked in a slow, deep breath. "Sir, if just one of these canisters was detonated over Manhattan, it could poison hundreds of thousands and render the entire island uninhabitable for thirty years."

"Jesus." Morrison paused for a moment, staring at the screen again before returning to his chair, the man clearly shaken. "Where is it now?" he asked, his voice subdued.

Leroux smiled. "About the only good news I've got for you today, sir. We found him."

Morrison looked up, his mood clearly brightening. "How?"

"We intercepted a phone call made in the clear. Apparently the Chechen leader, this Vok, is dropping SVR names along the way to get past border security. During the exchange something was handed over—an envelope"—the image appeared showing the handoff—"and we think it contains some document or something of that nature, as a universal pass. But at the Azerbaijan border I guess someone didn't believe him, so decided to make a phone call to validate the document. From that phone call we've been able to pick up their trail and now know exactly where they are."

"And that is?"

"They'll be entering disputed Syrian territory within the next four days."

Morrison rose, a broad smile on his face. "Excellent work, everyone. You've earned your paychecks today." He turned to Leroux. "I'm going to talk to the White House and see if we can arrange an op to retrieve the Cesium before it's too late."

"And Kane?"

Morrison put a hand on Leroux's shoulder. "He's the toughest man I know. He'll figure a way out, of that I have no doubt."

Morrison left the op center, everyone all smiles at the compliment they had just received except Leroux, who dropped into his chair, praying to God his friend was still alive.

Outside Al-Raqqah, Syria

Sometimes playing games with superpowers backfired, and Dawson just hoped today wasn't going to be yet another example of that very thing. He peered through his scope at the scene below, a group of men on the edge of town waiting, six of them clearly armed, the other two who seemed to be in charge, sitting in two of four chairs placed around a table by the new arrivals.

They were definitely waiting for someone.

Intel said this would be where the sale of the missing Cesium would take place, and from his briefing, he knew they had to recover it at all costs, the potential human toll unimaginable.

And in the White House's infinite wisdom, it decided to inform the Russians that their missing nuclear material was about to be retrieved, and not to conduct any bombing missions in the area as there would be friendly forces present.

The Russians had turned it around on the White House, insisting they accompany any mission otherwise they couldn't guarantee the safety of American troops on the ground.

The White House had agreed.

The attempt to embarrass had backfired.

American Special Forces were constantly conducting operations in the area, and there was no need to inform the Russians of any specifics, beyond that they were there. This had been a continuation of the tit-for-tat game playing out on the world stage leading everyone toward a second Cold War in which Russia wasn't hampered by the flaws of communism.

It was a standoff that could lead to serious bloodshed if someone didn't figure out quickly how to deal with the belligerent Russian leader.

And goading him would never work.

"Here they come. Ten o'clock."

Dawson shifted his view to see where Sergeant Carl "Niner" Sung had indicated and spotted two vehicles approaching, one stopping several miles back, the other continuing forward, toward the town. The vehicle came to a stop about fifty feet from the table set out for the transaction, the men seated behind it rising to greet their guests.

Four men exited the vehicle, three with weapons, one with none obvious, and the only one to step forward.

"Is that him?"

"It does not appear so," said the heavily accented voice to his left, Major Zolotov, the Russian lead on the mission. There were eight from each country, split into two teams of six plus two sniper teams, all deployed around the site, ready to engage on Dawson's signal, it decided somebody had to be in ultimate command.

If only the major knew my rank.

While everyone's focus was on the exchange, he redirected his attention to the second vehicle that had held back.

"They're gone."

Zolotov grunted. "It doesn't matter. Look."

Dawson refocused on the table, a case produced and opened, it impossible to tell from this angle if it was what they were after, yet it was obviously what those gathered below were there for. He rose to his knees. "This is Zero-One. Execute in three—two—one—execute!"

Two shots rang out from opposite sides of the gathered terrorists, two guards dropping, two more shots fired before their bodies even hit the ground. Dawson and his group of six including Sergeant Will "Spock"

Lightman and Sergeant Leon "Atlas" James, sprinted toward the distracted hostiles, the other team approaching from the other side.

In range, Dawson raised his MP5 and squeezed the trigger, taking out one of the new arrivals hiding behind the wheel of his vehicle, the Russians pouring a steady stream of fire on the proceedings, leaving little doubt to the enemy where their location was.

Fools!

It was an arrogant method of engagement, underestimating one's enemy, putting everyone at risk. He glanced over at Atlas who was shaking his head, his weapon raised, yet to take a shot, there nothing left to shoot at.

Arriving at the scene, Dawson, using hand signals, ordered a perimeter established while Atlas and Spock grabbed the case, bringing out testing equipment to confirm the contents. Atlas glanced up from the display and gave a thumbs up.

"This is it."

Dawson approached, the Cyrillic writing plain to anyone. The Cyrillic writing on three canisters.

There's supposed to be six.

A shot rang out behind him and he spun around, Zolotov having put a bullet in a wounded hostile. It was clear the Russians wanted no prisoners, probably so no one could identify their crooked SVR agents. Dawson jerked a thumb over his shoulder, at the case. "You guys in the habit of losing this stuff?"

Zolotov stepped over to the table then nodded, raising a radio to his mouth. "Now."

The thump of helicopter rotors sounded in the distance, rapidly approaching, the betrayal Dawson had fully expected, and told the colonel would happen, now underway. He activated his comm. "Beetlejuice."

Zolotov raised his weapon, aiming it at Dawson, Spock and Atlas returning the favor. "What does this mean, this Beetlejuice?"

Dawson held his hands out to his side, motioning for everyone to remain calm. "Simply signaling those back home what's happening here."

Two Russian Hinds, probably the most intimidating looking helicopters ever built, cleared a nearby ridge, coming to a hover several hundred feet away, several more rushing over the town as half a dozen troops dropped from each. Dawson checked to the east then west and saw his sniper team of Niner and Jimmy led by gunpoint.

Zolotov flicked his AK-9 assault rifle. "Your weapons, please. And your communications equipment."

Dawson nodded to the others and they slowly rid themselves of the tools of their trade. Dawson held up his knife. "And this?"

"That, you can keep."

Dawson sneered a smile. "You're so generous."

His team of eight was lined up against a wall, half a dozen Russian troops holding weapons on them as the case was taken, the remaining troops loading into several choppers that had landed.

Zolotov stared at Dawson. "Do you want to know why?"

Dawson shook his head. "No need. I already know."

"Why?"

"You're Russian."

"And what is that supposed to mean?"

"It means you can't be trusted. Now you've just proven to Washington what those of us on the ground have been telling them for years."

"And what is that?"

"That the Soviet Union is back."

Zolotov laughed, a broad smile on his face. "I like you, American. It's too bad you are right. We might have shared some vodka and toasted our fallen comrades together." He frowned, lowering his weapon and stepping closer to Dawson. "I'm supposed to kill you"—he tipped his head toward the hostiles—"with their weapons."

"Then why don't you just get it over with?"

Zolotov smiled. "Because I have what we came for, the terrorists are dead, and I only kill people I don't like." He pointed up at the sky. "I leave that to others. Say your goodbyes, gentlemen, you're dead already."

Zolotov jogged to the final chopper waiting and climbed aboard, though not before snapping a casual salute at Dawson's team. The Hind lifted off, banking sharply to the right and disappearing quickly over the rise. Dawson pointed in the same direction, knowing full well what the warning meant. "Run as fast as you can and don't look back."

They all pushed off the wall, sprinting hard, Spock in the lead, the bastard fast, as the screech of fighters in the distance, rapidly approaching, filled their ears. They crested the rise just as the first Sukhoi Su-34 tore overhead, missiles erupting from its weapons pods. Dawson glanced back to see Atlas, the largest and slowest, just reaching the top of the hill, the rest already down the other side.

"Hit the deck!" shouted Dawson and they all dropped, Atlas flying forward as massive explosions rocked the town behind them, the ground vibrating in protest. "Move! Move! Move!" Everyone was back on their feet as three more Su-34s thundered overhead, more missiles loosed.

"Over there!" shouted Spock, pointing to a rock outcropping. Dawson turned, making a beeline for the cover, shoving everyone inside the cluster of rocks before crouching down and squeezing in himself. They were on the edge of a large number of boulders, the only cover in the area, but an area large enough that he hoped the Russians wouldn't decide to take them out.

They didn't.

The pounding of the town lasted for about ten minutes before the last of the Su-34s left, leaving nothing but the wails of those who had managed to survive.

Dawson stepped out first, surveying the thick black smoke over the crest. Niner emerged from their cover, standing beside him.

"Nobody was meant to survive that."

Dawson nodded. "No, *we* weren't."

"Now what?"

Dawson looked at the others then pointed up. "Everybody wave to the eye in the sky."

Everyone did, and within moments, Atlas pointed to the south. "There it is."

They all turned to see an RQ-7 Shadow UAV racing toward them, lower than it would usually travel, its operator, tucked away safely, perhaps stateside, rocking it from side to side, letting them know they had been spotted.

Atlas' impossibly deep voice rumbled. "The Russians really need to start understanding that just because their president can't see it, doesn't mean it isn't there."

Dawson chuckled then sat down, knowing their retrieval team was only moments away, his Beetlejuice code word the trigger for their departure.

Never trust the Russians.

Al-Raqqah, Syria

"No! Please no! I'll do anything you ask, I swear!"

Amira Shadid sobbed uncontrollably, her two daughters clinging to her legs as her arms stretched toward her pleading husband. A large group of ISIL soldiers, all laughing at their predicament, surrounded them as their leader, a man whose name she did not know, taunted her beloved. Another man, his face covered by a keffiyeh, his hand badly scarred, directed two others as they stacked tires around her husband.

She dropped to her knees, crawling forward. "Please, sir, I'll do what you ask, I'll do anything, just don't kill my husband!"

The leader pointed at her, shouting at her husband. "Your women, they will fetch a good price at the market in Al-Mayadeen. They will service our warriors for years to come!"

His men laughed, several comments about her body and those of her daughters thrown her way.

Yet she could barely hear them now. The panic that gripped her was overwhelming as she held her young daughters tight to her sides. They were too young, far too young to even understand what these barbarians were saying, too young to know the evil that men were capable of when it came to women they had no respect for.

It was the new reality she had lived under since ISIL had taken her town. Women had no rights, they treated as the property of their men. Her husband had joined them out of self-preservation, the only reason they were all alive today.

But yesterday she had refused a request, and sealed his fate.

"I'm sorry!" she cried, looking at her husband as he stood helpless, tires piled to his neck.

He stared at her, tears staining his face, terror filling his eyes as he tried to get one last look at his girls. "I love you, I love you all! Never forget that!"

"Oh, how sweet," taunted the leader, approaching her husband, a book of matches in his hand as the scarred man doused the tires with gasoline. "Tender words in your final moments."

Her husband turned to the man. "Get this over with, you pig! This is not the work of Allah! When you die, you will burn in eternal damnation for what you have done here today!"

"Please!" she cried, "Please stop! I'll do what you want! Anything you want!"

The leader eyeballed her. "You had your chance." He tossed the book of matches to the scarred man who removed one, striking it then tossing it at the tires. The gasoline exploded, flames stretching toward the heavens as her husband screamed in agony. His daughters screeched in horror as she tried to cover their eyes, trying to prevent their innocent minds from seeing the evil Shaytan's work carried out.

Yet she couldn't tear her own eyes away.

The horror imprinted on her mind forever.

Until the day she died.

Her husband's cries of agony stopped and her head dropped to her chest as she thanked Allah for taking him quickly, for ending his pain.

Something in the distance had her staring up, as did the others gathered, their laughing and cheering, their shouts of Allahu Akbar, forgotten as several large helicopters whipped by overhead.

Orders were shouted, lost to the rush of blood pounding in her ears, all she could hear beyond that were the crackling flames that was her husband, the love of her life, the father of her two daughters, and her sole provider.

They might as well have killed us all.

She sat on the ground, her daughters holding her, sobbing, not sure of what was going on, as the soldiers rushed around, shouting.

Then there was a loud roar and the ground shook.

And Allah had answered her prayers.

Please take us too.

Tarek Nazari raised his weapon and opened fire as the Russian fighter streaked across the sky. It was a near futile effort, though Allah willing, he might just get a lucky shot off that took down the infidel. Missile after missile pounded the town, a curious turn of events considering it was unimportant, and even housed a small hospital on the outskirts run by infidels. It was tolerated, as it meant a steady source of supplies they could steal when necessary, and skilled doctors were always welcome after a battle.

Yet why the Russians were here today was strange. His men's presence was nothing new, though another group had come through the town earlier, he himself having checked their IDs. When he had seen the first worked for the Caliph himself, he had immediately waved them through.

That must be why the Russians are here.

He glanced toward the woman and her daughters, turning to grab them when the building behind him erupted in flames, the blast knocking him off his feet. Dazed, he lay still for a moment as shrieks and cries surrounded him, the bombing incessant, the Russians seemingly determined to flatten the entire town for some reason.

Could the new arrivals be that important?

He shook his head, trying to regain his senses as he pushed himself to his knees, staring at the devastation around him. Almost every building was flattened, most of his men lay scattered about, dead or dying.

And the woman and her daughters were nowhere to be seen.

Instead, only a pile of rubble where they had once huddled together.

Operations Center 3, CIA Headquarters, Langley, Virginia

"They double-crossed us, but I can confirm it's only half the shipment."

Leroux and his team sat at their stations in silence as the Delta operator filled them in on what had happened, Director Morrison taking the lead on the questioning.

"So the Russians have it?"

"Yes, sir."

Morrison nodded. "Well, you'll be interested to know that the Russians have reported that you were all killed during the assault by the terrorists and that they would be recovering your bodies after their air assault is complete."

"They pounded the town pretty hard, sir. Something tells me they'll use that as an excuse for why they couldn't find our bodies."

"Why do you think the Russian Major left you alive?"

"I got a sense he had some honor left in him."

"Lucky for you."

There was a chuckle. "Yes, sir, absolutely. Did you correct them?"

"Negative. The White House is pissed so I think they're going to let the Kremlin hang themselves a little while longer."

"Well, maybe they'll learn you can't trust them."

Morrison smiled. "Eventually."

"Sir, has there been any word from you know who?"

Leroux knew Kane had once served with these men, and they had been the ones who brought Kane in on his current mission. If he were them, he would be extremely concerned, perhaps even feeling responsible for his fate.

"Not yet. All we know is that based on the footage you transmitted before you were betrayed, the ISIL members that were there for the sale have links to the cell he is supposed to have infiltrated."

"Christ, I hope he wasn't killed in that bombing."

"Let's hope not."

"Do we know where the Chechen leader is?"

"We tracked the second vehicle to Al-Mayadeen, but lost them there."

"I think it's safe to assume they had the other half of the Cesium."

"Agreed."

Leroux frowned. "Which means ISIL now has enough radioactive material to contaminate pretty much any city in the world."

Al-Raqqah, Syria

Amira groaned. Every part of her body was in pain. Her head throbbed, her mouth was dry, and she could see nothing. Or almost nothing. There was a dull orange glow surrounding her, though that was it. She tried to move but couldn't. As her eyes adjusted, she realized she was lying on her stomach, something heavy pressing down on her back.

The girls!

"Maya! Rima!"

A whimper to her left, another to her right had her breathing a brief sigh of relief. They were alive, though what condition they were in she had no clue. There were shouts nearby, the sound of men running back and forth in confusion, but she didn't dare call out for help.

Allah may not have answered her prayers the way she wanted, yet he had delivered them from evil, at least temporarily.

She sucked in a deep breath and felt whatever was on her back move.

So she could lift it.

She drew her arms in then pushed up, whatever was on her back rolling off and painfully hitting her leg.

She yelped.

The girls whimpered.

"It's okay, Mommy's coming."

She sat up on her knees, looking about. She was surrounded by rubble, the building behind her apparently having collapsed on them or around them, it a miracle from Allah that she was still alive. Gingerly testing her arms and legs, she could feel no broken bones.

She turned, searching for her youngest, Rima, barely eight years old. "Rima, honey, where are you?"

"Over here, Mommy!"

The girl began to sob and terror rushed through Amira as she realized someone might hear them, and their misery continue. "It's okay, dear, just be quiet, we don't want anyone to hear us, okay?"

"O-okay."

She groped in the dark, her eyes adjusting to the dim light, most of it provided by the fires burning around them and a quarter-moon overhead. She spotted the corner of her daughter's dress and quickly removed the rubble lying atop her. Before she had a chance to check her over, Rima had leapt into her arms, hugging her tightly.

"Are you okay? Do you hurt anywhere?"

"I'm thirsty."

Amira smiled, squeezing her tightly then letting go, quickly checking for broken bones in the dark, squeezing everything, listening for a gasp or a cry.

Nothing.

"Let's find your sister."

"I'm here."

Amira turned to see the shadow of Maya standing behind them. "Are you okay?"

Nothing.

"You have to speak, honey, I can't see you."

"I'm okay."

Amira rose, taking both girls by the hand. "We must leave quickly and quietly, understood?"

"Yes, Mommy," replied Rima.

"What about Daddy?"

Amira looked back and could see the tires still burning in the village square. She squeezed her eyes shut and turned away.

"He is with Allah now."

"Can we go with Allah?" asked Rima.

Amira bent down and gave her a kiss on the top of her head. "Not today, sweetie, not today. Today Allah watches over us, and we must not waste His gift. Now let's go. Quickly and quietly."

She picked her way through the rubble, toward the edge of town, knowing that this was her one chance of escaping the clutches of those who had killed her husband, and those who would happily turn them all into sex slaves.

Even her precious little girls.

Al-Raqqah, Syria

Nazari stared into the fire as his friend jabbed at it with his scarred hand, a long stick prompting hisses of protest from the burning embers. The Russians had killed many of his men in the air raid earlier in the day, and all of the group sent from Al-Raqqah as well. The woman and her children had escaped, though he had sent some men after her, he hopeful he would hear back soon that they had been found.

A new group had already arrived, led by Kanaan, a man he had dealt with for years now, a man he respected and trusted, and their regional commander. He had apparently successfully completed the transaction interrupted by the Russians.

A transaction he had yet to reveal the details of.

But the plan he was briefing them on was incredible.

Bold.

Worthy of dying for.

For should they succeed, they would surely die.

"Do you think it can be done?" asked one of the others.

Kanaan nodded. "Absolutely. Never doubt your ability to succeed when Allah is on your side. Our brothers never doubted they would succeed on 9/11, though I think they never thought they would be so successful."

"It was a glorious victory," agreed Nazari, his head bobbing as he chewed on a piece of lamb. "And if what you propose should succeed, this victory could be even greater."

"I agree," said Kanaan. "We will deliver a mighty weapon into the infidel's stronghold and shake their faith to the core."

"What is it?" asked another.

Kanaan shook his head. "I can say only this. It has the power to change everything. No longer will the war only be fought here in our home. After we succeed, the war will be in the infidel's cities and homes. And with Allah's help, we will be victorious!"

Shouts of Allahu Akbar filled the night until Kanaan raised his hands, silencing those gathered.

"Where will the blow be struck?" asked Nazari, taking a sip of water.

"In America."

"How many of us?"

"All who sit here tonight," replied Kanaan, his arm stretching out to the others. "But we are but a small part. Thousands will be sent, including our new friend here." He slapped the back of an American convert that had been sitting beside him the entire time, saying nothing since introduced as a loyal servant of Allah, a man who had apparently been with them for less than two weeks though had already fought in several battles, proving his loyalty and fervent faith.

But Nazari didn't trust converts.

There was a reason Islam demanded the death of all converts *from* Islam. There was, after all, only one true path to God, and if you left that path, you were wasting His gift, therefore you forfeited the right to the life He had granted.

And to switch to Islam late in life was a wonderful thing, but a man who switched his faith once could switch back. And to have him on a mission as important as this seemed foolish.

Though he was wise enough to keep his concerns to himself.

Kanaan clearly trusted the man, and having a white American might just help them.

"When do we leave?" he asked.

"Tonight."

Tell Abiad, Syrian-Turkish Border

Amira held her daughters' hands tightly. It hadn't taken long to reach the border with Turkey, their hometown close, and with the recent air campaign ramping up with the Russians involved, they had simply joined the stream of misery heading for safety.

But they were hungry, thirsty, sore, exhausted.

And the little ones were cranky.

She wished her husband was here with them, he always having a way with the girls that quieted them down during troubling times.

And there had been so many of those.

The girls were too young to really remember what living in peace was like. Syria hadn't been so bad, in fact, from her perspective as a schoolteacher, it had been quite good. They had a nice little home, were never hungry, and had a happy life until the civil war.

Things had quickly spiraled downhill from there.

At first she had thought overthrowing the Syrian leadership would be a good thing, yet when the fundamentalists had taken over much of her area, she realized she was wrong.

Terribly wrong.

Then things became worse.

ISIL.

She was a good Muslim, a devout Muslim. She believed in the supremacy of Islam over all other religions, and its destiny—the establishment of the Global Caliphate, though she didn't agree with all the violence that seemed to come with that dream.

She could never understand how others could be so hostile toward her chosen religion. Didn't Christians feel their religion was better than the Jewish, an improvement over what had come before? Then why was it so hard to believe what had come last was also an improvement? If Allah had delivered his last words to the Prophet Mohammad, then why couldn't the world simply accept the latest and last word from God? Wouldn't it be better for everyone simply to have one faith, one belief? Wouldn't there then be peace?

She had to admit it made no sense to her, but then again, she knew from her books that there were over seven billion on the planet, and less than two billion of them followed the teachings of the Prophet.

If all the others must die!

She shivered with the thought.

She could see the border ahead, a large, long fence stretching in both directions, loud speakers pleading for calm. She had never been to Turkey before, and had frankly never heard anything good about it, it a Muslim state that had abandoned the true fundamentals of Islam.

Complete implementation of Sharia.

Then again, so had her native Syria.

Until the fundamentalists had taken over.

She was confused. She could admit that to herself. She believed in the Koran, though if Islam was meant to be so wonderful, then why was life under it so often horrible?

Angry young men.

She looked about. Almost everyone within sight was a young man. It made no sense. She spotted a woman to her left staring at her and pushed her way through the throng of testosterone. "Hello!" she called.

The woman smiled. "Hello! How are you?"

Amira reached the woman to find her with two young children of her own and her husband. "Tired. What is going on here?"

The woman shook her head. "I don't know. It's so strange. Where are the families?" She held out her hand. "I'm Jodee Basara. This is my husband, Sami."

"I'm Amira Shadid." She cocked an ear. "Can you hear what they are saying?"

"I think they're saying they're only taking families," said Sami. "We need to get closer." He stepped forward, talking to some men ahead of them but she couldn't hear what was said. She looked at the mass of men blocking their way, quickly losing hope.

"Please! Let us through! We have children!"

Her futile pleas fell on deaf ears.

Or so she thought.

One of the young men Sami had been talking to turned back and stared at them. She knew she looked rough. Filthy, sweaty, not the lady she liked to present to the world.

And her children appeared even more pathetic.

As did her new friends.

The young man slapped the shoulders of several of those around him, words she couldn't hear quickly exchanged, then something miraculous happened.

"Come, follow us!"

A wedge of young men formed in front of them, shoving through the crowd, pushing those in front to the sides. There were protests at first, but as they saw what the men were trying to do, the crowd relented, even joining in, several more families fed into the center of the wedge. Amira's chest swelled with pride in the good displayed by those around her, thanking them as she passed, her girls waving to the wall of flesh surrounding them.

It didn't take long for them to reach the border, the Turkish guards on the other side pointing at them and waving them ahead.

She turned to the young man who had orchestrated their salvation.

"Thank you! Thank you so much! You are good boys!"

The young man beamed and stood aside, letting them through.

As Amira stepped into Turkish territory, she overflowed with a sense of relief.

And foreboding.

Were they truly safe here?

And what would they do now, now that they were refugees in a country she knew little about?

Tell Abiad, Syrian-Turkish Border

Kane dropped a shoulder and charged, several of his cell already engaging the Turkish soldiers guarding the border. He had no intention of killing any of the guards, nor did they seem to have any intention likewise. They were merely putting up a half-hearted attempt to stem the flow, Turkey seemingly resigned to housing over two million refugees.

His aim was to get through so he could pass on his intel.

It had been almost two weeks since he had been out of contact, and he now knew enough that could help. As had been suspected by the various intelligence agencies, the refugee crisis would be used as cover to infiltrate perhaps thousands of terrorists into the Western democracies. From the bits and pieces he was able to glean—his Arabic perfect, unbeknownst to the others—the vast majority of those infiltrating in this wave would be left as sleepers for future attacks.

But not his cell.

His cell had been assigned an immediate attack using what he could only assume was the Russian Cesium-137.

And that had to be stopped.

Yet right now he had absolutely no way of warning his country unless he could get away from his "brothers", at least for a few minutes. And that would only be of use if he could get his hands on a phone.

He elbowed a guard in the side of the head, sending him to the ground, then shoved another out of his way as he sprinted past the line, joining the hundreds who had already done so, pushing deeper into Turkish territory. He continued to race forward, past those in less shape, until he was about a mile inside the country, far enough that if caught, he'd be redirected to a refugee camp rather than the border.

Someone slapped him on the back and he spun around to see Nazari, his new cell commander, Kanaan having stayed behind, he apparently too valuable to risk on this mission.

I guess the leaders don't sacrifice themselves for their 72 virgins. Just the minions.

He had a brief flash of a bright yellow minion in a suicide vest.

Give it time. Hamas will have that on their kid's TV shows before long.

He could never understand the blind hatred by some of Israel for defending itself against an ocean of people that wanted it wiped from the face of the Earth. Over four times more money per capita had poured into the Palestinian territories than had been given to Germany during the Marshall plan.

And look at Germany now.

What was the difference between them and the Palestinians?

Perhaps it might have been that the beaten Germans, when allowed to vote again, wouldn't have promptly elected a Nazi government. Perhaps it was that the beaten Germans wouldn't have allowed remnants of the Nazi regime to continually attack its neighbors then cry foul when those neighbors retaliated.

The fear of many in the intelligence community was that it wouldn't matter too much longer. With the sanctions being lifted against Iran, and over one hundred billion dollars about to flood its coffers, the proxy war with Israel would heat up quickly, and once Iran successfully acquired the bomb, it could smuggle one into downtown Tel Aviv and solve the problem itself.

Triggering Israel to drop its estimated two hundred nukes on Iran and anyone else that had pissed it off, since it would be its last act.

If the Twelvers running Iran wanted their Armageddon, this might be the very real way of attaining it.

Kane regarded Nazari, his eyes filled with just a bit of craziness that those enjoying an adrenaline rush, and who were just a bit touched, displayed.

This is someone who would definitely strap on the vest.

"We made it!"

Kane nodded, searching about to see if any of the others had. Judging from the tepid response of the troops, he suspected they would all get across unless someone did something stupid like try to take a gun.

But Nazari had been explicit in his instructions, and from what Kane had seen, everyone within sight had followed them.

Someone shouted to their right and Kane turned to see several of their cell waving as they walked toward them, and within minutes they had all gathered.

"Where now?" asked one.

"We make for the coast. A boat has already been arranged to take us to Greece."

Kane started to walk with the others, Nazari leading the way. If there was one part of this journey that might be dangerous, it would be the boat ride across the Aegean.

Thousands had drowned already.

And thousands more would die before the crisis was over.

And he didn't want to become part of the statistic.

At least not before he delivered his intel.

Kilis Refugee Camp, Turkey

"I'll give you two hundred American dollars for your daughters."

Amira stared at the man, horrified, unable to believe she had heard the man correctly. "What? What did you say?"

"I said I'll give you two hundred dollars for your daughters." He scrutinized little Rima. "Okay, two-fifty, but I can go no higher."

Amira put her arms around her daughters, holding them tight against her side. "There's no amount of money you can offer me for my children. Who would ever sell their own flesh and blood?"

"You'd be surprised," said the man, stepping closer, Amira backing away. He reached for Maya but Amira swatted the man's hand.

"Don't you dare touch them!"

He glared at her, then smiled, his rotting teeth a testament to his character. "You should take the money. Eventually someone will come in the night and simply take them from you, then you'll get nothing."

"You stay away from us!" she cried, picking up both of her girls and rushing back toward Jodee's family who were holding their position in a registration line while she had sought a bathroom for Rima.

"But Mommy, I have to pee!"

"Just hold it a little longer, honey."

She spotted Jodee who waved. She rushed up to them, feeling slightly safer with Sami there. "We have to get out of here!"

"Why?" asked Jodee.

"Someone just tried to buy my children!"

Sami's eyes narrowed. "Really?" He shook his head. "I took a stroll a few minutes ago and talked to some of the other men. Apparently children are getting kidnapped in the night. All girls."

"What are they doing with them?"

"Selling them into the slave market. Sex slaves. A young, healthy girl fetches thousands of dollars on the black market. The younger the better. They groom them into whatever they want."

"That's disgusting!" cried Jodee.

Her husband nodded in agreement. "Unfortunately, it's reality." He lowered his voice. "But that's not all."

"What?" asked Amira, terrified to think what could be worse than her daughters sold off to a life of rape and torture.

"There's a rumor going around that they're going to send us all back to Syria. Anyone who registers here today is going to be sent back."

A pit formed in her stomach. "But where will they send us?"

"Probably into government controlled territory."

"We'll be thrown in prison if they find out where we're from!"

Sami nodded. "The regime basically treats anyone from the eastern half of the country as enemies of the party." He looked at his wife. "We can't stay here, we need to get out of this camp and head for the coast."

His wife's eyes narrowed. "Why the coast? Won't we be trapped there?"

He shook his head. "No, we'll take a boat across to Greece. We'll be safe once we get there."

Jodee turned to Amira. "What do you think?"

Amira wasn't sure. They were genuine refugees, and her understanding was that a refugee was supposed to declare their status at the first safe haven, and this appeared to be safe—at least from the ravages of war, if not from slave traders. "Who is spreading these rumors? Can they be trusted?"

Sami shrugged. "I don't know, and you're right, I'm not sure I believe it anyway." He tilted his head at the children. "But staying here puts them at risk, as you've already seen. I think we need to take our chances elsewhere."

"But how do we get out? How can we afford to get across on a boat?"

Sami leaned closer to her, lowering his voice to barely a whisper. "I have money. I was a dentist before this and have been planning our escape for some time."

"But what about us? We have no money."

"You're with us now. Allah will provide."

Tears welled in Amira's eyes as she hugged him then his wife. "You are such good people. I thank Allah at every chance for bringing us together."

"Allahu Akbar," smiled Sami, putting an arm around his wife's shoulders.

Amira smiled, wiping her eyes, happy to hear those two sacred words said calmly for once, rather than in a psychotic fervor.

"Allahu Akbar."

Northern Greece

It was almost too easy.

Comically easy.

It was Greece's revenge on the rest of Europe for the horrendous conditions imposed on them for bailout money. Kane could almost hear the politicians in Athens laughing at the situation. The humanitarian crisis was dire, of that there was no doubt, and Greece was in no position financially to deal with it.

Yet instead of imposing a naval blockade, which they could, they continued to rescue the refugees and allow them to flood their territory by the thousands each day.

And each day they put them on trains and buses and sent them north to the borders of Bulgaria and Macedonia.

At first these governments, wanting to look good to the masters in Berlin and the other capitals of Europe, agreed to take the refugees in, under the promise they would receive monetary support as they processed them and sent them on their way to the Mecca for most of these people.

Germany.

The great Germany, twice the oppressor of Europe, was now the orchestrator of its ultimate doom with their Chancellor's promise to take in almost one million refugees this year alone. It wasn't until the reality of this had begun to settle in that the other governments in Europe reacted with outrage, blaming Germany for creating the crisis. The vast majority of these refugees were not refugees at all, but merely economic migrants, something Kane himself could attest to. He had heard dozens of different dialects of Arabic since he had joined the masses moving north, most of which were not Syrian or Iraqi. He had even heard Farsi far too often for it to be a chance encounter.

There were clearly hundreds if not many thousands of Iranians among these refugees.

He thought of the Germans, still blaming themselves for what happened over seventy years ago, their leaders willing to destroy the culture they had created after the war, all for the sake of looking like great humanitarians in the face of the greatest crisis Europe had faced since the Second World War.

Though what many didn't realize was Germany had an extremely generous refugee policy, a policy that allowed refugees to bring their families in to join them.

So one million refugees actually meant as many as seven million by some estimates.

And that was just based upon those expected to arrive by Christmas.

The train he and much of his group, including Nazari, were riding on was jam packed, far beyond the safety limits he was sure. It almost reminded him of the Tokyo subway during rush hour, poor families terrified the wall of flesh pressed together might smother their children.

Yet there were acts of kindness he had witnessed all along the way. These weren't all bad people, far from it. In fact, whether they were refugees or not, he'd feel confident in saying 99% of them were kindhearted people who tried to be good human beings, helping others when they could, especially the women and children.

But he had also seen the ugly side, including young Muslim men refusing to take bags of food because there was a Red Cross symbol on them.

Where did they think they were going? If they felt that strongly about their hatred for anything Christian, why were they desperately trying to get to the heartland of Christendom?

Europe was heading for a crisis, and how it would come out of it in the end, he had no idea, only that a continent that had enjoyed relative peace for seventy years was most likely going to lose its innocence once again. If millions of Muslims arrived, all demanding the services foolishly promised, then family reunification, then reasonable accommodation based upon their distinct belief systems, he feared civil war and strife that could see the Nazi regime's solutions to such problems return.

How do you deport thirty or forty million people, many of whom were born in your country?

"This is it," said Nazari, slapping him on the shoulder as the train came to a halt, snapping him out of his reverie. He flowed off the train with the others, getting off much calmer than getting on. "Cameras!" hissed Nazari, turning his head quickly to the left. Kane did the same, desperate to look at the news crews and get his face on their footage, but surrounded by those of his cell, he couldn't risk being seen ignoring Nazari's warning.

A wise warning, for Langley and every intelligence agency in the Western world would be analyzing every piece of footage they could get their hands on to try and identify any known terrorists, their computers mapping facial recognition points for everyone. And even if they didn't identify someone, it would be stored, and in the future if they were caught doing something untoward, their face would be run, they'd be identified, then everyone they were travelling with traced as well.

But only if their faces were captured.

He stole a quick glance over his shoulder.

"Turn your head!" hissed Nazari and Kane's head swiveled back, a wide-eyed expression on his face that would have done his high school drama teacher proud.

"Sorry, I don't know what made me do that."

Nazari grabbed him by his sleeve and pulled him forward. "You Americans are always so eager to get on camera."

Kane chuckled, trying to break the tension, the man already clearly not trusting him. "It's one of the many reasons their society must fall."

Nazari slapped him on the back, smiling slightly. "If you don't keep screwing up, Allah willing, it will be so."

Kane nodded. "Allahu Akbar."

Aegean Sea between Turkey and Greece

"We're going to sink!"

Amira held onto her daughters as tightly as she could with one arm, the other arm hooked around the railing encircling the waterlogged boat, the driving rain and wind making it impossible to see ahead, the screams of terror surrounding her nearly drowned out by the howl of the storm. Both Maya and Rima had their arms wrapped around her legs, their whimpers going unheard, their heaving chests torturing her with each sudden inhalation.

But they were alive.

For now.

Crossing Turkey and getting a boat had been relatively easy, though only because of Sami's money. The man had been true to his word, using his precious stash of foreign currency, mostly Euros, British Pounds and American Dollars, to get them all out of the refugee camp—a modest bribe to a guard—then transport to the coast—a not so modest bribe—then passage on a boat.

Where the only one available was the rickety affair they were now on due to his funds having to cover seven people instead of just four.

She had felt overridden by guilt when they had heard the price for safe passage on a boat they all felt they could trust to get them there. He had enough for his family, and Sami had looked at her and she had stared at him, dread filling her eyes as she silently pleaded for him to find another way, not to abandon her and her children after having come so far.

"There's seven of us. We need something cheaper."

Another man had been called over, the café they had met their prospective boat captain at seemingly teeming with profit mongers, and a deal struck.

She squeezed her eyes shut as she realized that if they should all die here today, it would be her fault.

Sami was just ahead of her, he holding one child and the railing, his wife the other. They weren't going to fall overboard, though the waves kept sweeping over them. The concern now shouted by the captain at the helm was that they were overloaded and going to sink.

"She's Christian!" shouted someone to her right. Her head spun toward the man who was now pointing at a woman, huddled at her husband's feet, praying, a crucifix in her hand, a look of horror on her face at having been discovered.

"Throw her overboard!" yelled someone else. "Why should we die so infidels can be saved!"

"Throw the dirty Christian off!"

Amira stared up at the Captain, hoping he'd do something to stop this, but instead he simply turned his back on the entire proceeding. She watched in horror as several young men approached, slipping and sliding on the deck, risking their own lives as they seemed determined to take others'.

The woman's husband swung his free hand at the first man, making contact, his would be attacker falling onto the slick deck, sliding back as the prow rose steeply, dumping everyone off their feet who didn't have a good hold of something.

Yet it didn't stop them. More converged on the man and he was quickly overpowered, his screams, his pleas, barely heard above the angry, desperate shouts of the others.

And then they stopped, his flailing body tossed overboard, his wife's scream tearing across the deck, then silenced, as she too joined her husband in the roiling sea. Amira looked back to try and spot them, and for a moment thought she saw a hand, though couldn't be certain.

To her horror the young men weren't done, joined by more as they made their way around the boat, there only about thirty souls aboard, challenging each to recite passages from the Koran, any who hesitated attacked and tossed overboard. She again stared up at the Captain who seemed careful to avoid looking at what was going on, and she felt sick to her stomach as the men who had taken charge approached Sami and his family.

She had to admit she felt bad for those dying, though a small part of her was relieved that someone had taken action. Was it right that they should all die, or did it make sense to sacrifice some so that the others could live? And how should it be decided who should live and who should die? Should it be men? Women? The elderly? How was that any less discriminatory than choosing by religion?

Her mouth suddenly filled with bile and she pushed her head over the side of the railing, heaving several times, her children crying out, gripping her legs tighter. She thanked Allah that she was Muslim, that she was one of the followers of the Prophet's teachings, and she would be spared the culling.

And prayed for those misguided souls sacrificed to save her and her children.

Already she could sense the boat was faring better, the Captain seeming less agitated, but still not stopping the murders happening around him. She stared up at him, pleading silently for him to look her way, and he did.

And they made eye contact.

"That's enough!" he shouted, the young men who had taken control stopping just as they approached her, Sami having passed the test. "We should be fine now."

They continued for several more hours, land finally spotted, bypassing the safer Greek islands and heading for the mainland. The Captain pulled into shallow waters, smaller boats rushing out to meet them and take them ashore, their own deathtrap roaring away the moment the last foot left its deck.

As her feet hit land for the first time in hours, she dropped to her knees and began to pray, thanking Allah for sparing their lives and for the sacrifices the kafirs had made, praying their souls would be allowed entry into paradise even if they weren't worthy in some people's eyes.

Jodee patted her shoulder. "Come, we need to get moving."

She nodded and rose, taking her children by the hands when several vehicles with flashing blue lights arrived on a road just ahead, soldiers or police pouring out. Several people screamed, others shouted, the young men sprinting away, she and her travelling companions instead simply standing there, exhausted, soaked, and hungry, resigned to whatever fate had in store for them.

It turned out it was a ride to a refugee-processing center.

Processing took hours, their photos taken, their names and other relevant information recorded before they were finally pointed toward a tent-filled camp.

"What now?" she asked the woman who had processed them, a woman who spoke passable Arabic.

"Now you wait."

"For how long?"

The woman shrugged. "However long it takes." She pointed toward a road leading away from the camp, a long line of people slowly walking down it, away from the area. "If I were you, I'd follow them and get to Germany. Those fools are taking everyone."

"But how? That would take months."

The woman shook her head. "There's trains and buses. You might be waiting a while though, since it seems almost everyone arriving are young men and they're not exactly letting the women and children on first."

Amira glanced around and noticed the same thing she had noticed in Turkey.

A sea of young, well-built men.

She shivered.

Though whether it was from her still soaked clothes or a sense of foreboding, she couldn't say.

"If we stay here?"

The woman shrugged again. "Can't say. But we don't want you." She pointed toward the camp. "Move along."

Amira nodded, spotting Sami and his family waiting for her.

"What do you think?" she asked, nodding toward the camp.

"I was told we should try to get to Germany." Sami pointed toward the long column of people heading away from the camp. "That's where they're going."

Amira looked back at the lines of people being processed, knowing that if they delayed too long, those people could very well be ahead of them, waiting for the same trains to Germany. She turned back to the others. "I was told the same thing."

Jodee eyed the guards who were doing nothing to force anyone into the camps. "Do you get the sense that they want us to leave? To go to Germany?"

Amira nodded. "Mine told me as much."

Sami picked up one of his children. "I don't want to stay where I'm not welcome. Let's get moving."

Amira took her children by the hand and followed, merging into the crowd heading inland, not sure if they were making the right decision.

Food, water, shelter and clean clothes all were available on the other side of the fence.

She feared they might all regret the path they had just chosen.

Miratovac, Serbia

Kane allowed himself to be shoved aboard the bus, he pressed so tightly against the man in front of him he could feel the guy's ass pulse. It was a good thing he wasn't a homophobe or he might be a little uncomfortable right now. He looked behind him, at the surging mass of flesh outside, there thousands desperately clamoring to get aboard the limited number of buses that were waiting to take them across Serbia and into Hungary.

Why doesn't someone organize this?

His stomach churned with guilt at having made it aboard, there women and children outside, unable to compete with the young men who were willing to stop at nothing to get aboard. The Greeks, Macedonians and Serbs had made it crystal clear to everyone that the Germans were taking everyone, and offering generous refugee benefits including food, shelter, health care and an income. It would sound almost ridiculous if he didn't know it was true, and these desperate people, fleeing war and economic strife, were willing to believe anything.

What had become abundantly clear was that nobody wanted these people. The Turks didn't want them, the Greeks didn't, and the Macedonians and Serbians certainly didn't. It was obvious that the poorer countries of Europe were desperate to shift the mass of humanity to the richer north, with Germany being the hub of the insanity.

He watched as the guards stood by, letting the young men flood the buses, and realized why they were allowing this to happen.

Families weren't threats.

Young men were, and the sooner they moved along on their journey, the sooner they were someone else's problem. Some families were brought to the front of the lines before the buses arrived, and he spotted one of those families now, sitting huddled together, a woman and her two children, another family of four behind her.

All terrified.

All relieved to have a seat.

He smiled at the woman then winked at the two little girls. The woman smiled shyly back at him, her two daughters burying their heads in her lap before their mother suddenly went pale, fear washing over her face as she quickly turned away.

He glanced back to see if anyone was looking at her but saw nothing.

I wonder what that was about.

Amira had lost track of how many days she had been travelling. Her body was aching all over, she was hungry, thirsty, filthy, and terrified of an uncertain future.

I wish Adnan was here!

Things would be so much better if he were. Her husband would be the one doing all the worrying, and she'd be able to just take care of the children. If he were still alive, he'd be able to fight the young men for food and water, some of the fools throwing it back at the aid workers all because of a Red Cross symbol.

It was ridiculous.

It was scary.

Who are these people that would turn down food?

Only fundamentalists would, and if fundamentalists surrounded them, she wondered how Germany would react when they arrived.

She watched as more young men boarded the bus, pressing their way to the back, she thankful at least to have a seat, the aid workers at least prioritizing some of the families before the buses had arrived. She glanced up as a young man approached, his smile almost infectious, he giving a quick wink to her daughters.

He looks European!

She returned the smile, slightly, it frowned upon to interact with strange men, quickly breaking eye contact and staring past him. Her heart slammed into her ribcage, a lump forming in her throat as her stomach flipped with fright, the man who had ordered her husband burned alive standing not five feet from her. She quickly turned her head, lifting the scarf that covered her head up, over her mouth and nose, debating whether she should get off the bus and risk having him see her.

She began to stand then the bus jerked forward, knocking her back into her seat, those aboard cheering. She glanced up and saw the man standing right behind the friendly man, his expression emotionless, there no happiness there.

Only evil.

She turned away, not sure of what to do. She couldn't tell anybody without drawing attention to herself, and even if she were willing to risk it, there was nobody she could tell. There appeared to be a bus driver and two guards at the front, and that was it. She had no way of reaching them, and no reason to believe any of them spoke Arabic or English.

Yet she had to tell someone.

Didn't she?

After all, if the murderer of her husband was here, then how many more members of ISIL were there?

Horgos, Serbian-Hungarian Border

Kane spotted the camera crew to the right as he stepped off the bus. He immediately raised his hand, blocking his face, then dropped it, glancing over at the reporters for just a split second before turning away.

"Cameras!" he hissed, Nazari immediately turning his head away, Kane successfully avoiding any suspicion since he had been the first to give the warning. He just hoped that his actions would appear suspicious enough to anyone back home reviewing the footage to flag him for special attention.

If someone there were to analyze his face, an alert would be triggered and Langley notified, they the only ones who would know his true identity. At least then they'd know he was alive and where he had been at a specific date and time.

And then knowing them, they'd try to intercept him, possibly with a brush pass where he could exchange some intel.

"Something's going on!"

He turned toward where Nazari was pointing, the Hungarian border only a few hundred feet away, their bus already having left. Hundreds of riot police were rushing toward the border, creating a human barrier as several large trucks roared up.

Kane squinted as he tried to make sense of what he was seeing.

Shit!

It was a massive spool of chain link. He looked and could see posts extending as far as the eye could see to the left and right, the Hungarians obviously having been busy preparing to fence off their border. It wouldn't stop the refugees, that was for certain, though it could definitely slow them down.

"If we're going to cross, then we've got to do it now!" said Nazari to the others of their cell who had clustered together. He pushed himself up off the ground, using the shoulders of two of his men. "They're trying to keep us out! We must run! Now, before it's too late!"

He dropped down as the shouts were repeated, the message quickly spreading through the crowd, the panicked surge toward the border only taking seconds to begin. It was a true stampede in every sense of the word, a mass of flesh, chaotic, only concerned for itself.

And mostly young men.

Women and children cried out in terror but there was nothing he could do, he himself caught up in the surge, forced to move with it or face being trampled himself. He glanced to his left and spotted the woman from earlier, her anguished face as she tried to stumble along with her two children, heartbreaking.

Then one of them fell from her arms.

He shoved through the crowd, perpendicular to the flow, tossing a few elbows to get through, finally reaching the woman, now bent over, trying to pick up her youngest daughter. Kane yanked her to her feet then picked up the screaming child, tossing her over his shoulder. He took the woman by the hand and pushed forward, with the flow. His grip on the woman was like iron as those around them tried to break the link in their own desperate attempt to reach the border before it was too late.

He heard several distinctive pops and cursed.

Teargas!

He spotted Nazari just ahead, along with several of the others, the line of riot police still holding firm against the crowd now slamming against their shields. The teargas began to burn his eyes but there was nothing he could do about that now.

They cleared the unfinished fence.

He pointed to the left, down the fence line, away from the cordon of police officers and toward some thick woods on the Hungarian side.

"That way! Understand?"

She nodded as he handed her daughter back. "Thank you. Thank you so much."

Kane smiled, the woman's English near perfect. He pointed again. "Go, quickly, and don't stop. Get into the woods then go farther inland."

She nodded, her eyes wide but grateful, another family rushing up beside them, the man eyeing him with suspicion before they all headed for the trees.

Kane watched for a moment as they cleared the length of the police line, dozens of others figuring out the same weakness, the woods soon flooding with fleeing refugees. Kane continued forward, quickly spotting Nazari and the others as they broke through the line, realizing it was strong when you pushed on it, but rather weak when you pulled.

The line broke, the police falling back to regroup, yet it was too late. Kane raced forward, tossing an elbow at one officer who tried to stop him, then was through.

Still with no way to contact home.

Outside Roszke, Hungary

Amira's muscles screamed in protest as she carried both of her girls into the woods, having cleared the line of police trying to stop them. She didn't know who the kind stranger was, yet he had saved their lives, she was sure of it. She glanced over her shoulder but he was nowhere in sight, it odd that he didn't go in this direction as well.

The woods were thick, dark, damp, and quickly filled with the wails of desperate souls as her daughters whimpered, their eyes burning from the teargas, as were hers. Jodee's family was just ahead of her, her husband pushing through the undergrowth before they came upon a clearing, a small farmhouse and barn greeting them. An old man was working on his tractor, the hood opened as he tinkered. He turned back to see them rushing toward the farmhouse, Sami quickly turning away from him.

The man stepped down from the tractor, his hands pressed on his hips, appearing displeased to say the least.

Then Rima cried out in pain.

And the man's stern face broke.

He walked toward them, waving for them to come, pointing at the barn. Sami hesitated, looking at his wife then Amira.

"We need help, we need to wash this stuff out of the girls' eyes," said Amira.

"But can we trust him?"

"Can we afford not to?"

Sami nodded and they ran toward the man as others began to emerge from the woods, all taking a beeline away from the farm. The man held open the door, urging them inside, closing it behind him. He said something none of them understood, probably in Hungarian. He motioned for them to come in deeper and he grabbed a glass bottle of milk, probably extremely fresh, considering he had several dairy cows mooing only feet away.

He said something, pointing at his eyes then at the bottle.

Sami shook his head, pulling his daughters back.

"English?" asked the man.

Amira smiled, her head bobbing rapidly. "Yes, I speak English."

"The milk will take away the pain. Just pour it in their eyes."

Amira nodded, remembering she had heard the same thing somewhere, and immediately had her daughters lie down, on their sides. The man began to pour the milk on their eyes, Rima first, she protesting vigorously until it began to take effect.

"It works!" she cried, Maya immediately shuffling toward her, wanting her turn, the other children dropping to the ground and rolling on their sides. The farmer treated them all within minutes then left, leaving Amira immediately to begin to fear where he had gone. Was he calling the authorities? Was he going to turn them in?

The barn door opened again and he returned with a pitcher of milk, a loaf of bread with butter, and some cheese. They attacked the food as the farmer sat on a milking stool.

"You can't stay here."

She looked at him and nodded. "We know. Where should we go?"

"Germany. They're taking everyone." He pointed to the far side of the barn. "Go in that direction, opposite where you came from. You'll reach a road. Turn left and follow that. There's a refugee collection point there with buses and trains. Once you reach there, they won't send you back.

He rose, their meal finished, and opened the rear door of the barn. "Now go, and good luck."

She smiled at him, bowing slightly. "Thank you, sir."

He waved his hand. "No need. It's the Christian thing to do."

She stepped outside and into the fading light, a pit in her stomach as she thought back on how Christians had helped her along the way. Here, today, by providing them brief sanctuary, and before, on the sea, when they had been sacrificed to save the rest.

Are we truly so much better than them?

Sopron, Hungarian-Austrian Border

The rumor among the tens of thousands gathered at the Austrian border was that the Hungarians had had enough. They were erecting a fence along their entire southern border, and building a corridor through the country to funnel everyone north.

The generosity the press and politicians of Western Europe espoused was spent, the population beginning to fight back against the influx.

Kane waved his American passport over his head, one of the Austrian border guards spotting him and waving him through. He was directed to a small building where those using the border legitimately were being screened, the refugees processed by the UN and other agencies, the gates of Western Europe finally reached.

And Germany only one hop away.

There would be no escaping getting processed this time, so Nazari had ordered him to use his passport to get through in case they were somehow stopped. At least one member of the cell would get through to carry out their plans.

He was certain Nazari didn't trust him, though at this point he didn't have much choice. And as soon as Kane could acquire a cellphone, he'd be able to make contact and warn Langley of the hundreds if not thousands of infiltrators among the sea of misery migrating northward.

Yet that might be easier said than done.

"American?" asked the guard sitting behind the desk. He studied Kane up and down, motioning for him to sit. "You look like hell!"

Kane smiled weakly. "You have no idea what I've been through. There are no buses or trains, at least not packed with these people"—he jerked a thumb over his shoulder—"and my rental was stolen by some of them two days ago. I've had to walk ever since."

The guard slammed a stamp down on the passport, handing it back. "You're lucky they didn't find out you're American. They might have killed you."

Kane nodded, rising. "Any idea where I can rent a car?"

The man shook his head. "I'm afraid you're going to have to walk." He pointed to the road. "Only a few kilometers. Should be nothing after what you've been through."

Kane waved his passport at the man. "Thanks."

The man turned away, calling the next person up as Kane exited the building, his passport already tucked away. He stared up at the brilliant blue sky, breathing in the crisp fresh air of Austria.

And frowned.

The stench of misery filled his nostrils and he glanced to his right at the thousands shuffling along. He looked about for any communications source, but saw nothing, this outpost intentionally chosen for its remoteness, it seemed. It would appear the Austrians, like everyone else along this journey, wanted as little interaction as possible between the refugees and their populace.

He turned to his right and noticed that the new arrivals were being split, some taken toward what appeared to be a refugee camp, the rest, the majority, sent up the very road he had been directed to.

"The camp is only accepting families!" announced someone over a PA in Arabic. "Keep moving north. There will be a train to take you to the next camp. You will be processed there."

The announcement repeated itself and Kane shrugged, heading up the road, an Austrian police officer waving him into the crowd. He didn't dare show his American passport to gain privileged access to the opposite side of the road, it most likely gaining him no such advantage, and possibly getting him killed.

A hand slapped him on his back and he turned to see Nazari walking behind him, several of the others nearby.

"Well, that was easier than we were expecting."

Kane nodded. "Apparently. What now?" he asked, still not giving Nazari any indication he spoke Arabic.

"There's a train. We'll take that to the next camp then try to get through to Germany."

Kane nodded, falling in behind Nazari who set a brisk pace at the outer edge of the crowd, his fundamentalist zeal fueling him forward.

Leaving Kane to curse, his chance at contacting Langley lost.

Sopron, Hungarian-Austrian Border

Amira sat frozen, unable to tear her eyes away from the hand that gripped the seat in front of her. A tear rolled down her cheek then shame washed through her as she felt her bladder let loose, a steady stream of urine flowing down her legs, soaking her abaya and pooling on the floor.

"Mommy! You—"

Rima's cry snapped her back to reality as she quickly slapped a hand over her young daughter's mouth, silencing her. She pushed her daughters to the side of the bench seat and thanked Allah that the entire train reeked of much worse than what she had just done.

A woman sitting across from her elbowed her husband and pointed, both glaring at her. She turned her head, the shame of being caught overwhelming.

But it hadn't been a bladder held too long that had caused this.

It had been fear.

Pure, unadulterated, fear.

For the horribly scarred hand that gripped the seat in front of her, she was certain was the same hand that had directed the tires to be fit over her husband, who had soaked her beloved in gasoline, and who had tossed the match that had set him ablaze.

A man whose face she had never seen.

Yet who had seen hers.

"Mommy, why?"

"Please, Mommy had an accident," she hissed, trying to silence Maya now. "Just keep quiet and look out the window."

"Take this."

Her head spun, terror in her eyes, a young man handing her a bundled up scarf. He motioned toward the puddle on the floor and she took it, smiling shyly. "Th-thank you," she whispered, her voice breaking as she tried to keep her face out of view of the man who was standing with his back to them.

"Throw it out the window when you are done," said the man who then turned his back to her, blocking the view of those across from her.

They may be young, but they're good boys.

This one reminded her of one of her students. In fact, they all did, especially after the restoration of the Caliphate, women not allowed to go to school. She had been allowed to continue teaching, it felt English would help the Islamic warriors in their battle with the infidel.

It had kept them fed.

She bent over and first used the scarf to clean herself under her robes as best she could, though it was a mostly futile effort. Dropping it on the floor, she used her foot to move it around, sopping up most of the thick yellow fluid, it clear she was dehydrated.

"Open the window for Mommy."

Maya complied, stepping back as Amira reached down and lifted the dripping cloth, shoving it out the window. Somebody yelped farther down the train, apparently sprayed with some of the waste.

Her daughters giggled.

She hugged them both, glancing back at the young man and nodding her thanks with a smile. He said nothing, returning the acknowledgement, then continued speaking to some other men standing with him.

She returned her focus to the hand, still only inches away from her, daring a glance up the arm, to the neck, then the side of the man's face, though from a poor angle, not even able to see his nose.

He turned.

She dropped her head fast, lifting up her scarf to cover her mouth and nose, turning in her seat and facing the window, gathering her daughters close as she felt her bladder release again, though this time, thankfully, there was nothing left.

The train jerked slightly and she sensed it begin to slow. Maya reached up and wiped the tears from her mother's cheeks, tears she hadn't noticed.

She smiled and kissed Maya's forehead. "What would Mommy do without you?" Maya beamed and Rima jealously wiggled her way between the two of them. Amira hugged them both, hard, as the train came to a stop. She let those standing leave first, the hand gripping the chair in front of her gone when she dared to look.

Someone touched her shoulder.

She flinched.

"Oh, dear, I'm sorry I startled you."

She looked up at Jodee who immediately appeared concerned.

"What's wrong? You look terrified!"

Amira quickly shook her head, saying nothing, instead getting up and urging her girls into the aisle. Sami led the way and they were soon off the train and across another border, a red and white flag flapping overhead, a flag she didn't recognize, though they were supposed to be heading to Austria, and she knew her globe well enough to know Germany was next.

Things seemed more organized here, less frantic, perhaps because everyone knew they were close to their destination of Germany where they would finally find sanctuary. It also seemed better organized, there hundreds of people in bright yellow vests guiding the new arrivals, the families being singled out and brought into what appeared to be a tidy tent-city, the young men that had been her concern all along, redirected down a roadway.

The two families stood in the same line and eventually one of those in the bright vest reached them with two others in tow. The woman held up a piece of paper with various languages displaying what she assumed was the same message since the Arabic and English matched.

Please point at your language.

Sami pointed at the Arabic. Amira decided to try something different, perhaps her skills giving her an advantage over most of the others gathered here. She pointed at English.

The woman's eyebrows popped. "English? Really?"

Amira nodded. "Arabic is my first language, of course, but I taught English."

The woman's head bounced in appreciation of her skills, turning back to the others, one handing her a clipboard with some forms attached to it, and a pencil. She passed it to Sami who took it, quickly beginning to fill out the papers. She reached back for another clipboard and handed it to Amira.

"Fill this out then take it to that line over there," she said, pointing at a very short line.

"What about my friends?" she asked, placing a hand on Jodee's shoulder.

"They'll be okay, but they should stay in this line. Once you're processed, you'll see them again inside."

"We'd like to stay together." She motioned toward the tents. "In the same tent, if possible."

The woman eyed her then pursed her lips, as if deciding whether the extra effort was worth her time. She nodded slightly. "You'll be through first and be handed a tent assignment. Wait near the head of this line, and when your friends arrive, tell the processor the tent number you're in, and we'll see what we can do."

She smiled at the woman who quickly moved on, then translated for the others.

"I'll see you soon, okay?"

Jodee smiled, her husband grunting as he continued with the paperwork. Amira took the girls and headed for the shorter line, then began filling out the paperwork, it not the first time she had done so, though each country seemed to have their own set of questions.

It was finally her turn and she handed over her paper to the man sitting behind a table. He quickly read through it, typing the information into a computer. "So you were a school teacher?"

"Yes. English."

"That's good, that's going to help you. Not so much in Germany, but Canada, the UK and the United States are taking some refugees, and might show a preference for people who can speak the language."

"Anywhere my children are safe." She thought about his words. *Some. Might.* It all sounded so uncertain. "But what about Germany? Shouldn't I try to get my family there, in case Canada or America say no? I thought they were taking at least a million people."

The man nodded, hitting a button, apparently done entering the information into the computer. "Something like that, but they're starting to wake up to the fact that that promise was idiocy."

She stared at him, puzzled. "But why wouldn't everyone want to help? Look at these people. Look at us! We're innocent victims here, just trying to find someplace safe to live."

The man looked up at her from his chair, apparently unimpressed. "Would you want a million Christians moving into your neighborhood?"

Her cheeks flushed and she cast her eyes down, ashamed at the realization he was right. She wouldn't like it, not one bit. Not necessarily because she didn't like Christians, but more because their ways were so different from hers. They prayed differently, on different days, at different times. Their laws and beliefs and symbols were different, their holidays simply incompatible, and it seemed, wherever they went, there was always conflict.

He was right.

And she could see the Germans perhaps feeling the same way.

"Wh-what should I do?"

He leaned forward. "Look, you're here, you're safe. Wait for us to find you a host country. We'll do a security clearance on you and your children." She stared at him, her eyes slightly wide. "Don't worry, I'm sure you've got nothing to worry about, it's the young men we're more interested in, they're the ones more likely to be terrorists, not women and children like yourself."

The mention of the word sent her pulse racing, her head swiveling to see if anyone was looking her way who shouldn't be. These people were concerned with security, concerned with keeping terrorists out.

And these people controlled her future.

She lowered her voice, leaning over the table.

"What if I told you I know of at least two members of ISIL that were travelling with me?"

Traiskirchen Refugee Camp, Austria

Alexis took a long swig of her ice-cold bottle of water. She had just finished an eight-hour shift processing refugees and was dead tired. It was an emotionally and physically draining experience, though one she wouldn't trade for the world. She had initially wanted to go to Turkey and help there, but her father had essentially forbidden it.

For many daughters that would have been enough to make sure it absolutely happened, but her father had the power to actually stop her.

Austria had been the compromise.

And the need here was still great.

A two-month leave of absence was arranged at her job and she had boarded a plane from JFK two weeks ago, arriving in Austria, then the camp, within a day. Training and acclimatization followed, and she had to admit, it was a culture shock. There were a good number of English speakers here, though it was her knowledge of Arabic and Farsi that had got her the job, languages her father had encouraged her to learn when she had discovered she had a knack for it and had asked him which ones to spend time on.

"Chinese, because they'll probably rule the world one day, Russian, because we'll probably be at war with them one day, Arabic, because knowing a few lines from the Koran might save you one day, and Farsi, because they'll probably kill us all one day."

She had laughed until she realized he was serious. "I was thinking more French or Spanish."

Her father had dismissed the suggestions with a flick of his wrist. "They're no threat."

"Has anyone else noticed how many young men have been crossing here?"

She returned her attention to the conversation, a group of volunteers sitting around one of the many picnic tables set apart from the refugees, a man named Jeff dominating the discourse.

"Yeah, I ran a quick report. It's over seventy percent," said another named Tomas. "That's insane."

"No wonder they're so concerned back home about terrorists infiltrating. Too many of these guys look like they should be on the cover of Men's Health."

"And under all those robes, I can't tell if any of the women should be on the cover of Maxim!"

The men laughed, Alexis rolling her eyes at one of the other women.

Yet they were right to be concerned. Her father had warned her that there were almost definitely going to be terrorists in the group, and to report anything she found suspicious to her superiors.

"This isn't a joke. You know my job. You know what I do for a living. I can't tell you specifics, but be careful, even in Austria. If you see something, don't try to stop it, just report it. These people will do anything to reach their goal, including killing a nosy American."

"So I shouldn't drop your name?"

He had appeared horrified at the thought. "Definitely not!"

"Don't worry, Dad, I'm not an idiot."

He had grunted, leaving her to think he might just think she was.

Jeff continued. "Did you read that news report that ISIL has claimed they're sending over half a million fighters with the refugees? Can you imagine what would happen even if they just sent a thousand?"

"It would be mayhem," muttered the joker, Tomas.

"Do you think they'll catch them?" asked one of the women.

Jeff laughed. "Don't you mean *we*? We're the ones on the frontlines here. We process the paperwork, assume they're telling us the truth, then pass it on for the CIA or whoever to check out. They might catch some, but this kneejerk reaction around the world is causing things to move too quickly. There's a process and it's being ignored or streamlined too much."

"Yeah, just bring them in then worry about the consequences later." Tomas took a drink. "This entire situation is ridiculous. Troy anyone? Just today some woman was swearing up and down that two men who killed her husband were among the refugees travelling with her."

Jeff's head bobbed in furious agreement. "That's the problem, they'll say anything if they think it will get them further along."

Alexis put her bottle down. "Why didn't you believe her?"

Tomas looked at her. "Because I hear the same bullshit day in and day out. Someone is always trying to bribe me with cash, sex or intel. You can't trust desperate people." He leaned forward. "Listen, I don't blame them, I'd be doing exactly the same thing they are—"

"I don't think the sex thing would work for you!" laughed Jeff.

"Hey, it might work on you. I've seen you staring at my dick in the shower."

Jeff flushed, Tomas saving him from a sputtered, nonsensical retort questioning his sexuality, instead returned his attention to Alexis. "Like I was saying, I would do the same thing, but I would also expect the people I was conning not to trust me."

"So you don't believe her?" asked Alexis.

"Not for a second."

"Was her husband with her?"

"No, according to her he's dead, remember?"

Alexis smiled. "I know that. But don't you think that suggests he actually *is* dead?"

Tomas shrugged. "Could be, or he went on ahead, or he sent her on ahead."

Alexis tilted her head slightly. "I don't know. These cultures are pretty tight as a family unit, not like us. I'm not sure if they'd split up like that. We're not discriminating against families without fathers, we're discriminating against men without families."

Tomas shrugged again. "Or the husband went on ahead, knowing Germany's refugee policy allows for family reunification. She never heard from him, got desperate, and left on her own with the kids."

Alexis had to agree it was a definite possibility, and perhaps the wife was afraid to say her husband was already in Germany, thinking it might put her in a different queue that could delay her escape.

Yet her father had said to report anything suspicious.

And he was the National Clandestine Service Chief for the CIA.

So he knew his stuff.

More than these testosterone laden fools who were treating this entire situation as a chance to get laid, it apparently rutting season at the volunteer camp.

"I'd like to talk to her if possible."

"You're welcome to, but I processed several hundred people today. I have no clue who she is."

"But she's in the computer?"

"Yup."

"What's your last name, I'll look her up."

"Schmidt. And yours?"

"Morrison."

Hotel Palazzio, Munich, Germany

There was a knock at the door, a coded two-one-two, Nazari rising to answer it then embracing the two men who entered. Kane continued to let them think he didn't understand Arabic, and merely rose to shake their hands, no one seeming to trust him.

Once they had arrived at the Austrian-German border it had been easy to get into Germany, contacts across the border picking them up and delivering them to Munich. A steady stream from their cell continued to arrive, there apparently hotel rooms around the city filled with fighters ready for the next phase.

Nazari sat down next to him, a broad smile on his face. "This is good," he said in English.

Kane nodded. "How many do you think will get through?"

"Enough. Allah willing, more than enough." He pointed at the room. "Look, almost everyone from our cell has made it through." He looked at Kane. "Allah is clearly on our side."

Kane's head bobbed in agreement. "It would appear so. When will we be told the plan?"

Nazari stared at him, his eyes narrowed slightly. "You will know when you need to know. And when it is executed, America and Europe will crumble from the chaos we will bring." He turned to the group, speaking in Arabic. "Tomorrow we leave for Frankfurt. I want everyone showered, groomed, well rested, and fed. We are no longer refugees." He pointed to a pile of clothing delivered by their contact. "Fresh clothes." The men attacked the pile as Nazari rose. "I think *I'll* shower first."

He left Kane to "wonder" what was going on, not bothering to translate, and the men to take their pick of the clothes, Kane thankful that soon the stench that filled the cramped room would be lessened as weeks of sweat, grime, shit, spit and every other lovely excretion caked on their bodies would be washed away.

Somebody is going to have to burn these clothes.

He closed his eyes.

And fumigate the room.

Traiskirchen Refugee Camp, Austria

Alexis Morrison read the number on the side of the tent then tapped her foot on the piece of wood at the entranceway, meant to give them something dry to step on should the ground turn into a mud pit as it had in some places.

"I'm looking for Amira Shadid."

A woman's head poked out, her face etched with fear, the wide eyes and pink cheeks suggesting to Alexis' untrained eye the woman was certainly scared of something, but then, everyone here was probably terrified of being sent back.

"Are you Amira Shadid?"

The woman nodded, stepping out of the tent, two little girls, on their hands and knees, sticking their heads out. Alexis smiled at them and gave them a little wave. "Hello!" They disappeared instantly. She looked at Amira. "My name is Alexis Morrison, I'm one of the volunteers here. You told one of my colleagues something that I would like to talk to you further about."

Amira went ghost white. "Not here," she hissed.

Alexis was prepared for this. "Oh, if you want to talk about the special nutritional requirements your daughter has, we can do that in private. Follow me."

The woman's eyes flared for a second then narrowed, a slight smile of relief pulling at the corners of her mouth as she clearly understood the ruse. She poked her head in the tent and told someone inside that she'd be gone a few minutes and to please watch the children. They walked in silence for several minutes before reaching the cordoned off section separating the refugees from the no-go area of the volunteers. This small area allowed them to interact with the refugees in private, away from prying eyes and ears.

Alexis stepped inside the tent, several lamps on, it already late evening, and motioned for Amira to sit in one of the chairs, she taking the other. She put her tablet computer on the table in front of her along with a notepad and pen.

"You know why we're here?"

Amira nodded, hesitantly. "About my husband. About who killed him."

"Yes. Please, tell me everything."

The story laid out before her was heartbreaking, terrifying, inspiring. It was the story of a courageous woman who had taken charge and saved her children after suffering an unimaginable loss and untold horrors and trials along the way. It was the story of not only the physical dangers of the journey, but the mental anguish of being forced to relive the horrors of that fateful night that had changed her life forever as she realized the very men that had committed the foul deed were among those she was traveling with.

And she believed every word of it. From the kind white man to the murder of the Christians.

Every word.

Yet her belief meant nothing.

She needed proof.

She needed something verifiable.

"Would you recognize them?"

Amira nodded. "One of them, yes. The other, only his hand."

There's thousands. Tens of thousands. Millions!

Flipping through unfiltered pictures of the refugees would be a complete waste of time, and that was assuming these men had even been processed. If they were indeed terrorists, they most likely would have tried to avoid it.

So a face couldn't verify her story.

She smiled, realizing what she needed.

"When did your husband die? You said it was during an air raid?"

Amira nodded and gave her a date. An exact date.

Alexis' eyes narrowed. "Do you even know what day it is today?"

Amira shook her head.

"Then how do you know what date your husband died?"

"I may not know what day it is today, but I will never forget the day my husband died."

Alexis nodded, the woman's words ringing true.

How could anyone forget?

She quickly wrote her contact info on the pad and tore off the sheet, handing it to Amira.

"Whatever you do, don't leave the camp without contacting me first, understood?"

The woman nodded, her hands shaking as she reached for the paper. "I-I won't."

Alexis led her back into the camp, directing her toward her tent, before returning to the segregated area.

Now to talk to Dad.

Morrison Residence, River Oaks Drive, McLean, Virginia

Leif Morrison took a sip of his scotch, his eyebrows popping in surprise. Kane had somehow bypassed all of his security and left the bottle, with a card, on the antique mahogany desk in his den months ago as a thank you for his assistance with the Chinese national, Lee Fang.

And tonight he had decided he would open it in his honor, his agent missing now for weeks and, he feared, very much dead.

Fantastic!

He picked up the bottle, reading the label.

Glen Breton Ice.

Nova Scotia?

"Huh."

His wife Cheryl looked over at him, resting her Kindle on her lap. "What is it dear? Something wrong?"

He shook his head, returning the bottle to the end table. "No, but Scotland better start to worry."

"Excuse me?"

"Scotch talk, dear."

"Tuning out." She glanced at the television, CNN on low, a report on the crisis in Europe playing. "What do you think of this?"

He glanced at the screen, savoring another sip. He swallowed. "You don't want to know."

"That bad?"

"Potentially." He sighed. "The news isn't getting vetted properly. Look at what happened in Canada. A politician blamed the government for the death of that little Syrian boy. Turns out it was all lies. The family had never made a refugee claim yet the press ran with it including the New York Times. Now the truth is starting to come out, and the more reports that come across my desk, the more I realize my cynical nature is probably guiding me in the right direction on this one." He motioned toward the screen, the ice in his glass clinking. "Like this guy getting off the bus. Why is he hiding his face from the cameras. Something like that makes no sense to me."

"Maybe you should check him out?"

Morrison chuckled. "Believe me, dear, every single scrap of footage we can get our hands on is being analyzed. That guy will be singled out." He took another sip. "And now the press is finally starting to report on some of the things that have come across my desk, like refugees rioting, some carrying ISIL flags, an Austrian woman being dragged out of her car and assaulted, food being turned down because it was from a Christian group. Christ, hon, you'd have to be a fool to let this go unchecked."

The phone rang, cutting off his rant.

Cheryl read the call display. "It's Alexis!" She grabbed the phone from its charging station and answered. "Hello, honey, how are you? Is everything okay?"

A few moments of quick pleasantries were exchanged before a look of disappointment crossed his wife's face. "She wants to talk to you."

His eyes narrowed. "Is it my birthday?"

"Ha ha. Enjoy it while you can."

He took the phone, giving his wife a wink. "Hiya, kiddo, want to talk to the old man, huh?"

"Hey Dad, can you find out if there was an airstrike at a specific date and time in a specific location?"

Morrison put his drink down.

"You've got my attention."

CIA Headquarters, Langley, Virginia

"The meatloaf isn't bad today."

Leroux glanced at Sherrie White's plate. "Looks like just the right amount of burn on it."

Sherrie nodded, stabbing the block of ground meat with her fork. "That's the key. A little crispy on the outside, moist and juicy on the inside." She stuck another bite in her mouth and chewed. "Or I'm just craving good ole American food."

"How's the training going?"

"If someone had told me that I'd need to learn how to identify and *enjoy* pretty much every food and drink from around the world, I might have thought twice about taking the job. Do you know that I ate actual scorpions today?"

Leroux covered his mouth, his stomach churning. "How about we skip the dirty talk."

Sherrie beamed a smile at him, reaching over and patting his hand. "You okay, dear?"

He smiled at her, taking a drink of water. "I'll live. I'm just glad this mac and cheese is fairly bland."

Sherrie pushed the salt and pepper shakers toward him. "I'm always telling you that you need to add seasoning."

Leroux eyed the shakers. "I always thought it was an insult to the chef to do that."

Sherrie laughed. "Yeah, Chef Ramsey will bite your head off and teach you a few new swearwords, but here, I think you're safe."

"Uh huh." He shook on some salt.

"Don't forget the pepper."

He gave her a look. Then shook some on. He shoved his fork into the mass and swirled it around a bit then took a bite, nodding in appreciation.

"See, told you."

"Right as usual."

"Never forget it." Sherrie leaned back, patting her impossibly flat stomach. "I'm stuffed."

"Already?"

"Hey, I've been eating all day. This was just a palette cleanser."

"What are you eating tomorrow?"

"The delicacies of Mother Russia."

"Ahh, borscht and vodka."

Sherrie smiled. "What the hell is borscht anyway?"

"Something pickled, I think. I think they pickle everything over there."

"Including their livers."

Leroux snorted in mid chew, grabbing for his napkin. He swallowed. "In America, you eat food. In Soviet Russia, food eats you?"

"Oh, don't get me started on the Soviet Russia jokes. Yakov Smirnoff is like required viewing." She checked her watch. "Do you want me to wait up for you?" She leaned forward. "Maybe I can 'welcome' you home?"

Leroux flushed, nearly dropping his fork as he felt a shoeless foot run up his leg. He looked around, the crowd light at this time of night, but the fine dining table cloths that might hide her game of footsies were nowhere to be found at this CIA cafeteria.

He cleared his throat, reaching down and blocking her foot.

She appeared hurt.

"You're going to get us in trouble," he hissed.

She bit her finger. "But it'd be worth it."

"It would be, but then we'd both be unemployed, I wouldn't be allowed to violate people's privacy, and you wouldn't be allowed to kill them for what I found. And what fun would that be?"

Her foot dropped as she laughed, leaning back in her chair and crossing her arms. "Okay, you're right, life would be boring." She tapped her watch. "So, am I waiting up for you?"

He shook his head. "No, I don't know when I'm coming home. We're processing so much footage trying to identify possible terrorists, everyone is working overtime."

"How's it looking?"

"Let's just say, disturbing. We're getting dozens of hits. There's no doubt there's infiltrators."

"And what's being done about it?"

Leroux swallowed another bite of his mac and cheese then wiped the corners of his mouth. "We pass it up the chain and I assume it gets shared with the Five Eyes but I don't know. It might explain why those countries have been reluctant to admit the refugees too quickly, and with the agreements signed between the intelligence agencies, they can't release that data so their public is in the dark."

"Might help wake up some people if they knew the truth."

"True, but it would also tip off the terrorists that we know they're coming. I can only hope someone is trying to round them up, quietly."

His phone danced across the table and he read the message, sighing. "Chief wants me."

Sherrie pushed her almost untouched meal back a few inches. "I guess you better go then."

He rose and leaned over, giving her a kiss. "Love you."

"Love you too," she replied, smacking his ass as he turned to bus their trays.

One of his junior staff members, Randy Child, grinned at him and Leroux flushed.

Why oh why did it have to be him that saw that?

Traiskirchen Refugee Camp, Austria

Alexis awoke with a start, bolting upright in her cot as she tried to figure out what woke her. Her boob vibrated. She reached in and grabbed the phone, it a trick she had read somewhere—where she couldn't remember—to keep your phone safe from being stolen in shared accommodations, and to wake you if you were expecting an important call.

It definitely worked.

She eagerly swiped the display, the caller ID indicating it was her father.

"Hi Dad, just a second." She slipped on a robe and some flip-flops then quickly exited the sleeping quarters. "Okay, I can talk. Did you find out anything?"

"I'm fine, thank you."

She smiled. "Sorry. How are you?" she asked with an exaggerated cheerfulness.

Her father laughed, it a sound she missed terribly since being stuck here. The living conditions were miserable, though tolerable compared to what the refugees were living with, but sacrificing the comforts of home was tough, especially for someone who had grown up quite well off. They weren't rich, though they weren't hurting by any means, her father's various jobs paying quite well over the years, as had her mother's.

"I'm okay, and you?"

She surveyed the camp, the morning sun just making its presence known on the horizon. "Almost ready to tackle a new day."

"Sorry for calling you so early, but I'm in meetings all day tomorrow so I figured I'd pass this on right away."

She glanced at her phone. "Isn't it almost midnight there?"

"You know me, I never go to bed early."

"Uh huh. What did you find?"

"You didn't hear this from me, but yes, there was an airstrike at the location you provided. It wasn't us, it was the Russians, which is the only reason I'm telling you this because we only classify our own missions."

Alexis sighed, relieved. "So she's telling the truth."

"Don't be so hasty. Never take what a desperate person says at face value. She *could* be telling the truth, but she could also be lying. But I'll tell you this, if there's any chance she *is* telling the truth, we need to find these men. They're hardcore. We're going to need specifics on where and when she saw them and what they look like. You up for the job?"

A flush of pride swept through her, goosebumps raising every hair on her body as she realized her father was asking for her help. It was as if with that one, simple question, he had shown her he was proud of her, that he had confidence in her.

That he finally thought of her as an adult.

"Absolutely."

Operations Center 3, CIA Headquarters, Langley, Virginia

Chris Leroux pinched the bridge of his nose, his tired eyes closed, the Sandman still doing a number under his eyelids. He hadn't left until three last night, and then he had been paged to return only hours later, there a priority tasking Director Morrison wanted his team to handle.

"Any luck?"

Leroux flinched in his chair, uncertain of whether he had fallen asleep, the sound of his boss standing directly behind him shocking him wide-awake, his desperate desire for a Red Bull a fading memory, it no longer needed.

"S-sorry, sir. Umm, I really hope I wasn't asleep."

Morrison laughed, taking a spare chair beside him. "Never admit to your boss that you might have been sleeping. Just say you were thinking about something work related."

Leroux smiled sheepishly. "Yeah, that would probably have been smarter."

Morrison winked. "That's why you're here and not in the field."

Leroux grunted. "I think there's a few more reasons." He nodded toward the photos flipping by on several monitors spanning the front of the operations center. "We've found a few hits around the timeframes your daughter reported and we're pulling hundreds of faces, but the witness isn't sure of her dates and times, so it's proving to be a larger dataset than we'd like—we haven't even found *her* yet. And that doesn't mean we haven't seen her. If she wasn't looking in the direction of a camera, or her face was covered, we've got nothing to work with. We're sending everything over in real-time to Austria but there haven't been any hits reported back yet." He sighed. "It's like looking for a needle in a haystack."

"Found her!"

Morrison smiled at Leroux. "I guess your team was just waiting for me to arrive."

Leroux flushed, still not used to having a boss who joked around. They both rose and walked over to Marc Therrien's station. "What have you got?" asked Morrison.

Therrien pointed at the main screen, video footage of a woman boarding a bus with two children playing, facial recognition points mapped and compared to the digital photo taken by Morrison's daughter earlier. "It's a match. We now have a date and time to work with."

"Excellent work," said Leroux. "Send this to Austria, let's see if our witness can spot any of the men she reported seeing."

Traiskirchen Refugee Camp, Austria

I look horrible!

Tears flooded Amira's eyes as she watched the footage of her and her children boarding the bus. It was the first time she had actually seen herself, mirrors nowhere to be found along her journey, and it was heart wrenching. She had always taken great efforts to make herself appear kempt, well groomed—generally respectable. And she never would have allowed her children, even after a day of play, to look the way they did.

They looked unworthy of taking part in civil society.

The footage zoomed in on her face and she gasped. "I-I've aged ten years!"

Her husband wouldn't recognize the woman that she now stared at. Her skin was dry and weathered, her lips cracked with deep lines around her eyes, a tuft of her hair that had escaped her chador appearing dry and split.

She turned away, it too much.

"You've been through a lot," said the woman helping her. "There's no shame to be had here."

Amira nodded, glancing briefly at the beautiful woman, her hair and makeup impeccable, her clothes clean and pressed. She glanced down at her own ratty clothes and frowned. She had finally been able to bathe, one of the most joyous experiences since the death of her husband, and she had washed her clothes, but she still was a disgrace.

Yet the woman was right.

It wasn't her fault.

It was the terrorists they were now trying to identify who were to blame.

For all of this.

She looked back at the screen. "Please, continue."

The woman clicked the computer and another image appeared, a man's face highlighted. Amira shook her head and another image appeared, then another, and another. Her mind began to drift as face after face flashed past, her eyes glazing over when her heart thumped and she quickly inhaled.

The woman stopped.

"Do you recognize him?"

Amira's conscious mind quickly caught up, her eyes focusing on the face.

Fear gripped her as she realized the moment she confirmed his identity, she would have officially cooperated with the enemy.

And her life would be forfeit should they find out.

She nodded. "That's him. That's the man who killed my husband."

The woman leaned closer, staring at her. "Are you sure?"

Amira turned, meeting her stare. "Would you ever forget?"

InterCityHotel, Frankfurt, Germany

A knock at the door silenced the room, everyone turning as Nazari peered through the peephole then waved them off, opening the door. A man stepped inside, the door closed, hugs exchanged.

Everyone rose, including Kane. Almost his entire cell had made it, including several he had only heard of and never met.

It was disturbing.

They had done nothing special, had no help from anyone beyond the prearranged boat from Turkey, any additional help not provided until they had made it to Germany, which begged the question: how many other cells had also arrived with such ease?

He silently prayed his cell had received special treatment in Turkey due to their specific mission, but arranging a boat was easy with money, and ISIL was extremely well financed. It wouldn't be outside the realm of possibility that the rhetoric preached to them by Nazari of thousands sent may actually be fact. He didn't for a moment believe the half million number he had heard bandied about, it a ridiculous notion, but hundreds? Absolutely. Thousands? Possible if not probable.

And this new arrival was holding up a bag as if he were Santa Claus, perhaps the worst possible comparison his mind could have come up with.

"I come bearing gifts, my friends!"

Or not.

He opened the cloth bag, reached inside then pulled out his hand with a flourish. "New passports and IDs for everyone!"

Nazari quickly ended a round of cheers and Allahu Akbars.

"Silence you fools! Do you want people to know we are here?"

Sheepish looks were exchanged, Kane disappointed that Nazari continued to prove his intelligence. Though the Germans were fools on the refugee front, they were not when it came to terrorism, and would take seriously any report of a bunch of Middle Eastern men shouting Allahu Akbar in a hotel room only miles from the busiest airport in the country.

He had yet to have a moment to himself though had managed to get his face on a few cameras, especially since they had arrived in Germany, there so many traffic cameras, ATM cameras and such, that surely some had picked him up.

He just hoped Langley was looking for him.

Protocol would suggest he had already been designated MIA, but until they had some sort of proof, a star wouldn't be going up on the wall at Headquarters, and people like his buddy Chris would keep searching.

I wonder if Fang is worrying about me.

The thought of her filled his stomach with butterflies as he watched the passports being handed out, and his reaction to the memory of her was so strange for him, he realized that for once in his life he actually had genuine feelings for a woman.

It felt kind of good.

The new arrival stared at him. "I don't have one for him."

Kane pretended not to understand.

"He's American. He already has a passport." Nazari turned to him, switching to English. "Show him your passport."

Kane nodded, producing the artificially aged document produced by Langley. "All set," he said, smiling.

The man nodded, eying him with suspicion.

Christ, does no one here trust me?

The passports handed out, the man reached into his bag, pulling out a sheaf of papers. "Boarding passes!"

One person yelled out Allahu before cutting himself off, several snickers escaping from the others.

"When do we leave?" asked one of the men.

The man held up the passes, waving them in the air. "Tomorrow you arrive in New York City, Allah willing."

Smiles and murmured exclamations of excitement spread through the room.

Nazari smiled. "And then Armageddon begins."

Operations Center 3, CIA Headquarters, Langley, Virginia

"Okay. Map that, let's see if we know him."

Therrien nodded, quickly plotting the facial recognition points and sending the image through their database, Leroux returning to his station to notify Morrison.

"Got him."

Leroux felt his chest tighten. If they had a hit that fast, then this was a serious character. "Put it on the screen." Therrien hit a few keys as Leroux sent a message to Morrison about the positive hit.

"Syrian national named Tarek Nazari. According to information we have from several hacked Syrian databases, he was born April 7th, 1979. Educated in England. Huh, Oxford."

Leroux's eyebrows popped. "Family?"

"His father was a senior member of the regime's cabinet but fell out of favor when the troubles began."

"Status?"

"Officially, unknown. Unofficially, it's suspected he was executed."

Child spun in his chair. "That's enough reason for someone to go loco on their daddy's former boss."

Leroux nodded. "What do we have on his recent activities?"

Therrien quickly scanned the file, his eyes widening as he did. He blocked the text and sent it to the screen. "He's been linked to half a dozen executions of Western hostages and at least a dozen beheadings. This guy is hardcore. They like to use him I think because he speaks perfect English."

Leroux shook his head. "Lovely."

Morrison entered the operations center, immediately staring at the screen. "Is that him?"

Leroux rose. "Yes, sir. Tarek Nazari. This guy's a piece of work, dozens of executions linked to him. Educated in England, speaks perfect English, father was part of the regime in Syria but is thought to have been executed."

Morrison frowned. "And where is he now?"

"That photo was taken in Serbia almost two weeks ago. We assume he's on his way to Germany then possibly here, but we can't be certain."

Morrison pointed at the screen. "Let's identify everyone he was travelling with and try to trace his route. That bus stopped somewhere, let's see if we can catch him getting off."

"Yes, sir."

"Umm, sir, is that who I think it is?"

Both Leroux and Morrison turned toward Therrien, who nodded toward the screen. Leroux looked to see an isolated video clip of a man getting off a bus, his face covered then his hand removed, his face revealed for a moment before he turned away.

Leroux's heart skipped a beat.

"Isolate the face, freeze it on the best angle," he said, his voice barely a whisper as he stepped down, closer to the screens, Morrison at his side. Therrien advanced through the video, a frame at a time, before Leroux snapped his fingers. "There!" He grinned at Morrison. "He's alive!"

There was no doubt it was Kane, weathered and dirty, yet absolutely recognizable. Leroux couldn't stop smiling, resisting the urge to jump up and down, the elation he felt demanding a release.

"What are we looking at?" asked a more serious Morrison.

"I estimated the time it would take the bus to reach its destination then pulled the images from that time and found this. This is later the same day at the Serbian-Hungarian border."

Leroux glanced back at Therrien, the smile beginning to hurt his cheeks. "Good work." His brain caught up with what was said. "Wait a minute, he was on the same bus as the woman?"

Therrien nodded, then pointed. "And look who he's with."

The photo of Kane zoomed out, showing the crowd exiting the bus, Therrien isolating another man, his face hidden, but whose clothing matched exactly those of Tarek Nazari as he boarded the bus earlier.

"Christ," muttered Leroux. Kane had clearly infiltrated one of the terrorist cells, and the fact they hadn't heard from him meant he had no comms capability. They needed to reach him somehow.

He dropped in the nearest chair, Morrison on the phone, his words drowned out in the fog of relief. Kane was pretty much his only friend, a man who had taken him under his wing in high school and protected him from the bullies while Leroux tutored him. They had become good friends in high school though lost touch when Kane had left for college. Their chance encounter at Langley years later had rekindled the friendship. Kane had been his friend, his protector, and had also forced he and Sherrie back together after a budding romance had broken apart for reasons he had long ago forgiven Sherrie for, they not her fault.

If it weren't for Dylan Kane, his life would be a shadow of what it was today.

"—an extraction team in theater immediately."

Leroux tuned back into Morrison's conversation.

"Okay, keep me posted."

Morrison replaced the phone in its cradle and turned to Leroux. "You okay?"

Leroux nodded. "Is it wise to extract him?"

Morrison shook his head. "Hard to say. He's clearly successfully infiltrated one of the cells, and he clearly has no way to communicate with us or he would have by now. We need to know what he knows, otherwise any intel he's gathered is useless."

Leroux nodded, his mind racing as he tried to think of a way to get the intel without blowing Kane's cover and putting his life at risk.

He smiled.

"I've got an idea, but it requires people he can trust. And finding out where he is now."

Embassy of the United States, Ankara, Turkey

"You know what I miss the sound of?"

Dawson looked over at Niner. "What?"

"Church bells. I can't remember the last time I heard them."

Atlas' voice rumbled across the room, it small yet comfortable, provided to them while they waited for transportation to the Akinci Air Base then back home. "What made you think of that?"

Niner nodded toward the window. "The calls for prayers over those loudspeakers. You hear it all the time. But I can't remember the last time I heard church bells. I think I used to hear them as a kid, then again, maybe I'm remembering it from movies or TV."

Spock cocked an eyebrow. "With the amount of TV you watch, I think most of your childhood is probably false memories."

Niner whipped a coaster at him, Spock easily catching it without moving anything but his arm, placing it on the table beside him. "Throw something bigger next time, little man."

Atlas chuckled. "He'd need some muscle for that."

Niner gave him a look. "Hey, I may not be a human Michelin man like you, but I'm wiry."

"Uh huh. Maybe they should have put a lean Asian at the end of Ghostbusters then."

Niner smacked his forehead. "Dude, you and I have to sit down for an Essentials Eighties Movie Marathon. That was the Stay Puft Marshmallow Man, not the Michelin man."

Atlas shrugged. "Huh. What do you know, I don't care."

Niner's head lolled toward Dawson. "Can we leave him behind next time?"

"I might leave one of you behind."

"Hey, I can't believe you'd even consider blaming me for his ignorance of pop culture. I'm Korean, from a starving family, and I know everything about American culture."

Everyone groaned, Atlas shaking his head. "You're as American as I am, born in Florida, with relatives living in a nice, modern country like South Korea. And the next time I hear you bring that up, I'm going to plant you like a damned human vegetable in the dirt then piss on you to see if you grow."

"I could use a few extra inches." Niner held up a finger, cutting off Atlas' retort. "Hey, no locker room talk!"

Atlas chuckled, Spock snickering, Dawson watching the door as someone rapped twice then opened it. A Marine corporal stepped inside. "Sir, call for you." He pointed to the phone. "You can take it there, line three."

Dawson nodded, the room becoming silent as their mission to review Embassy security was complete, this call unexpected since almost no one knew they were there. He picked up the phone as the door closed. "This is White."

"Good morning, Sergeant Major. Busy?"

Dawson smiled as he recognized Colonel Thomas Clancy's voice. Clancy was the commander of Delta and one of the few senior officers he actually completely trusted, Clancy having proven on more than one occasion he believed firmly in the 'no man left behind' doctrine that soldiers relied upon in the field. Sometimes Washington brass were too quick to abandon the principle for Special Forces teams when their political taskmasters felt they were about to be embarrassed, but Clancy never did.

He was a soldier's soldier, and his men would fight and die for him if he asked them to.

"Not busy, sir, just waiting for our ride home."

"Well, sorry to change your plans on you, but you're needed in Germany."

"They visiting the French again?"

Clancy chuckled. "No, but a friend of ours might need extraction."

Hotel InterContinental, Frankfurt, Germany

Cindy Robinson held her brush tight, leaning closer to the mirror as she sang Taylor Swift's Shake it Off at the top of her lungs, perfectly mimicking the dance moves from the music video. It was her favorite song of the moment, and she loved it, regardless of whether her father thought almost all music made today was shit and in twenty years forgotten, whereas the Beatles, Rolling Stones and Kiss would be remembered forever.

Whatever!

She hit a high note perfectly—in her mind—wondering if she should try out for American Idol.

Wasn't it cancelled or something?

She shrugged, tossing her brush on the counter and grabbing her towel, drying herself off as her phone rang. She read the call display.

Argh!

It was her mother. She debated letting it go to voicemail, but the woman would simply keep calling her back.

She swiped her thumb, putting the call on speaker.

"Hi Mom!"

"Hi sweetie, how are you?"

"Kind of busy, getting ready for my flight."

"Where are you?"

"I already told you. Frankfurt."

"And you're going to be home in time for your birthday?"

"Yes, Mawm."

"Well make sure you're not late. It's a big one, your twenty-first! Oh God, it seems like only yesterday we were bringing you home from the hospital. You were four weeks premature and we were so scared. But look how you turned out."

Cindy flashed herself in the mirror, grinning.

Yeah, look at it!

There was a knock at her door, saving her from the same story she had heard twenty-one times before. "Gotta go, Mom, breakfast is here."

"Okay dear, have a safe flight."

She ended the call and headed for the door, humming her song, a few lyrics escaping aloud. She checked her towel, making sure she wouldn't give the room service guy a thrill he couldn't handle, and opened the door.

A hand reached forward, something gripped in it. She gasped at a clicking sound under her chin, an odd smell filling her nostrils as something pressed into her chest with excruciating pain. She shuddered to the ground, every muscle in her body tensing as a young woman stepped inside, kicking the door closed behind her, then pressing a foul smelling rag against her mouth.

"I'm sorry about this," said the woman.

And it was strange.

She actually believed her.

Frankfurt am Main International Airport, Frankfurt, Germany

Amira examined herself in the large mirror that occupied much of one wall of the small room she and her children were waiting in, the young woman who had helped them along, Alexis Morrison, sitting with them. The transformation was remarkable, and she finally felt human again. They were all dressed in new, clean clothes, they all had been able to shower and groom themselves properly, they all had full bellies, and her children were smiling for the first time since their father died.

She might be about to escape the chaos, but it was clear to her the American woman was scared. It had apparently been decided that she and her family should go to America for safety reasons, and refugee status had already been granted. After watching the news almost every waking moment in the hotel room they had spent the night in, she was happy to escape what appeared to be a looming crisis in Europe, elements of the population beginning to fight back against the influx of her people. Fences were going up, populations were protesting, some governments blaming Germany. If they hadn't left when they did, they might never have escaped. There was a genuine fear that terrorists might be mixed in with the new arrivals, yet to her, it seemed the reaction was more anti-Muslim than anything else.

When her journey had begun, she might not have understood that reaction. But now that she was here, now that there definitely were terrorists in the mix, and now that she had seen firsthand what could happen to the infidels at the hands of her own people, she completely understood the reaction.

Hopefully America will be better.

She stared at herself in the mirror, her traditional abaya flowing over her body, her chador covering her hair and framing her plain, unadorned face, then stole a quick glance at Alexis with her modern Western dress, stylish hair and makeup. The contrast was striking.

Will we fit in there?

She couldn't see how. She didn't want to change who she was, she didn't want to compromise her commitment to her religion. She loved being a Muslim, genuinely did believe it was the one true religion destined to be worshipped by all mankind. She didn't agree with the violence often associated with it, though she did believe in the goal, and with America being the greatest opponent to the cause, she wasn't sure if she could ever call it home.

"Do we have to stay?"

Alexis looked up from her cellphone. "Excuse me?"

"Do we have to stay in America?"

Alexis' eyes widened, clearly surprised. "Umm, I suppose not. Do you mean you don't want to go now?"

Amira shook her head. "No, we definitely need to go now. But I mean, can we leave later, if peace returns to my homeland?"

Alexis smiled, though Amira had the distinct impression the woman couldn't understand why anyone would want to return to Syria. "Of course you can. We're doing this for *your* safety. You're not being forced to go." She paused, leaning forward. "You don't feel like you're being forced, do you?"

Amira sighed, gazing down at her hands. "Not by you, no."

But she *was* being forced. Forced by those who would destroy her country, then forced by those same people seemingly following her along the way, and now due to her breaking her silence, people trying to help keep her safe by sweeping her off to the other side of the world, her home so far, it might as well be on another planet.

There was a knock on the door then it opened, a man stepping inside. "We're ready."

Alexis rose. "Time to get on the airplane."

Amira gathered up the coloring books and crayons occupying her children, then walked out of the room, holding her children's hands as they were led through a corridor lined with offices before exiting through a thick door, a wall of sound hitting her the moment it opened.

They stepped out into the terminal, to her right the security screeners she had cleared hours before, to her left thousands of people rushing in all directions, guards with machine guns strolling by as if nothing were out of the ordinary.

Something was barked in what she assumed was German and she jumped, stepping out of the way of several guards marching a man toward the door she had just left.

She gasped when she saw who it was.

The friendly white man who had smiled at her on the bus and saved their lives.

Today there was no smile at all.

Frankfurt am Main International Airport, Frankfurt, Germany

Kane had to admit he was impressed. The logistics of the operation were substantial, and expertly executed. Anyone who dismissed ISIL as only a regional threat were sadly mistaken. Everyone in his cell had been provided with passports, boarding passes to various planes, background information on their new identities, worn luggage, worn clothing and scuffed up toiletries. It was clear that this was well planned, well organized and under development for some time.

He just wondered how many times the scene in his hotel room last night had been repeated.

In his group, he was the only one travelling as himself, or so they thought. He was using his CIA issued passport and he had just used it to check in, which should mean someone at Langley would be taking notice about now. Hopefully that would mean some sort of contact in New York when he landed.

The others were travelling on new passports from various European countries not requiring a visa to travel to the US. Unless somehow flagged, he fully expected them to get through, and unless he could get a message to his handlers quickly, there'd be no finding them once they left JFK.

Something had to be done, but again, he was never alone, Nazari only half a dozen spots behind him in line.

"Sir, will you come with us, please?"

Kane looked up at a guard holding his passport. "Huh?" He glanced past the guard to see two imposing officers behind him, submachine guns at the ready. "Why?"

"You've been randomly selected for a full search."

"Are you kidding me? I'm American. Besides, I've got a flight to catch, I don't have time for this."

"You won't miss your flight if you cooperate. Please come with me."

"But—"

"Sir, you will be placed under arrest if you do not come now."

Kane sighed, dropping his head slightly, his shoulders slumping. He stole a quick glance toward Nazari who was trying not to react, but Kane had spent enough time with the man to recognize the look of concern in his eyes.

"Fine!" he said, stepping away from the tray containing his personal items—all provided last night—raising his hands to his shoulders. "But I still say this is ridiculous. How can I possibly fit any profile?"

"This way."

Kane followed the man, the two armed guards walking slightly behind him, many of those in the immediate vicinity staring at him. The lead guard ordered a group out of the way of the door they were heading toward. Kane looked at them, a Muslim woman with her two children, a shocked look on her face as she stared at him. She seemed familiar and he had to think for a moment before he recognized her.

The woman from the bus and the Hungarian border!

He gave no indication he recognized her, not wanting to cause her any trouble, instead simply keeping the pissed off expression on his face, knowing that the moment he cleared this door, he could get word to Langley.

If anyone would listen to him.

The door closed behind him and he glanced back to make sure Nazari hadn't somehow managed to follow him.

Clear.

"I need access to a phone immediately. I'm a—"

"In here." The man held out a hand, directing him into a room to the right.

"Listen, my name is—"

"Now."

A guard shoved him from behind and he stumbled into the room, the door closing behind him.

"Well, well, well, look what the cat dragged in."

Dylan smiled as Dawson and Niner rose from behind the room's lone table. He stepped forward and gave Dawson a hug, then Niner. "You have no idea how good it is to see you guys."

"Likewise," said Dawson as they all took seats. "Langley thought you might be dead."

"We knew you weren't."

Kane looked at Niner. "I appreciate that."

Niner bowed slightly then waved his hands. "Don't get me wrong, it's not because we thought you were too good to get yourself killed, just that we weren't that lucky."

Kane chuckled. "I love you too, Niner."

Niner kissed the air. "Back at you, big boy."

Kane slumped in his chair, relaxing for the first time in weeks. "You have no idea how nice it is to hear an American voice that isn't some nutbar convert hell bent on destroying the country that gave him the freedom to worship the religion of his choice."

Dawson jerked a thumb at Niner. "He's a nutbar but he's harmless."

Kane chuckled at Niner's pout. "How did you find me?"

"You were spotted on some footage and tracked to Germany, then someone bought a plane ticket in your cover's name yesterday so we were able to arrange this little meeting." Dawson leaned forward, becoming all business. "What can you tell us?"

"I successfully infiltrated the cell I was tasked with. Eight of us were sent here and at least six arrived successfully and are leaving for the US today."

"How many do you think we're dealing with?" asked Dawson as he scribbled notes.

"According to what I've been able to gather, hundreds if not thousands have been sent, and if all but two of my cell made it to the rendezvous, then…" Kane shrugged. "I hate to guess, but it's going to be a Charlie-Foxtrot, that's for sure." He jabbed the table in the direction of Dawson's notepad. "Here's the problem. These guys are experts at misinformation. I have no way of knowing if it was just our cell that was sent, or if it was actually hundreds or thousands. All I can say is this. Other than a pre-arranged boat waiting for us in Turkey, we received no help until we got to Germany." He looked from Niner to Dawson, leaning back in his chair. "It was just too damned easy."

Niner frowned. "Which means it could have been just as easy for any number of others."

"Exactly."

Dawson tapped the pad with his pen. "Do you want out?"

Kane shook his head. "No way. We're supposed to be picked up when we land then taken somewhere. I'm hoping from there I can get a handle on what's going on, perhaps be able to track down the other cells." He leaned forward. "Look, this goes way beyond just a terrorist attack. The chatter from the others is that we're to deliver a major blow using some sort of weapon that I can only assume is the missing Cesium we've been looking for. I'm staying in until we recover that."

"Good, I would have called you a pussy if you wanted out," said Niner, straight-faced.

"They're always looking for new recruits if you want to join me."

"Naw, I'm too pretty to be a terrorist."

"You do have girlish good looks."

Niner's jaw dropped and his hand pressed against his chest. "Just because I'm dainty doesn't mean I'm feminine."

Dawson pushed a small case toward Kane. "Langley wanted me to give you this."

Kane immediately recognized the case and flipped it open.

Trackers!

"Swallow the red one," said Dawson, pushing a glass of water toward him. "Langley says they'll be able to track you for about forty-eight hours." He pointed toward the case. "The others will stick to pretty much everything. Use them as you see fit."

Kane nodded, swallowing the red pill, wondering if it would truly reveal the truth. He put the glass down then took each of the half-dozen trackers, carefully sticking them inside his shirt cuff.

Dawson glanced at his watch. "Time's up. Last chance to get out."

Kane rose, shaking his head. "Too many lives are at stake. I'm in this until the end."

Frankfurt am Main International Airport, Frankfurt, Germany

Nazari sat on a bench across from the door he had seen the American enter almost ten minutes ago. He had spotted several of the others go by, everyone ignoring each other, and had noticed some from other cells he recognized from joint operations. It appeared the leadership was trying to get a large number through all at once, which made sense. Catch one today and then they'll be watching like hawks tomorrow.

Send *everyone* today…

The door opened for not the first time, but this time the American emerged, appearing none too pleased.

Nazari wasn't sure if he could trust the man, he simply not liking Americans, Muslim or not. Even the Muslim Americans seemed to have a superiority complex, as if they thought they were somehow better than the others, always trying to tell the true Muslims how things should be done, more often complaining about the conditions, many of them not lasting too long.

Yet this one hadn't complained, hadn't tried to tell him how to run the show. He had simply followed orders.

Perhaps he is *a true Muslim.*

He watched the American rush toward his gate and rose, following him at a slight distance, not wanting to trigger any suspicions, he having no doubt cameras were following the man should they be interested in him. The American had been out of sight for about ten minutes. Long enough he supposed for a strip search, especially if he were quick about getting his clothes off and back on.

Also more than enough time to make a phone call should he be a spy.

Nazari came up behind him on the moving sidewalk, slowing just before he reached him. "Problems?"

The American didn't turn, instead covering his mouth. "No, but stay away from me, they might still be watching."

"Excuse me," said Nazari, the American stepping aside as Nazari continued down the moving sidewalk, passing other travelers as he put distance between him and the American. The response had been exactly what he would expect out of a loyal recruit.

Though it was also the exact response a trained spy would probably give as well.

They should have never made me take him.

He trusted every man under his command. They would die for the cause, without hesitation, and would never betray him or their brothers.

But this American?

This convert?

He didn't know, and that simply wasn't acceptable. A commander had to trust his men. He decided at that moment that when they reached their destination, he'd request the American, and any other converts, be removed from the mission.

And if the American did turn out to be a spy?

He'd skin him alive.

Delta Airlines Flight DL107

Frankfurt am Main International Airport, Frankfurt, Germany

CIA Agent Sherrie White glanced over her shoulder and smiled at the Captain as he emerged from the galley, a glass of water in his hand. And his eyes on her ass. He gave her a quick wink before disappearing back in the cabin, though not before checking her out again.

And she couldn't blame him.

It is *a great ass.*

It had been a whirlwind of activity getting here, Langley sending her out late last night as soon as Kane's ticket had been purchased. She felt bad about the flight attendant she had waylaid this morning, yet it had been necessary, it simply too late to get someone on the plane in an official capacity. Yes, she could have been placed aboard as a passenger, but passengers didn't get to roam the aisles and the other restricted areas of the plane.

Flight attendants did.

Young Cindy Robinson had been chosen because she had been assigned a solo room and had nothing on her resume on file with the airline that suggested she'd be able to resist a trained agent. Even a lucky punch couldn't be risked as it might give Sherrie a black eye, which would make her too conspicuous for the mission.

Cindy had been neutralized, drugged so she'd be out long enough for the flight to reach New York, her room service order cancelled, her hotel booked an extra day with a Do Not Disturb notice, breakfast cancelled, and a phone call placed faking an illness.

Langley had hacked the airline's computer to assign a newly created flight attendant as a last minute substitute.

Her.

A friendly face for Kane, and backup on the flight should he need it for some reason. There were several agents on board, none of whom he had met. All would be able to come to his aid should he need it, but she was his conduit to that help in case he couldn't simply come out and ask for it.

She reached out for Kane's boarding pass, smiling at him as she had every other passenger so far. Glancing at his seat assignment, she pointed to the far side of the aircraft. "Aisle seat, far side. Have a good flight, sir." Kane nodded, murmuring a thank you, not giving any indication he recognized her, and she leaving it at that, continuing her job. Her crash course in being a flight attendant was a manual emailed to her by Langley for just such an occasion, this apparently a scenario the eggheads back home had cooked up before.

She took the next boarding pass handed to her, repeating the procedure, each person's face and pass captured by a camera in her broach, the image immediately relayed to Langley and run through their databases. They apparently only knew one face that had been travelling with Kane, and she felt her heart race slightly as the man approached. She directed him to his seat. "Have a nice flight, sir."

"Thank you."

She made a mental note as to what Tarek Nazari's seat assignment was, then finished greeting the passengers, every face now captured and sent.

And hopefully identified by the time they reached American soil.

Then we take them down.

Lufthansa Flight LH400

Frankfurt am Main International Airport, Frankfurt, Germany

Amira buckled Maya in, Alexis taking care of Rima, the two of them chitchatting about everything around them, Rima seeming to have taken to the American woman whose Arabic was excellent if heavily accented. She pulled her own belt tight and leaned her head back against the seat, closing her eyes, not sure of what to expect. This was her first time on an airplane, and she was at once scared and excited.

With all the terror she had experienced over the past weeks, she decided excitement was what she should be focusing on. This was a new experience, and who knew if she'd ever get to experience it again.

A smile spread across her face as the sound of her children's giggles filled her ears. It was so good to hear them happy. Maya was old enough that she would probably never forget what had happened to her father, but Rima might in time. It would sadden her to think her youngest would forget her father, though it was probably for the best. She would do everything she could to keep his memory alive in her mind, as long as it wouldn't rekindle the nightmare of that day when he had died.

Her smile faded as those minutes played out like a horror movie.

She opened her eyes.

And gasped.

A man was staring at her as he walked down the aisle, his hands gripping the back of each seat as he passed, first his left, then his right, then his left again. She didn't recognize him, though she had the distinct impression he recognized her.

His right hand reached up and he placed a finger to his lips.

A finger attached to a deeply scarred hand.

She paled, nearly fainting.

Then he went by.

Amira gripped the armrests with both hands, her entire body shaking as she desperately squeezed down below, trying to avoid a repeat of the last time she had been so frightened.

He had seen her.

He had recognized her.

And he had warned her.

She glanced over at Alexis, showing the girls the safety guide, desperately wanting to tell her what had just happened.

But stopped herself.

If you tell her, she might try to do something.

She closed her eyes, trying to control her rapid breathing.

And he might kill us all.

Tears filled her eyes, collecting in the corners as all hope faded inside.

After all this, I'm dead anyway.

Delta Airlines Flight DL107

Frankfurt am Main International Airport, Frankfurt, Germany

Kane walked down the aisle toward the bathrooms, having spotted Sherrie White working away as if she were a pro, the initial drink service just completed. He had to admit he was surprised and pleased to see her. She was a terrific woman and had done wonders for his best friend's self-esteem, she truly seeming to love him deeply. He imagined Leroux thought of her as out of his league, he too hard on himself. The guy wasn't bad looking by any stretch of the imagination, just painfully shy.

He had been thrilled to find out Morrison had promoted him, and with both Morrison and Sherrie championing his friend, he had heard through the grapevine, and experienced firsthand, his capabilities.

He was growing up. Coming out of his shell.

And with the way Kane barely glanced at the flight attendants in their form-fitting outfits, he had to wonder if he was growing up as well, thoughts of Fang continually invading his thoughts.

The past weeks had been lonely. Painfully lonely, more so than usual. He had been on ops for weeks, even months, and none had bothered him like this one. In the past, he had simply been bored, but this time he had actually felt lonely.

He missed her.

It was strange, since he had barely spent any time with her, yet he kept reliving those few precious moments over and over when he found himself sitting by himself, perhaps surrounded by the others in his cell, chattering away in Arabic as he pretended not to understand. He would take mental notes of anything said of interest, but the reality was they were all just as much in the dark as he was.

He passed Nazari's seat, ignoring him, the man perhaps the only one who truly knew what was going on, and even then he had his doubts. It was his belief that when they arrived at their destination, only then would Nazari get the true picture, and perhaps the rest of them as well.

Compartmentalization.

Need to know.

Whatever you wanted to call it, it was effective. They had left Syria only knowing where to meet for the boat and the name of its captain, in case they were separated. This Captain had passed on the contact's name for when they arrived in Germany, Kane having the distinct impression that the boat had been reserved for repeated voyages carrying only ISIL members.

And in Germany, they had been taken to prearranged hotels in Munich, then transported to Frankfurt and told nothing until their new identities had arrived. Everyone was now travelling in pairs, and with him travelling with Nazari, he had been told nothing about who they were to meet in New York.

He was as much clueless today as he had been weeks ago.

All he knew was the threat was real, and perhaps unstoppable.

Sherrie spotted him coming, walking toward him and bumping into him slightly.

"I'm so sorry, sir. Legs are a little wobbly today."

"No worries," he said, smiling down at her. She beamed a smile that must melt Leroux's heart, then pressed something into his hand. He gave no reaction, instead stepping past her and entering the bathroom. He locked the door and opened his hand to find an earpiece. He quickly took care of business, not knowing when he'd get another chance, and also giving Sherrie an opportunity to find a secure location to talk.

He pushed the bud into his ear.

"You there?"

"Yes. You okay?"

"For now. Surprised to see you."

"Langley wanted a familiar face onboard just in case you needed help. There's three other agents disguised as passengers with Air Marshall designations, so they're armed. What's your plan?"

Kane could hear the eagerness in her voice, the young woman desperate for some action. He remembered that zeal from the start of his career, but unlike her, he had several years of Army experience to help temper that adrenaline.

After seeing death too many times, you weren't as eager to get into the fight unless it was absolutely necessary.

And here it wasn't.

In fact, it could be extremely dangerous.

"Nothing. We're just going to let this play out. I have no idea how many are on the plane besides Nazari, and it's just too dangerous. We'll land in New York and you guys can use the tracker on me to see where we go."

"Keep the earpiece, at least then you can communicate."

"Negative. If they search me they'll find it, then not only am I dead, they'll know we're onto them and they'll scatter."

"Of course, you're right. Sorry."

Kane smiled, checking his teeth in the mirror. "So, how's Chris?"

"Worried about you and relieved to know you're alive."

Kane turned away from the mirror, leaning against the sink. "Give him a big sloppy kiss from me."

"I'll do more than that."

"Umm, if you do, don't mention it's from me."

There was a giggle.

"Has Langley had any luck identifying anyone yet?"

"Not that I know of, but beyond basic status reports, I'm out of the loop for now. We've stepped up security at the major airports without it being obvious, and every passenger is being reviewed, but even your guy Nazari has impeccable credentials. His ticket was bought as a single ticket, by a credit card only used once, from an IP address only used once."

"These guys are smart."

"Too damned smart. And beyond his face, we have nothing to really check against. Langley is finding some hits in their database among the refugees, but frankly we don't know who to look for."

"It would make sense they'd send low profile people for the most part, people who hadn't been on camera. We're just going to have to hope we get lucky at the New York rendezvous."

"Fingers crossed."

"Okay, I'm going to ditch the earpiece. Tell Langley to be ready to move on a moment's notice."

"Without comms, how will you let them know?"

A burst of air blew from Kane's mouth. "No idea, but I'll think of something."

"Good luck."

"You too."

Kane removed the earpiece and stuffed it under the rubber floor mat surrounding the toilet, just in case he might need it again.

He returned to his seat, again ignoring Nazari, instead scrutinizing the other passengers.

Wondering who were the agents.

And who else might be a terrorist.

Lufthansa Flight LH400, Somewhere over the Atlantic Ocean

Amira had to pee. Desperately. She had hoped to hold it, not to leave the safety of her seat, but they were barely halfway through the flight and she could wait no longer. She turned to Alexis.

"I have to use the bathroom."

"Do you want me to come with you?"

Amira shook her head. "No, I need you to stay with the children."

Alexis nodded, looking at the two youngsters, sound asleep, the excitement of the day wearing them out, thankfully. "No problem. Take your time."

Amira rose, heading quickly for the bathroom, trying not to look at anyone, praying she didn't see the man who had helped murder her husband, otherwise she might create another embarrassing mess. She reached the bathroom without incident, thanking Allah there was no lineup. She quickly finished her business and splashed some cold water on her face, staring at her pale visage in the mirror.

She held out her hand.

It was shaking.

Just get to America, then you'll be free of them.

She fixed her chador then unlocked the door, turning the handle. Someone on the other side pushed the door open, the handle ripping from her hand as she yelped, the scarred man stepping inside, placing his disfigured hand over her mouth as he shoved her back, closing the door behind him. Still gripping her face, he locked the door then raised a finger.

"You scream, you die. Understood?"

She shook out a nod, her entire body ready to give way, only his hand holding her up now.

"Do I know you?"

His question puzzled her. *He* had stared at *her*. Shouldn't that mean he knew her? But if he didn't recognize her, didn't remember who she was, she might just be able to convince him he didn't.

"You d-don't," she said, her voice muffled by the hand still over her mouth.

He removed it and shook his head. "No, I recognize you from somewhere and you definitely know me, the way you reacted to me looking at you."

"Y-you frightened me. Y-your hand."

He stared at her, suddenly grabbing her by the chin and shoving her head to the left, then the right, trying to get as good a look at her as possible. He pursed his lips, his nostrils flaring. "No, I've definitely seen your face before, and you definitely recognized me."

She had to think quickly. Where could she possibly tell him they knew each other from, something that wouldn't tie her back to the death of her husband. And it suddenly occurred to her. "Y-your hand. I recognize it from the bus in Hungary. You stood just in front of me. That must b-be where you saw m-me."

He nodded slowly, still moving her chin from side to side, then glanced over at her left hand, gripping the wall.

He snatched it, squeezing the wedding ring. A sneer emerged from one side of his mouth. "You were in Al-Raqqah." The sneer spread. "You're the teacher. I killed your coward of a husband."

Tears filled her eyes, she desperate to defend her husband's honor, yet she resisted, knowing her life was in this man's hands. "I-if you kill me or hurt me, they'll know."

The man smiled, a wicked, evil smile, his eyes narrow and piercing. "If you tell anyone, we'll blow up the plane and your children will be dead."

Every muscle in her body went slack as her world threatened to go dark, his grip tightening on her face as he kept her upright.

He smacked her.

She immediately returned to reality, the stinging in her cheek enough to focus her.

"Do we understand each other?"

She nodded.

He jabbed a finger in her chest. "Do as you're told and your children will survive. If you don't, you and your children will be reunited with your husband, very soon." He leaned closer. "And so will the rest of your family back home." He let her go and she collapsed onto the toilet. He bent over, tilting up her face with the scarred hand. "Remember why your husband died. You may think you escaped, but you never did."

She slumped against the side of the tiny room, the world fading rapidly.

Alexis checked her watch, growing more concerned by the minute, Amira still not having returned from the bathroom. She glanced back for the umpteenth time and breathed a sigh of relief as she finally spotted the woman making her way to her seat. She reached over and moved the lap belt out of the way.

Amira dropped into her seat and Alexis frowned, the woman pale and sweating. "What's wrong?"

Amira shook her head a little too rapidly. "Nothing."

Something was definitely wrong. One didn't need CIA training to know that. She leaned over, lowering her voice. "Amira, clearly something is wrong. Please tell me what it is so I can help."

Another rapid headshake. "Please, leave me alone, I just want to rest."

Alexis nodded, sitting back in her chair as Amira buckled her seatbelt and closed her eyes, her hands gripping the armrests tightly, her knuckles white. Something was wrong, of that there was no doubt. They were halfway into the flight so she doubted it was a sudden fear of flying.

She must have seen someone!

She gulped, her mouth suddenly dry as her heart began to race. She had no way of knowing if there were any terrorists onboard, and if they were easy to spot or identify before they got onboard, people like her father would have done so already.

But Amira was from the area.

She had seen them.

Met them.

And her clear terror suggested she had seen one again.

So they were all in danger.

She tried to stand, her lap belt yanking her back into her seat. She unbuckled it and rose, heading for the bathroom, eyeing the passengers, trying to spot the terrorist.

Yet it was of no use.

Easily half the plane appeared Middle Eastern to her but could be Italian for all she knew.

How can you know who to trust?

She suddenly understood why politically correct screening at airports was stupid. Why were they searching just as many little old Caucasian ladies as they were young Middle Eastern males?

She stepped into the bathroom and locked the door, pulling out her phone. She dialed her father, he immediately answering.

"Hello?"

"Daddy?" She dropped onto the toilet seat, battling an overwhelming urge to begin sobbing. "I think I might be in danger."

Operations Center 3, CIA Headquarters, Langley, Virginia

Morrison raced down the hallway, his sobbing daughter still on the phone pressed against his ear. He entered his code and the operations center door opened, he bursting inside, startling Leroux's team.

"Bring up the manifest for my daughter's flight, now!"

Leroux snapped his fingers and one of his staff attacked the keyboard, it clear they knew from his demeanor this was urgent. Those words from his daughter's mouth had forced an emotion forward that he had rarely felt.

Fear.

No father ever wants to hear his own daughter's voice filled with terror, fearing she was going to die. And in his business, he knew only too well how real that possibility was when dealing with these people.

These were fanatics.

With no morals.

No compassion.

No concern for who they hurt or killed, as long as they accomplished their goals.

And they wouldn't hesitate to blow up a plane.

If they could.

He just prayed they didn't have that capability.

"The manifest is on the monitor now, sir," said Therrien as Morrison stood in front of the screen, Leroux joining him.

"Show me where my daughter is seated."

A seating chart appeared beside the scrolling list of names, a flashing yellow dot indicating her seat.

"And the refugees."

Three more dots appeared, all in the same center row beside his daughter.

He put the phone closer to his mouth. "Honey, you said she went to the bathroom?"

"Yes."

"Which direction?"

"The rear."

"And she came back terrified?"

"Yes, but she won't say why. I think she saw someone she recognized."

Leroux snapped his fingers, his best analyst jumping into action, giving orders to his team. "Remove all the women and children." The list quickly dwindled, red X's appearing on over half the seats. Leroux tapped his chin. "Remove anyone who's on the return leg of a flight." Half of what remained disappeared.

"They're not going to send old men," said Morrison, realizing what Leroux was doing.

"Eliminate anyone over sixty." More names disappeared from the list, more red X's appearing on the seating plan. "How many are left?"

Therrien looked at his display. "Fifty-three, sir."

"What about visas?" asked Child. "Chances are we're dealing with fake passports, so they'd make them from a country that didn't need a visa, that way they'd avoid having to go to our embassy."

Leroux smiled, Child continuing to impress. "Good thinking." He nodded toward Therrien, another dozen disappearing. "Okay, start running everyone that remains. Concentrate on the Middle Eastern looking ones, but remember there's thousands of converts over there fighting, so it could just as easily be a white guy."

Faces quickly flipped by, facial recognition points plotted, databases searched, identities appearing, then nothing.

Morrison turned to Therrien. "Any red flags?"

"Negative. None."

"None?"

Therrien nodded and Leroux cursed. He turned to Morrison. "If there's a terrorist onboard, we have no idea who he is."

Morrison nodded. "And if we don't know who *he* is, then we don't know how many of his friends are with him."

Leroux looked at the screen. "Kane said there could be hundreds or maybe even thousands on the way." He turned to Morrison. "What the hell are we going to do?"

Morrison slowly shook his head.

"I have no idea."

Delta Airlines Flight DL107

John F. Kennedy International Airport, New York City

"No, wait until everyone else is off."

Amira vehemently disagreed with Alexis' instructions, she desperately wanting to get off the plane as quickly as possible and out of the metal tube she had been trapped in for hours. The man who had helped kill her husband was seated behind her and he definitely knew where she was sitting. He could easily stab her or break her neck as he walked by and it would be over before anyone could stop him.

She leaned away from the aisle, closer to her children, trying to hide the fear from her face, the little ones excited for the adventure ahead of them though neither knew the hardships they would face in this ocean of Christianity where they didn't speak the language and would be forced to live a lifestyle they were never meant to live.

I want to go home.

It wasn't a possibility of course, at least not now. Perhaps in time, perhaps if the bombings stopped and the civil war ended. At this place, at this moment, she didn't really care who won, she just wanted to return to the town she had grown up in, to the school she had taught in, to the home she and her husband had lived in since they were married.

She wanted to bury her husband.

"Ok, let's go."

She glanced over her shoulder and saw the aisles empty, the man who had threatened her life obviously having deplaned with everyone else. She breathed a sigh of relief and rose, ushering the children out as Alexis rounded the next row of seats and took the lead, warily watching over her shoulders at the empty plane behind them, as if fearing someone might be hiding.

She knows.

They stepped out of the plane, past the last flight attendant who immediately turned away from the door, returning inside for some final task, leaving the four of them alone to traverse the empty jetway.

Something to her left emerged from the shadows and she screamed as a hand dropped hard, swinging something. She twisted away but it wasn't meant for her, Alexis crying out as a gut wrenching thud filled Amira's ears, her guardian collapsing to the floor. A hand grabbed her, spinning her around then clamping down on her mouth, cutting off her scream. She was hauled back into the shadows, her children staring at her, fear in their eyes, too terrified to yell themselves.

Her mouth was suddenly free and she sucked in a breath to yell for help when she felt his arm wrap around her neck, his other hand, his scarred hand, covering her mouth for a moment as her oxygen supply slowly cut off.

She couldn't scream now if she wanted to.

His hot, damp breath blew over her ear as he bent down, squeezing harder and harder.

"Remember your du—"

A gunshot rang out and the grip loosened, her husband's killer gasping. She wrenched herself free, rushing toward her children as two men in suits raced toward them, guns opening up on the man as he suddenly charged from the shadows, screaming "Allahu Akbar!"

He dropped to the floor, his eyes staring at her as if delivering one last message.

She turned her head, shielding her children from the sight.

"Are you okay?" asked one of the new arrivals, taking a knee beside her.

She nodded. "Yes." She motioned toward Alexis. "Check her. She was hit from behind."

The man shifted his attention to Alexis as heavy footfalls echoed through the closed jetway, more police and security arriving, ushering flight crew and a janitor away from the scene.

Alexis groaned and the man helped her to a sitting position.

"Are you okay?"

Alexis nodded, rubbing the back of her head. She looked at the dead body, then at Amira. "What happened?"

"He hit you."

Alexis held up her hand. "Help me up."

The man pulled her to her feet, keeping a steadying hand on her arm, her legs wobbly. "Are you sure you're okay to stand?"

Alexis nodded. "Yes." She drew a deep breath then glanced again at the dead terrorist. "So that's who you were scared of?"

Amira nodded, unable to look.

Alexis turned to the man in the suit, his partner guarding the body. "Who are you?"

"Your father sent us."

Amira stifled a gasp.

Her father?

She suddenly filled with doubts about this woman who had claimed to be helping the entire time. If her father could send armed men to meet their aircraft, then who was she?

And who was she working for?

And was anything she had said, the truth?

John F. Kennedy International Airport, New York City

"Welcome home."

Kane smiled at the CBP Officer with a tilt of his head. "Good to be home."

He calmly walked through the airport and waited at the carousel to pick up his luggage, it part of their instructions, all of them given one piece of luggage and roundtrip tickets to allay any suspicions. Middle Eastern men with no luggage and one-way tickets were a major red flag in this day and age.

And it was just as important to pick up that luggage, any unclaimed baggage easily linked back to their ticket, then their passport and their photo, making them identifiable.

He spotted the beat up piece of Samsonite issued to him and yanked it off the carousel, briskly dragging it toward the entrance and the pickup area. Exiting outside into a crisp fall day, he stood for a brief moment, enjoying the sounds and smells of home, something he enjoyed far too infrequently in his job.

It reeked of jet fuel and pollution with a side of pissed off tourist and New York cabby.

It was awesome.

"The seat's all wet!"

Kane turned to see an incredible looking blonde in an impossibly short skirt with stilettos that could double as weapons, climbing out of a Jaguar XK-8 convertible, her firm backside stained with something.

"Sorry about that, I just went through the carwash. Let me get you a towel." The driver, *not* in her league, rushed around with a hand towel, quickly drying up the seat.

"Why don't you get the roof fixed? This happened last time," said the woman as she tested the seat out with her hand, apparently satisfied.

"I tried, baby, I tried, but the dealership said that it's normal for convertibles."

"Having driven in many, I can assure you it's not," she said, pulling the door shut, leaving the poor bastard red and sweaty, glancing around to see if anyone had heard the exchange.

But no one except Kane appeared to have, a gaggle of reporters rushing into the terminal distracting everyone. He glanced at several of the security personnel who were listening to their comms a little closer than he would normally expect.

Something's up.

Peering down the line of waiting vehicles, he saw Nazari glance at him before climbing into a van. He walked toward the vehicle, the driver standing behind it. The man took his bag, saying nothing, and put it in the back, slamming the rear hatch shut. Kane climbed in beside Nazari and they were underway moments later.

"What's going on?" asked Nazari in English, as several police cars raced by.

"Someone was shot," replied the driver, a little heavy on the accelerator though not too much, drawing attention at this stage not wise.

"One of ours?"

The driver checked his mirror and changed lanes. "We don't know yet. It just happened a few minutes ago from what I can tell."

Nazari glanced over his shoulder and through the rear window, the airport quickly fading into the distance. "How many have made it?"

The driver smiled in his rearview mirror. "All but one."

Kane's eyes popped wide. "Excuse me?"

"You were the last I was assigned to pick up, and only one person didn't show up for the rendezvous. We're thinking it might be who was shot."

Nazari smiled at Kane, his eyes wide with zeal. "All but one!"

Kane grinned back. "How many is that?"

"More than enough." Nazari turned to face the driver, his smile still wide. "And the package?"

"Arrived yesterday."

"What's the package?" ventured Kane, needing to confirm once and for all if the Cesium he had been chasing was the actual weapon hinted of.

"Allah's vengeance."

Once again, no help at all.

Operations Center 3, CIA Headquarters, Langley, Virginia

"Your daughter is secure, sir."

Morrison breathed a sigh of relief, dropping into a spare chair in the operations center as Leroux's team continued to track Kane, the agents he had sent finally getting his daughter into a safe location at the airport. He looked over at Leroux. "Now I can tell my wife what happened."

Leroux smiled. "She still might kill you."

Morrison chuckled. "Wait 'til you have kids. If they don't kill you, your wife will."

Leroux flushed, turning away.

A little too soon, perhaps?

He decided to save his underling, Sonya Tong gazing at the poor guy longingly. "Status on the strike teams?"

Leroux threw himself back into the job, Morrison never regretting for a moment promoting the young man. "We have six rally points across the city. They'll start to redeploy as we narrow down their destination. This is an FBI show, so we're just bystanders on this one."

Morrison nodded, content to be on the sidelines for once. "I wouldn't want to be the one making the decision on this."

"Why not?" asked Child, immediately back peddling as Leroux shot him a look. "I mean, umm, why not, *sir*?" His head dropped onto his chest.

Needs to work on that brain to mouth filter.

"If they want to catch them all, then they can't take these guys down today. The ones that haven't arrived yet will just go to ground. But if we let these guys go and lose some of them…"

Child's head bobbed slowly. "You mean if they succeed, then the person who decided not to act would be blamed and probably lose their job."

Morrison smiled slightly, scrutinizing the young man. "Son, I don't think there's a person out there today who's worried about losing their job. They're worried about losing American lives on their watch."

Child cast his eyes down once again. "Of course, sir."

Leroux looked over at Morrison. "So whose shoulders is it on?"

Morrison sighed. "Today, I'm afraid it could all be on Dylan."

Rally Point Foxtrot, Manhattan, New York City

"Shit! Looks like we're heading for Jersey. Let's roll."

Niner put their Ford Expedition in gear and pulled out into traffic, at least a dozen other vehicles joining them as they redeployed, Kane's tracking device indicating he had left the city. This was an FBI operation though Delta had been called in due to their expertise in these situations, and with them being the only military unit permitted to operate on American soil, the President had been able to authorize bringing on the additional firepower.

Dawson had three four-man teams deployed, all of his Bravo Team, and Colonel Clancy had more on standby. Though Delta had a large number of operators, most were in forward operating positions. The idea here wasn't to flood the area with armed military, but merely to have a few units available for unusual situations. The FBI were well-trained and experienced, and Dawson had no doubt they'd be able to handle the situation, but with Kane involved, a man he and many of his men owed their lives to, he wanted to see this op through to the end.

And the FBI had already screwed up, all of the rally points in New York City, no one considering Jersey a target.

"We should have pulled him out," muttered Dawson, thinking about Kane driving into the lion's den, unarmed, with no comms.

Niner glanced at him before blasting through a red light, sirens and lights blaring. "He wouldn't have listened, and besides, would you have done it any different?"

Dawson scanned his side. "Clear right." Niner surged ahead. "No, I guess you're right. I'll just be happy when this op is over."

"How nasty do you think this is going to get?" asked Atlas from the backseat.

Dawson shrugged. "Who the hell knows? Kane was talking hundreds, possibly thousands. If he's going to a big meet, I can't see the FBI not hitting the place. And with that many guns, some of the good guys are going to get hurt. Or worse."

"Hang on!" Niner cranked the wheel to the left, taking a sharp turn, the tires shuddering in protest. He straightened them expertly, keeping up easily with the other vehicles. "Let's just hope he keeps his head down."

"Amen to that."

Rome Street, Newark, New Jersey

Kane had watched keenly out the windows of their van as they left New York City and crossed into New Jersey, hoping his tracker was still functional, these things sometimes failing. He had spotted no obvious security along the way beyond the occasional police officer or cruiser, nothing to suggest a massive deployment preparing to respond to whatever was about to happen.

Which was just what he would expect.

He had no doubt teams were deployed, though they'd be out of sight of any of the routes he would be expected to take, and more than likely, they'd be hidden away in parking structures, away from the prying eyes of the streets, redeploying as destinations were ruled out.

The big question was not where he was going, but what he was going to find when he got there. Both the driver and Nazari had been silent as to their destination and what awaited them. For all he knew, it could just be another hotel room, though when they rolled into an industrial section of town, he started to believe otherwise.

The driver turned off the road, heading directly toward a large, dilapidated warehouse, its massive delivery door rolling up, revealing a dark pit, nothing visible inside. They drove straight in, the driver not hitting the brakes until they had cleared the doors, then jamming them on. Kane heard the doors behind them slam to the ground, the warehouse suddenly flooded with light. He blinked several times before his eyes focused.

"Holy shit!"

He couldn't help it, and the reaction would be completely in character regardless, anyone, devout nutbar or undercover spy, would be shocked at what they saw. He opened his door and stepped out, his mouth agape. A quick count showed over two dozen vehicles, parked in pairs around the perimeter of the structure, all kinds of makes and models, all large enough to easily seat half a dozen men with equipment.

And there was a lot of equipment, organized on tables at one end. Dozens upon dozens of men were lined up, each being handed a large duffel bag, their names taken and then sent to a numbered vehicle, there already groups of men standing in front of many of the trucks and vans lining the perimeter.

Four men walked up to them, weapons raised, a fifth with an iPad, not bothering to raise his head. "Identify yourselves."

"Tarek Nazari."

The man's fingers flew over the screen and Kane caught a glimpse of a photo of Nazari. The man glanced up. "Welcome to America, my friend. The commander wants to see you right away." He pointed to a thickly bearded man in the center of the warehouse, surrounded by a gaggle of others who appeared equally devout. Nazari immediately left them, the man with the iPad turning his attention to Kane. "And you are?"

"Bryce Clearwater."

The man's eyes narrowed slightly at the English name, entering it on the touchscreen. "Ah, a convert!"

"Yes."

"Excellent! There is no shame in coming to Allah later in life." He pointed to the tables. "Get in line, gather your equipment, then report to your assigned vehicle. You're in number seventeen." He paused. "Do you speak Arabic?"

Kane shook his head. "I'm learning, but it's difficult."

"Not to worry, most everyone here speaks at least some English. Get your equipment and make friends. It's going to be a busy day."

Kane smiled, looking about. "It truly does appear that Allah is on our side. It looks like at least a hundred men!"

"One-hundred-thirteen have checked in so far."

Kane shook his head, his chest tightening as he forced the smile to stay on his face. "Incredible. Are we expecting more?"

"Only a few more. The Caliph decided to have everyone arrive in one day from various destinations around the world. Never did we expect it would work so well."

No, I don't think anyone would have thought it would.

"The Caliph is clearly wise. Bringing them in all at once left the Americans with no chance to increase their security if they had caught one of us."

"Exactly. Allah must indeed be pleased with what we are doing."

Kane reached into his cuff, pinching off one of the trackers. "We do His prophet's work."

The man nodded, looking toward the opening garage door. "America will never be the same when we are done." He began to walk toward the newly arriving SUV when Kane patted him on the back.

"Good luck, my friend."

The man glanced back at him with a smile. "And to you, brother."

Kane headed for the supply line, taking in as much as he could.

And it was overwhelming.

To think over one hundred men were gathered here, determined to destroy America from within, was shocking. What they could possibly need so many men for was what had him curious. His initial thoughts suggested a massive attack on a significant piece of real estate like the White House or Wall Street, but as he eyed the vehicles, he began to question that assumption. If they were going to attack a single target, it would make more sense to use far fewer vehicles, perhaps delivery trucks that might seat a dozen or more men in the back.

But two dozen individual vehicles?

It suggested to him dozens of smaller attacks.

Which would probably be far worse.

He just prayed whoever was watching overhead understood his message delivered by activating the tracker, it clear the vast majority had already arrived.

Attack now!

Operations Center 3, CIA Headquarters, Langley, Virginia

"The FBI is converging on the location now, but it's going to take time."

Leroux watched the feed from the FBI on one of their monitors, dots converging from all across the area, heading toward the one critical dot.

The one indicating Kane's location.

"Do we have eyes yet?"

"Yes, sir," replied Therrien, bringing up a drone feed on another monitor. A large warehouse filled a significant portion of the screen, the entire area industrial, which was good. If things went to pot, civilian casualties would hopefully be minimal, and if the Cesium was indeed there, if it were detonated, a warehouse district was a lot easier to deal with than pretty much any other location in the region.

But they needed to know how many they were dealing with.

"Switch to thermal."

The screen flashed and a massive blob of red filled much of the warehouse. He turned to Therrien. "Is there something wrong with the imager?"

Therrien's fingers flew over his keyboard as his head shook. "I don't know, sir, let me see if I can clean it up." His fingers froze as his gaze moved from his own terminal to the large screens at the front of the operations center. "Holy shit!"

Leroux turned back toward the screen and felt his heart nearly stop. "What the hell am I looking at?" The large mass of red and orange had resolved into dozens of smaller dots, spread out across the entire building.

Therrien's reply was almost a whisper. "I-I'm counting over one hundred targets inside, sir."

Leroux snapped his fingers. "Get me the Director. Now!" He turned to Therrien as Sonya grabbed her phone. "Does the FBI know?"

Therrien shook his head. "They should if they cleaned up the feed. I'm using their data stream."

Sonya held out the phone. "It's the Chief."

Leroux took the phone. "Sir, we're counting over one hundred hostiles at Kane's location."

"Jesus! Are you sure?"

"I'm looking at the drone feed now, sir. At least one hundred targets."

"Keep me posted through internal messaging. I'm going to a Presidential briefing right now."

"Yes, sir."

He handed the phone back to Sonya as he watched the single, pulsing red dot at the center of the image, representing the only friend he had in the world, surrounded by a sea of swarming hate.

Then there was a second dot.

"What's that?"

"One of the other trackers just activated," replied Child as the two dots continued to separate, it clear this wasn't a false signal or an accidental activation. "Kane must have activated it, sir."

Leroux sat in his chair, firing a quick message to Morrison as he watched the target move toward a newly arriving heat signature, some sort of vehicle, its engine hot. Whoever it was, they must have been important for Kane to risk planting a tracker.

Or was it a signal that they should begin the assault?

Conference Room 4, CIA Headquarters, Langley, Virginia

"We're estimating approximately one-hundred-twenty hostiles inside the warehouse. Our units are redeploying right now, but it's going to take some time. We had assumed the target would be in New York City, not Newark. A few units are on scene but we're keeping a low profile, just in case others are still arriving. We want to try and catch them all in one shot."

Morrison watched the talking heads on the screen, glancing down at his phone, the secure message from Leroux about the second tracking device causing him to bite his lip.

Is that a signal from Kane to hit them now?

"What's inside?" asked the Secretary of Homeland Security.

"Infrared suggests over two dozen vehicles, mostly vans and SUVs, and what could be a lot of small arms and submachine guns," replied the Director of the FBI, Bob Waters.

Dozens of vehicles.

He scrutinized the image from the drone, the outlines of the vehicles plain to see if you knew what to look for.

He did.

And all of them were parked neatly, all facing the large doors that lined one side of the warehouse, each with a cluster of men standing in front of them, clusters that continued to grow as the men gathered in the center continued to disperse.

And if they assumed five to six men per vehicle, at most 150 terrorists were expected.

And he had to hope at least some were still stuck in Europe.

The FBI was waiting for terrorists who were never going to arrive.

He decided he could wait no longer.

"Based upon the number and positioning of those vehicles, and the redistribution of the personnel inside, it looks to me like they're preparing to leave."

"That's not our assessment," replied Waters, his voice tinged with his usual attitude when dealing with Morrison, the man still pissed that Morrison had beaten him out for a job years ago.

"Can we take that chance? Perhaps it's better to hit them now and not risk them leaving."

"This is an FBI operation. While we're happy to have CIA observing, we'll run the show."

Morrison kept his facial expression in check. "Not trying to piss in your Corn Flakes, Bob, but this is the heaviest concentration of known terrorists we've ever had on home soil. All I'm saying is we should consider what might happen if we wait too long."

"If they leave, we'll stop them."

"And if some escape?"

"We found them once, we'll find them again."

"*You* found them? Interesting. I'll let my man inside that warehouse know who to thank."

Waters turned a delightful shade of red before President Starling cleared his throat. "Leif, I appreciate everything the CIA has done thus far, but this is the FBI's jurisdiction now. I have to go with them on this. We can't risk tipping them off before everyone has arrived."

"Of course, sir. I apologize. My concern is that they may leave first."

"Then we stop them," said Waters, having regained his voice.

"It could be a blood bath since we barely have any units in position."

Waters glared at the camera, his words seething. "I'm aware of that."

President Starling cut in again. "Gentlemen, let's hope they don't leave before our teams are in position, and if this does turn ugly, pray it's mostly their blood that is spilled."

"Amen to that, Mr. President."

Rome Street, Newark, New Jersey

Nazari was having a hard time keeping his breathing steady. He brimmed with pride, with joy, with an excitement he couldn't recall ever feeling. The mission they were about to execute was far beyond anything he could have ever hoped for, and his part in it was extremely important, an honor not lost on him.

It's too bad I won't get to enjoy the fruits of this, here.

It was indeed an honor to be asked to give one's life to further Allah's cause, and that is what had been asked of him today. He had always gone into battle knowing he could die, yet doing everything he could to not only honor himself and his god, but to avoid death as well.

But today, he knew he would be dead soon.

And he couldn't wait.

Jannah awaited him, his life of service to Allah about to be rewarded with eternal bliss no man could imagine.

He arrived at his vehicle, number eighteen, paired with number seventeen, most of the men here from his own cell back home, including the American convert who was smiling with the others, apparently as eager to get underway as he was.

He held up an iPad he had been given with his instructions, his smile broad, his chest filled with religious fervor. "Brothers. Friends. We have been given a glorious mission, and if executed properly, we will bring America to its knees, and in time, force the infidel out of our homeland, and once out, the Caliphate will be free to spread until it is too powerful to stop!"

He held up his hands, silencing the shouts of Allahu Akbar about to break out. He pointed to all the teams gathered, their own commanders giving a variation of the same briefing he was about to give. "There are twelve teams, each with ten men. Each vehicle will have four to six men in it, and each team has been assigned a different city across this unholy land."

"Where are we going, sir?"

Nazari almost snapped at the man who had interrupted, but the sincere eagerness in the man's eyes halted the harsh words about to erupt. "Washington, DC."

Smiles were exchanged with the knowledge they would get to attack the infidels' capital. He too had felt the same elation when he had read his briefing notes on the iPad, knowing it was men he had fought with and trained that would get the honor. The plan given to him was simple—the difficult part, getting here, already done.

"We will be leaving immediately. In three days, at noon Eastern Time, each team will split into individual members and from a safe location, shoot one random person, then get to safety. It is key that it is only *one* person, and it is even more important that you then are able to get to safety. If for some reason you can't safely take a shot, then *don't*. It is more important that you survive to take your shot the next day.

"Each day, at a coordinated time, you will shoot another random person. This person doesn't need to be high profile like a politician or police officer. The more common, the better. Women, children, whatever, it does not matter. As long as it is one person, at the prescribed time, and you are able to escape safely. By safely getting away, it leaves you able to continue your mission the next day so the terror the infidels will feel will continue for days and weeks and months if necessary. For as long as it takes for them to yield to our demands."

"How will we know when to stop?" asked one of his men.

"Each day, after the shootings have been completed, we will send an announcement to the American press, claiming responsibility, and reminding them of our demands—the complete withdrawal of all American and allied forces from the Middle East and Africa. The American economy will grind to a halt as people become too afraid to leave their homes, and that fear will dictate American policy. They will be forced to meet our demands, and at that time you will—"

A squawk of a megaphone sounded and everyone turned to see the commander standing on a table in the center of the warehouse. "Brothers, you are all being briefed by your cell leaders. This is the most ambitious plan we have ever devised, and the most ambitious plan since 9/11, when we showed the infidel he wasn't safe in his own home. By helping orchestrate the heaviest forced migration since World War Two, we have managed to infiltrate all of you here today, and should we succeed, hundreds and then thousands more will follow. We are paving the way for them, proving what is possible when Allah is on your side. In three days, when everyone is in position, our operation will begin, and the American infidels will begin to die. And more every day after. Your actions, your courage, your *faith*, will change the world forever, and your sacrifice, should it come to that, will be remembered forever as you enjoy your reward in the afterlife!

"The Americans will be forced to heed our demands as their people continue to die, continue to live their lives each day, wondering if it is their turn. My brothers, success is inevitable, because we are on God's side! Allahu Akbar!"

The roar that filled the warehouse hurt his ears, a pain he would happily endure for a lifetime to see such a joyous outpouring of one's beliefs among so many young, vital men. He found himself shouting the chant repeatedly, his fist pumping in the air, his eyes wide with a love for his God he doubted any Christian or Jew ever felt.

The commander stepped down from the table, someone else taking over, ordering silence and a continuation of the briefing, the wired, sweaty men at once disappointed to stop, yet eager to get on with their assignments.

Nazari held up his iPad, his still pumped men turning to face him, one of them unable to contain his excitement.

"It's going to be glorious!"

Nazari smiled. "Yes it is."

Too bad it was mostly bullshit.

New Jersey Turnpike, Newark, New Jersey

"Something's happening."

Dawson glanced back at Spock who had a laptop jacked into the drone feed over their target. "What?"

Spock shoved the laptop between the seats so Dawson could see it. "What does that look like to you?"

There were now thirteen completely distinct groups, each gathered about pairs of vehicles, the thirteenth, probably the central command, still in the middle of the warehouse. "Looks to me like they're getting briefed by their platoon leaders."

"That's what I was thinking."

"Sure, always trying to kiss up to the Big Dog," said Niner as the vehicle surged forward a little faster, he obviously picking up on the urgency of the moment and anticipating Dawson's now unnecessary order.

"I'd say they're getting ready to deploy." He activated his comm. "Control, Bravo Zero-One. It's our opinion they are about to deploy, over."

"Stand by Zero-One."

Dawson motioned with his finger at the road ahead and Niner floored it, dodging past the other FBI vehicles, they not displaying any indication they knew what was about to happen. He glanced at the others. "I've got a feeling we're about to be caught with our pants down."

"Zero-One, Control. Continue as previously instructed to Rally Point Sierra and await further instructions, out."

Dawson smashed a fist into the dash.

"They're not ready!"

Rome Street, Newark, New Jersey

Kane kept glancing about for some telltale sign of an assault and continued to be disappointed. If the shit hit the fan, he intended to hit the deck, roll under the truck to his right, and stay there until the shooting stopped. He wasn't going to risk being caught in the crossfire of what would be an absolute bloodbath.

There was no way these people were surrendering.

And still, there was nothing from those outside.

At least he assumed they were outside.

Maybe the tracker failed.

He returned his attention to Nazari who had continued his briefing now that all the ridiculous cheering had stopped. The man pointed at the duffel bags they had all been issued. "Inside each bag are body armor, a handgun with three magazines, and an iPhone."

All the tools a modern terrorist needs.

"What do we do for three days?" asked one of the men. "Washington is close to here, isn't it?"

Nazari nodded.

"Motel rooms have been arranged around the city for each of you. There will be no contact between any of you once we arrive. Each evening you will visit a website set up on your iPhone at 9pm Eastern and login. This will let our commanders know you are still alive. You will report your success or failure, and you will receive the time for the next day's coordinated attack, and the web address for the next day's login, along with resupply instructions. Each week you will be given a drop point for ammo and money, plus any other supplies you request. Remember, this changes each day in case one of you is captured and is valid for only fifteen minutes. If you are captured, ask for a lawyer, and hold out until 9:15 Eastern time. At that point, tell them whatever you want, the website will no longer be active and you will have no information that is of any use to them. The mission will continue, unimpeded."

Kane had to admit the level of organization was impressive, and in reality, not that difficult from a technical standpoint to implement. Websites were easy, phone apps as well, and seedy motels asked no questions when paid in cash.

This plan could work.

Which was terrifying.

He raised a hand. "Umm, how do we know when to stop?"

Nazari flicked his phone in the air. "The website will tell us."

"What if we can't login, like the Internet is down, or something?"

"Then continue to randomly kill, one person each day, at a random hour, just once per day. Make no attempt to find the others. In fact, if you ever see one of your brothers, you must ignore him, just in case you are being watched. Our success relies on anonymity. When you do your killings, make sure no one knows it is you, otherwise your description will go out and people will be watching for you." He waved the phone again. "Each of your phones has your new identity on it. Over the next three days you will memorize them."

Nazari opened the rear of one of the vehicles, a briefcase inside. He opened it, pulling out a pile of personalized envelopes, quickly handing them out. "Cash, IDs, hotel addresses, tonight's website and password. Each is unique to you. This has been planned for months, my brothers, and nothing can stop us now."

Kane nodded, worried the man might actually be right.

The megaphone squawked again and the order to depart was given. Nazari clapped his hands together. "Everyone in their assigned vehicles, and glory be to Allah!"

"Allahu Akbar!" was the reply as Kane climbed into the back seat of his assigned vehicle.

And Nazari into the other one.

Kane cursed as the doors rolled open and the vehicles started to stream out.

Where the hell is everybody?

Conference Room 4, CIA Headquarters, Langley, Virginia

Morrison continued to listen to Bob Waters drone on about the assets in the area and how they'd be in position for a takedown within ten minutes.

His phone vibrated and he read the message from Leroux.

"Shit."

Waters stopped. "Excuse me?"

Morrison ignored him. "Mr. President, it would appear we're too late. They're already leaving."

"Christ!" exclaimed Waters as empty chairs replaced faces, people scrambling for updates.

President Starling remained remarkably calm. "What do you recommend, Leif?"

"Mr. President, my people tell me that our operative tagged another target. I suggest we pick him up." Starling nodded as seats began to fill again. "Might I suggest one of the Delta teams? They have the most experience and are in the area. You know the man, sir, he was with you in Mozambique."

A slight smile appeared for a moment, then a hint of gloom, the President having suffered a great loss that day, a loss he clearly wasn't over. "Mr. *White*." He nodded firmly. "Yes. Give him the job. And Leif, I want your people coordinating the takedown."

Someone cleared their throat, probably Waters.

Starling leaned forward, raising a finger. "No jurisdictional bullshit on this one. Thousands of American lives are at stake." He rose from his chair. "Meeting adjourned."

Operations Center 3, CIA Headquarters, Langley, Virginia

Morrison threw open the operations center door and rushed inside, slightly out of breath, swearing to himself he would get back on the treadmill next week.

It's always next *week.*

"Establish comms with the Delta unit led by White."

Leroux turned to Therrien who began to establish contact.

"Do you still have eyes on that second tracking device?"

Leroux nodded. "Yes, sir. A vehicle with that signal left, separate from the others."

Morrison's eyes narrowed. "Separate?"

"Yes, sir. We think it might be their command cell. They were clustered near the center of the warehouse almost the entire time before leaving last. Someone at this end had to coordinate things. My guess is they've been here for weeks or months laying the groundwork." He turned to Sonya. "Replay the departure." Sonya's fingers flew over the keyboard and a replay of the thermal imaging showed on the main display. "As you can see, they were split off into twelve groups of about ten each in addition to the command cell. Each vehicle had four to six people and they all left within three minutes of each other, all heading off in different directions. At this point no two vehicles are together."

Morrison frowned. "So there was no way the FBI were going to be able to stop them after they left. I hate being right sometimes." He motioned toward the screen. "And this command cell? Where are they?"

Leroux pointed to the bottom right of the screen. "Heading back to Manhattan by the looks of it."

"And the Delta unit?"

Sonya's fingers tapped away, a green dot appearing several miles away.

"Good. I want them to take down that vehicle and capture whoever Kane tagged, alive."

Leroux's eyes widened slightly, his eyebrows climbing half an inch. "What about the FBI? Aren't they in command?"

"Not for this." Morrison pointed at the screen. "Not after that. The President wasn't happy they couldn't get their act together fast enough." Morrison turned to Therrien. "Got them?"

Therrien nodded. "Yes, sir. Bravo Zero-One is on the line."

Morrison pointed at the headset Therrien held out, looking at Leroux. "It's your show."

Approaching Rome Street, Newark, New Jersey

Dawson spun his finger in the air and Niner checked his mirrors, quickly pulling a U-turn, breaking away from the other vehicles still heading for the rendezvous point, the directive of no lights and sirens once they reached Jersey killing their progress.

They were no longer bound by those orders.

Niner blasted through the traffic with lights and sirens activated, toward the new target now showing on the display attached to the dash.

"What can you tell me, Control?"

"Dark brown Dodge Caravan, five hostiles inside, two in the front, three in the back. Intel suggests they are most likely armed."

"Secondary devices?"

"None indicated but be prepared for suicide vests or other IEDs."

Dawson began checking his gear as did the others in the rear, Spock reaching forward and making sure Niner was squared away as the skilled operator continued to guide them through traffic.

Dawson asked the all-important question.

"Do we want them dead or alive?"

"Alive would be preferred, at least for our target."

"Which one is he?"

"Hang on!" warned Niner, Dawson grabbing for the Oh Jesus Handle as they took a hard right.

"He's seated directly behind the passenger seat."

Dawson pursed his lips, checking his Glock then holstering it. "This goes a lot smoother if we eliminate the other four, Control."

"Standby, Zero-One."

Spock poked his head between the seats. "Guess that one was a bit above his paygrade."

Dawson nodded. "Recognize the voice?"

"Yup. But what's the CIA doing controlling an op on American soil? What happened to the FBI?"

Dawson shook his head. "I have a feeling someone wasn't happy with what just happened."

"The President?"

Dawson shrugged. "Possibly."

"Zero-One, Control. Use of deadly force is authorized. What's your ETA?"

Dawson glanced at the display.

"Two minutes."

Interstate 95, New Jersey

There were only four of them in the large SUV, leaving plenty of space for Kane to disassemble his weapon, it laying in pieces beside him on the backseat. The other occupant, whose name he didn't know—nobody had introduced themselves to anyone else—watched him.

"Do you remember your training?"

Kane grinned. "I'm American."

He rapidly reassembled the weapon, the eyes of the other passengers widening with each click and snap. Kane slapped the magazine in and put two bullets into the chest of the man beside him, then one in the back of the head of the man in the passenger seat.

He pointed the gun at the driver. "Stop the car."

The man turned, his eyes wide with rage, his nostrils flaring as he gripped the steering wheel tight. "I told them we couldn't trust Americans!"

"I guess Allah wasn't on your side after all."

"Nor yours!" The man spun the steering wheel hard to the left and the SUV turned then tipped, teetering on two wheels, tossing Kane against the side before physics completed the driver's intention, the SUV slamming onto its side, the windows shattering as they skidded along the pavement. The driver, with no seatbelt, was now mashed against his dead partner on the passenger side, screaming in Arabic his hatred of all things American in Arabic, as Kane, already having regained his balance, stood on the side of the SUV's interior, his feet straddling the now non-existent side window, one hand gripping the door handle now over his head, the other pointing his weapon at the driver.

"Goodbye."

He pumped two bullets into the driver who was no longer playing his part.

The SUV screeched to a halt, Kane relaxing, not a scratch on him.

"I guess He *was* on my side."

Operations Center 3, CIA Headquarters, Langley, Virginia

"Jesus!" exclaimed Child as they all watched in horror, the retasked drone providing live footage of Kane's vehicle skidding on its side before coming to a halt in a cloud of dust.

"Is he alive?" asked Morrison as he and Leroux stepped closer to the screen.

Leroux shook his head. "I can't see anything."

Morrison pointed at a secondary display, showing Kane's tracking device. "Does that still work if he's dead?"

Leroux nodded. "Yes, sir, until the battery dies."

"Look!" Sonya pointed at the main screen, the rear windshield suddenly bursting out, a pair of boots visible for a moment before a man climbed into view.

"Is that him?" asked Morrison.

Leroux pointed at the main display. "Zoom in." He glanced over at the display showing the thermal view and Kane's tracker. "The tracking device has him outside the vehicle. It's got to be him!"

The figure looked up at the sky, waving, the zoomed in face clearly Kane, flashing a grin. Leroux breathed a sigh of relief as cheers and laughter erupted from the others in the room, the tension of the moment broken. Kane was quickly swarmed by civilians rushing over to help in what they most likely assumed was a traffic accident. Someone handed him something and moments later Leroux's phone vibrated in his pocket.

He answered.

"Hello?"

"Hey, buddy, it's me. You watching?"

Leroux looked at Morrison, pointing at the screen then the phone. "Yeah, you okay?"

"Peachy. Here's the quick rundown."

"Just a sec, I'll put you on speaker." Leroux tapped his phone. "Okay, go ahead."

"Approximately one-hundred-twenty hostiles have successfully entered the country. They're deploying to twelve different cities. Attacks will begin in three days, centrally coordinated. Each hostile has been instructed to kill one random civilian each day." Leroux felt his chest tighten as he held out the phone, exchanging glances with the others in the room. He kept silent as Kane continued. "I've eliminated three hostiles and have a lot more intel to deliver. I tagged a guy, did you get that?"

"Yes. A Delta team is about to hit them."

"Good. Tell them the guy has an iPad with everyone's ID on it including names, photographs and assignments. It's essential they get that iPad before he has a chance to erase it."

"Understood." He turned to Child. "ETA on friendlies?"

Child nodded toward the drone feed. "FBI units are arriving at his location now."

Kane, apparently hearing Child's report, turned on the screen. "I see them. I'm going to get on a secure comm and give you guys a full report."

"What about the other vehicles?" asked Leroux. "Is it safe to hit them?"

"Affirmative, they're not scheduled for any contact for three days. Make sure you get them all at once though before the news starts reporting on it, otherwise they might decide to go down in a blaze of glory."

"Roger that. Get yourself secure, we're about to hit the other target."

Kane gave a thumbs up to the eye in the sky as armed FBI quickly surrounded him. Morrison leaned toward the phone.

"Dylan, I'll make a call before the cavity search begins."

Kane laughed, the call cut off.

Jersey City, New Jersey

"There they are."

Dawson pointed ahead, the dark brown Dodge Caravan about half a block ahead, the traffic fairly heavy though moving. He glanced at the map on his laptop. "Looks like they're heading for Manhattan."

"Zero-One, Control. Do you read, over?"

Dawson activated his comm. "Control, Zero-One. Go ahead, over."

"Zero-One, we've got new intel. The target has an iPad that must be retrieved intact, over."

That changes things.

"And the target?"

"Now considered secondary. Primary objective is the retrieval of the iPad. Intact. Do whatever is necessary to ensure that, including termination of the secondary target."

"Roger that. Zero-One, out."

Dawson glanced at the others. "This just got a bit easier and a bit harder."

Niner channeled his inner Connery. "Some things in here don't react well to bullets."

Dawson smiled. "Exactly." He pointed to the vehicle. "We better do this before they get to the interstate. Tablet computers don't react well to high-speed crashes either. Pull up behind, passenger side. Atlas, take out their rear tire."

Atlas nodded, screwing a suppressor in place as Niner guided them through the traffic as it slowed for a stoplight.

"This might be as good as it gets," said Niner, about half a car length farther back than they'd like.

"No problem," rumbled Atlas, taking aim.

Hadad's head rested on the glass, his eyes burning with fatigue as he watched the city flash by. He had been in New York once before when he was a student. He had once loved America, even aspired to live there, but when American weapons wielded by American trained Iraqi troops had killed his brother, he had joined the cause. The strike they were about to blow today and over the coming weeks would cripple his nemesis. It would punish the infidels for their part in his family's grief and their arrogance in thinking their religion was better than his.

Islam was a way of life, a form of governance, a complete legal system. There was no separating the religious aspect from the judicial or from the governmental. Islam answered to no one, only Allah. Who was man to say what was right and what was wrong when Allah had already told the Prophet what was and wasn't, over a thousand years ago? Once victorious, the entire world would live under Sharia law, would worship Allah as instructed by the Prophet, and would be governed by the Imams, who were wiser than any politician could hope to be, as Allah himself through the Koran and the Hadiths guided them.

It was so simple a life he couldn't understand why anyone would resist it. Who wouldn't want to live with their entire life mapped out so clearly? Say your prayers, listen to your leaders, and serve Allah and his followers. It would be a humble life. Women would obey their men so they had no reason to worry about making decisions like the women of the infidels. Men would serve their leaders, do the farming and the labor, and with Islam ruling the world, there would be no wars with the Jews and the Christians and the other kafirs all dead or converted. There would be no need for Wall

Street, greedy investors, capitalism or democracy. Life would be modest, people would live in peace, and the world could heal itself from the greed of man.

It had happened before as outlined in the Bible, when Allah had wiped the slate clean with the Great Flood. Today, that flood was in the form of His true believers, believers flooding the shores of Europe, immigrating to the infidel's strongholds, breeding at three and four times the rate of those around them, so that soon there would be nothing the infidel could do.

It was inevitable; the infidels' own foolish policies of political correctness, multiculturalism and open immigration destroying them in the end.

They had failed to learn from history.

Hadrian's Wall?

The fall of Rome?

And today they took another step on the path to Allah's will, and though he and the others with him might very well die, they would die for the only just cause there was.

A popping sound from behind them snapped him from his reverie as he felt the vehicle shift.

"What was that?"

The driver slammed his fist against the steering wheel. "I think we just got a flat tire."

Hadad closed his eyes, looking up to the heavens.

Allah, why would you do this to us?

"Let's see how many get out," said Dawson as Niner inched forward, traffic starting to move now that the light was green.

The dark brown van stayed put, Atlas' shot perfect.

Three doors opened and everyone stepped out except the man in the passenger seat.

Must be the leader.

"There's our target," said Spock as a man stepped out, iPad in hand.

Dawson grabbed the door handle. "Everyone see the iPad?"

A round of affirmatives.

"Let's take them. Execute in three… two…"

"Zoom in on that iPad! Now!"

Child quickly complied with Leroux's order, the screen resolving into a clean image of the iPad, revealing what Leroux had feared the moment he saw the way the man was holding it when he stepped out.

He cursed, activating his comm. "Come in Zero-One!"

"What is it?" asked Morrison, staring at the image, puzzled.

"It's a dead man's switch!" exclaimed Child as the doors of the Delta team's vehicle burst open, the four men stepping out before Leroux could warn them.

Dawson pumped two rounds into their target's head, rushing forward to catch the tablet before it hit the ground as Spock came about on his right, eliminating the target in the passenger seat. Niner and Atlas took the left flank, dropping the others, it all over in seconds.

It was then that the screams of the public, witness to what had just happened, began.

And the phones came out, not to call for help, but to record the aftermath.

Everyone wants their fifteen minutes.

Dawson pulled the iPad from their target's still tight grip, activating his comm. "Go ahead, Control." His eyes narrowed as a countdown began on the display.

A countdown from five.

"Bomb!" He spun, grabbing Spock and yanking him with him as they all scattered. The previously fascinated pedestrians resumed their screaming as they realized something was wrong, heavily armed men not running away unless there was a good reason. He dove behind a parked delivery truck, Spock dropping beside him.

Then nothing.

He glanced back, the brown van just sitting there, blood still oozing from its occupants. He looked at the iPad.

Its display was blank.

It was then that he finally made sense of the shouts in his ear.

"It's a dead man's switch. Don't let go of the iPad!"

Dawson rolled onto his back, staring up at the sky, holding the iPad display so the viewers at home could see it.

"I think it's too late."

Boyle Plaza, Jersey City, New Jersey

Nazari reached into his pocket, his phone, issued to him at the warehouse, vibrating. He entered his code and read the message, cursing. The driver glanced at him.

"What is it?"

Nazari shoved his phone back in his pocket. "We've been compromised."

"What do you mean?"

"The leadership has been taken, which means we were betrayed." His immediate suspect was the convert, though how he could have done it, he had no idea. The man was in another vehicle with other warriors loyal to the cause, who would never have given him an opportunity to do anything.

And how would he have had time?

"What do we do now?" asked the driver, those in the back already whispering among themselves, scared.

Nazari sighed. "It's time to reveal to you our true mission."

This silenced everyone, the driver's foot easing off the accelerator as he suddenly forgot what he was doing.

"You will have noticed that each team split into two, and if you knew your maps, you would know that we are *not* heading for Washington, DC. Half the teams are indeed heading for their assigned cities, but the other half are heading for our primary target, a mission, that once completed, will be even more glorious than anything accomplished before."

"Where are we going?"

"We will be rendezvousing with others who have been here for months, laying the groundwork for the biggest attack ever conceived. But now that we have been compromised, we must assume we are being watched." He motioned to the driver. "Watch the GPS and speed up. Your job is to deliver us to our destination as quickly as possible without attracting attention."

"Y-yes, sir."

The man refocused on the road ahead.

Nazari turned toward the others in the back. "All commanders just received the same message I did, as did all secondary vehicles. At this moment, all of the teams, not just the half originally assigned, are heading for our primary target, as we have to assume that we are all being tracked. With twenty-four teams now heading for the target, we are sure to get a significant number through."

"What's the target?"

Nazari smiled. "One with over twenty-thousand Americans including men, women and children." He took a deep breath, the fever filling him. "Today we strike fear in the hearts of Americans everywhere, at one of the symbols of their supreme decadence."

Interstate 95, New Jersey

Kane watched the monitors, dots across the zoomed out map continually updated as locations were radioed in, every vehicle tracked from the sky, not enough with actual tails on them. Yet something looked off.

"Are we sure this is right?"

The FBI tech nodded. "We're tracking twenty-five vehicles. Twelve appear to be heading out of the city, including yours, so eleven now. Delta took out the twenty-fifth vehicle we were tracking—"

"And the other twelve?"

"All appear to be heading into Manhattan."

Kane's eyes narrowed, the pattern his subconscious had picked up on now clear. "That doesn't make any sense. We were all assigned different cities. What about the second one on my team?"

"Heading into the city."

"So not toward Washington?"

The tech shook his head. "Negative. Not unless they're completely lost.

Kane inhaled, trying to make sense of what he was looking at. His team had definitely been heading for DC, and until the moment the door of his vehicle had closed, every instruction given had indicated Nazari's vehicle was too.

Which meant he had been deceived.

But to what end?

"Wait a minute." The tech pointed at the screen. "Some of them are changing direction."

"Which ones?"

"So far only the ones leaving the city."

Kane closed his eyes, tossing his head back. "The dead man's switch. It must have sent a signal to the others that they'd been compromised." He cursed, staring back at the screens, realizing he had been lied to the entire time. "Where are they headed now?"

"It looks like they're all heading back into the city. My guess is they're going to join up with the others, wherever they're going."

Kane shook his head, his fists squeezed tightly, desperate to belt something that didn't cost a fortune. He was a decoy. They all were. The leadership must have assumed they were compromised, so took those they couldn't be absolutely sure about and sent them on the decoy mission. If they had successfully reached their destination, even just some of them, it still would have created havoc.

But it was the primary plan that he was now concerned with, a plan that at the moment, nobody knew anything about.

And he should have.

It had never made sense, and until this moment, he hadn't realized it hadn't made sense. Twenty-four teams, splitting up upon arrival, sent to shoot individual targets in cities scattered about the country.

That meant bullets.

Not bombs.

Not dirty bombs.

What are they using the Cesium for?

"They have to have something big in mind."

"Like what?"

Kane tapped his chin, chewing on his lip. "What's happening today that would have lots of people?"

The tech grunted. "Umm, it's New York City. There's lots of people everywhere."

Kane checked his watch. "It won't be the financial district, it's a ghost town now."

"I thought the entire point of a dirty bomb was contamination."

Kane nodded. "Yeah, but they were talking about making demands and forcing the government to stop the bombings in ISIL territory and to withdraw."

The tech's head bobbed. "So hostages."

"That's what I'm thinking. Hostages with the Cesium weapon as the insurance."

"Christ. Where do you think they'll hit? I've got family here, you know!"

Kane's eyes squeezed shut, his head dropping back as he realized exactly what type of target they would hit.

"Who's playing tonight?"

Lower Bowl, Madison Square Garden, New York City

Wendy sat in her seat, her eight-year-old daughter beside her, her teenage son one more seat down. "These are great seats!" She had never been to a game before, it not something she could afford as a single mother, but a contest at the office had her with a set of three tickets only a dozen rows back.

"There's so many people!" exclaimed her daughter, her mouth full, her hotdog already under attack.

"It's exciting, isn't it?" She glanced at her son who was already on his cellphone, texting, pretending to be bored, but she knew better, his breathing a little faster than usual, his eyes a little wider, this one of the biggest outings they had ever been on as a family. She still couldn't believe she had won the contest, and to be frank, she was pretty sure when she won it had been rigged.

Who offers a prize of three *tickets?*

Everyone knew how hard things were for her since her husband had died from pancreatic cancer, their savings drained, their home sold, their lifestyle sinking from middle-income to poverty line almost overnight.

And it hadn't saved him in the end.

Yet she would do it all again, even knowing how difficult things would be, those precious few extra months with her husband, with her children's father, so important. It had given them the time to get to know each other again, to fall in love again, to say the things that needed to be said.

To get the closure.

And tonight they would all forget their troubles and enjoy an evening out on her friends, the "contest" even including cash for the concessions and shirts for the kids, both already wearing jerseys as they tugged at their drinks between bites of their hot dogs.

The crowd roared and she saw dozens of men in military uniforms standing in the audience, waving, her brain catching up to the announcer who had just asked the audience to thank their men in uniform. She clapped and added her own Whoop! Whoop! as her daughter joined in, her son blushing in embarrassment.

Teenagers!

The lights went low, music started to blare, and she put her arm around her daughter's shoulders as the crowd roared.

"Here they come!"

Exiting the Holland Tunnel, New York City, New York

Nazari stuffed his phone back in his pocket, his chest swelling with pride, his stomach with butterflies as he realized the enormity of the message he had just received and the plans he had just read.

He was in charge.

The leadership was presumed dead and he was the most senior commander to have made it across.

The entire plan, its success or failure, was now on his shoulders, the fate of the Islamic fight against the infidel his responsibility.

He sucked in a deep breath, closing his eyes as they continued toward their destination, the others chatting quietly in the back, the driver focused on his one task.

Islam will not fall should you fail.

The thought comforted him slightly. Allah had a plan, and it was in His hands whether they succeeded tonight. If they failed, then it was His will.

But he couldn't see Allah wanting them to fail.

If they should succeed, the Caliphate could expand, could grow stronger, could restore Islam to its former glory, and eventually fulfill its destiny.

And tonight could be an incredibly important step on that journey.

The Prophet had said the Mahdi would return when the Romans landed troops in Turkey or Syria, and they would be met by an army of Muslim warriors who would stand side-by-side with the converts, the Romans—or Westerners—demanding their return. The battle would be brutal, with two-thirds dying, but in the end they would be victorious over the infidel, the Mahdi would return to rule, subjugating the entire world, then the Day of

Judgement would come, with only the righteous, those who had fought for Islam, given eternal entry into paradise.

Could what we do tonight force the Romans to invade?

The thought sent chills up and down his spine.

"We're almost there."

Nazari's eyes focused once again on the road, glancing at the GPS indicating their arrival in less than ten minutes. The commanders on the ground had chosen the target well. The men he was about to take command of knew the plan, but they needed an iron fist who had proven himself in battle to make sure the plan was followed, to make the tough decisions that less experienced men might hesitate to make.

He pointed at a sign. "Go to the service entrance." He turned to those in the back seat. "Weapons ready. Be prepared to shoot the guards, but wait for my order."

The men suddenly became all business, these seasoned veterans of the conflict back home. The driver lowered all the windows as they were flagged down at the gate, one of the officers holding an iPad, reading their license plate.

He smiled.

"Welcome, Commander!" he said, stepping over to the passenger side window. "They're waiting for you inside. Straight ahead, to the left, and through the large doors. One of our men will be there to guide you."

"Thank you."

"Allahu Akbar!"

Nazari smiled.

"Allahu Akbar!"

Operations Center 3, CIA Headquarters, Langley, Virginia

"Nazari's van has just arrived at Madison Square Garden. There's a basketball game tonight, estimated twenty thousand in attendance."

Leroux looked at Morrison who was shaking his head at Therrien's report. He turned to Therrien. "Has it started?"

Therrien nodded. "Just did."

"Shit." He scrutinized the display, the terrorist vehicles continuing to converge. "Why hasn't the FBI taken any of them down?"

Morrison's lips were pressed together tight, they now thin white lines.

He was pissed.

He reached in his pocket and pulled up something on it, reading a message on his phone. He turned to Therrien, handing him the device. "Here's the login information. Bring up that video conference, now."

Therrien nodded, his eyes slightly wide as he keyed in the information, half the display switching to a grid of images, including the President. The director of the FBI, Bob Waters, was already speaking.

Morrison cut in.

"Why hasn't the FBI stopped any of the vehicles?"

Waters stopped, turning his head, apparently looking at his own display to see that Morrison was standing in an operations center, surrounded by staff. "Is your end secure?"

"I trust my people. And I repeat, why haven't you stopped any of the vehicles?"

Waters reddened. "As I was explaining to the *President*, we feel they are all converging on a single location and we will hit them at that time so we can take them all at once."

Morrison shook his head. "You fool! If you'd stop sticking your head so far up your ass to say hello to your ego, you might actually be able to see what the hell is going on for once. Hasn't your staff told you where they are heading?"

Waters was a nice burgundy now. "I'll be attending an update as soon as this briefing is over. Until such—"

Morrison waved a hand, dismissing the man. "Mr. President, they are converging on Madison Square Garden. There's a basketball game there with twenty-thousand fans in attendance. If we allow one-hundred-twenty terrorists to arrive at that location, it will be a blood bath that will make 9/11 look like a regular day in the inner city."

Waters rapidly paled. "I-I didn't know. I—"

The President cut him off. "Leif, can your team handle this?"

"Yes, sir."

"You're in charge."

"Yes, Mr. President." Morrison turned, pointing at Therrien. "Clear that screen."

Approaching Madison Square Garden, New York City

Kane listened to Leroux as he provided a rapid update, the FBI driver blasting through the evening traffic, taking sidewalks when needed. All that mattered now was reaching the stadium.

"FBI is hitting everything they can right now, but it's too late," reported Leroux. "By the time the order was given, over a dozen vehicles had already entered the premises, with most of the rest within a couple of blocks."

"Did we get *any*?"

"Eight."

"Eight? Are you kidding me?"

"I wish I was, Dylan. At least it means about forty less hostiles to deal with."

Kane shook his head. "You're forgetting one thing."

"What's that?"

"If this was the plan all along, how many were already there?"

Leroux cursed. "What's your plan?"

Kane pointed to the approaching corner, telling the driver to stop.

"I'm going to join my brothers."

Loading Dock, Madison Square Garden, New York City

"Welcome, Commander. I'm Mohammad Bata."

Nazari smiled, shaking hands with the leader of the advance team, quickly surveying the massive delivery area. Nearby, dead bodies were loaded into an empty cube van, at least a dozen inside so far. "Tarek Nazari. Status?"

"As you already saw, we have taken the rear gate and replaced it with our own people. They'll let the rest in then block it with a few vehicles before joining us inside." Bata pointed at the van. "These were the people inside the loading dock area. We managed to take it with little resistance and no alarms raised."

Nazari nodded toward a security camera. "The cameras?"

"Our man on the inside overrode them for the rear gate and loading dock areas before we arrived. He's ready to take over all the cameras as we begin our assault."

"Where is he?"

Bata grinned, pointing up. "In an air vent. He was able to cut through to gain access to the security lines." Bata shook his head. "These Americans are fools. All of the plans are filed with the government, accessible to anyone with the right, shall we say, access?"

Nazari's head bobbed slowly as he walked toward the far end of the loading dock, more vehicles pulling in, his men quickly filling the area. "They certainly are arrogant. It will be their downfall." He turned back to Bata. "Supplies?"

Bata pointed at two large cube vans, men already handing out additional ammunition to the new arrivals. "Everything we need. If this turns into a long mission, there is plenty of food and water in the stadium, and there's no way the authorities will prevent us from accessing it since we'll have thousands of hostages."

Nazari watched with satisfaction as more vehicles arrived, there now almost a hundred men available to him, all donning loose fitting jerseys hanging almost to their knees, their weapons and body armor well hidden. "And the plan?"

"We have twenty men spread throughout the facility, ready to execute the plan on your command. My men—your men—are well trained and have been rehearsing this mission for weeks. The new arrivals will supplement the teams already here then help secure the stadium once we have taken the arena."

"Excellent. Nothing changes, we just have more people. We also have to assume they know we're here but haven't had a chance to react yet. Are you ready?"

"Yes, sir."

"Then proceed."

Bata motioned to another man who handed him a megaphone. "Team leads, report!" A dozen men broke away from what they were doing, lining up behind them, each the head of their own column. "Everyone else, line up behind a team lead, make them even. Now!"

There was a mad scramble as almost one hundred men, dressed as super-fans, rushed to comply, a dozen columns formed within a minute.

Bata smiled at Nazari, raising the megaphone. "You will follow your team lead to your assigned position and you will follow his orders. Do not speak anything but English, don't touch your weapons, and most of all remember to look happy!"

Nazari stifled a laugh as he watched one hundred adrenaline-fueled soldiers of Allah force smiles on their faces.

It seemed unnatural.

He took the megaphone. "Forget the smiles, you look like you're visiting your mother-in-law's." Laughter and genuine smiles. "That's better. Now remember that feeling. You don't need to look happy, just don't look like you hate everyone around you! Remember, follow your team leads, obey their orders, and wait for the signal. You've been training for this and Allah is on our side! Allahu Akbar!"

Operations Center 3, CIA Headquarters, Langley, Virginia

"How many made it in?"

Leroux read the count estimate on one of the displays. "Fifteen vehicles in total. Our count from the infrared scans is seventy-two, and according to your report, all with small arms and vests."

"And God knows what else inside." Kane's voice wasn't steady, one screen showing a drone image of him sprinting toward the stadium. "Better have NYPD shut down all traffic coming into the area. There's no way these guys are going to be able to secure the entire stadium, so there's going to be a lot of panicked people fleeing. We want them to be able to get away as easily as possible."

"What about hostiles being among them?"

"No, don't worry about that. If their goal was to mingle, they'd be doing it already." Leroux winced as Kane dodged what appeared to be an errant cab, insults exchanged. "These guys are converging to make a statement. I don't think any of them plan on leaving here alive."

A pit formed in Leroux's stomach. "It's a suicide mission?"

"That's my guess."

Child grunted, shaking his head. "Allah better prepare a whole lot of virgins."

Approaching Madison Square Garden, New York City

Spock brought the SUV to a halt near an FBI mobile command post that had just arrived a block away from the stadium. NYPD were converging on the area, blocking off streets, vehicles already in the two-block perimeter guided out of the panic zone they expected any minute now.

There was no stopping this.

It was happening.

Now their goal was to help get as many of those who managed to flee, to safety, and bring this to a swift conclusion with as few civilian casualties as possible.

As for the terrorists?

Bring lots of body bags.

A UH-60 Black Hawk helicopter thundered overhead, a group of soldiers rappelling to the street below, Dawson immediately recognizing his best friend and second-in-command, Master Sergeant Mike "Red" Belme. Dawson waved as he stepped out of the SUV, Red and the others quickly joining them.

"What's the word?" asked Red, following Dawson as he headed for the command post, stepping into the back.

"I've been given command of the assault, Langley is coordinating intel. We've got an estimated one-hundred hostiles inside with a possible dirty bomb."

"What's the plan?"

"We infiltrate as quickly as possible before they secure the building."

Red nodded. "Resources?"

"NYPD is sealing off the area. Bravo Team is on site plus more Delta units are inbound but won't be here before we make entry. FBI has several SWAT teams that we'll be deploying to the entrances to take out any obvious targets."

"Can we stop it?"

"No way. This is going to get bad before it gets better."

Red frowned. "So people are dying."

"Absolutely. All we can hope to control is how many."

Loading Dock, Madison Square Garden, New York City

Nazari glanced at his phone, the last status message arriving.

Everyone was in place.

He tapped the button, sending the signal, and Bata hauled open the door. Nazari stepped through, taking the lead, half a dozen men with him as they marched through the hall, people jumping out of their way, not sure of what to make of them.

They weren't his concern.

There would be plenty of time to kill civilians, right now their objective was to eliminate resistance and reach the arena. A police officer rounded the corner and his eyes bulged as Nazari pulled his weapon out from under his jersey, putting two rounds in the man, he falling to the ground, gasping for breath. Nazari walked up to him and put a final bullet in the man's head.

And the stunned silence at the first two bullets gave way to panic as those in the area realized they had indeed heard what they thought they had.

Screams filled the concrete halls as people raced to get away from what, they could not possibly know. They would be the ones to survive, those few who weren't watching the game, those who were out getting food and drink or using the bathroom.

Or just late.

They were the lucky ones.

And their panic would hamper the response of the security teams.

Which was exactly what they needed.

Lower Bowl, Madison Square Garden, New York City

Brian Parker leapt to his feet, cheering as a three pointer landed, then dropped back into his seat, exchanging an excited glance with his buddies. They were all on leave from the USS San Antonio, heading back to the Middle East in three days. His brother-in-law, who he couldn't stand—not because he wasn't a nice guy, but because he was laying it to his sister, which just wasn't right for some reason—had got him four tickets to the game, so close to the action he could smell Spike Lee's cologne if the man had been there today.

It was one of the best days of his life.

They had all agreed not to wear their uniforms tonight. While they loved the appreciation quite often shown, tonight they just wanted to be four guys out on the town for a good time, not four servicemen.

The other team scored.

A woman screamed.

They all laughed.

"Somebody's taking it too seriously."

Someone else screamed and Parker's smile disappeared, recognizing fear when he heard it. So did the others. Gunshots sounded behind them and the play slowed as some of the players stopped, turning toward the loud reports. Suddenly dozens of men rushed from the gates and down the stairs.

"Let's get the hell out of here!" shouted somebody from the floor, the teams bolting, staff and courtside spectators following, the crowd panicking as screams and cries replaced the excitement of moments before. More gunfire erupted and Parker rose, heading for the aisle to help when his friend Chuck Wilson grabbed him by the arm.

"Are you crazy! Look how many there are!"

Parker yanked his arm loose but stopped. There were dozens already on the floor, the players having managed to evacuate it appeared, but the audience trapped, most of their gates blocked.

Wilson pulled him back into his seat.

For there was nothing they could do.

It was already over.

Wendy screamed as the woman in front of her was shot, collapsing at her feet as a man wielding some sort of machinegun rushed past, screaming something in what she assumed was Arabic, his weapon belching lead at anything in his way.

Someone grabbed her from behind and she shrieked again.

"Don't worry, I won't hurt you."

She looked to see a man in uniform, pulling her away from the aisle, another one urging people to get down, both she remembered having stood up earlier to accept the applause of the crowd they were now trying to save. In her immediate area people were bobbing up and down with uncertainty, one minute wanting to race for the exit, the next hitting the floor as more shots rang out.

"Just stay down," said the man, talking into her ear so he could be heard over the mayhem. "They want hostages. Don't give them any reason to single you out. Don't make eye contact, don't make any sound. If they ask you a question, answer them, but keep it short. Keep toward the middle of a section; they'll most likely take people from the sides. Keep your kids calm, especially your daughter."

Wendy glanced at her daughter who was shaking uncontrollably, her hotdog forgotten in her hand, her young eyes wide with terror, staring at the body of a man draped over a seat in the row ahead of them.

The man took Wendy by the shoulders, staring in her eyes. "Are you okay?"

She shook out a nod.

"Good, take care of yourself."

The man immediately turned, his attention now focused on a little girl, wailing, her hand still holding that of her father, who sat slumped over in his seat, the back of his head missing.

We're all going to die!

Outside Madison Square Garden, New York City

It was absolute mayhem.

Thousands were streaming out of the exits, screaming, crying, shoving their way past those who were too slow to keep up with the panicked flow. Dawson could only watch as those knocked off balance were trampled, he and the others pushing through the crowd, trying to get into the stadium before it was too late and those who would do his country harm had full control.

They had quickly switched to civilian clothes, their weapons hidden, their body armor under jerseys confiscated from fans outside. His twelve member team, the best of the best, were attempting access at various points as the NYPD directed the flow of fleeing spectators away from the immediate vicinity, FBI SWAT teams still arriving though holding back, he deciding to keep them out of sight until the majority of those fleeing were out of weapons range.

He stuck to the sides as best he could, redirecting people into the center of the throng with well-placed shoves and shoulders, pushing as quickly as he could toward the entrance. He reached it, pushing through the doors as hundreds continued to stream past, he thanking God for every one of those that escaped, no matter how terrified they were.

It meant they would live.

NYPD was clearing the area and radiological teams were on their way, it expected that if this should go sour, Cesium-137 could cover the entire area.

But if that happened, they would have failed.

And failure wasn't acceptable.

He hugged the wall, continuing to push through the crowds as he scanned the area, ignoring anything coming toward him with the flow. It was the ones going against the flow, the ones standing still, that were of interest to him.

They would be the hostiles.

Though he had yet to spot one, Niner the only other person pushing through like he was.

Wait a minute.

He spotted a man, standing in the corner, letting the crowds surge by, doing nothing. He appeared Middle Eastern and was watching the crowd, there excitement on his face, but no panic. The man turned toward Dawson.

Dawson spun, bending over slightly, faking a leg cramp. He glanced carefully behind him, the man having continued to turn, no longer looking toward him.

Dawson surged forward, drawing his knife, clearing the last few civilians and plunging it deep in the man's neck, arterial spray spurting over the crowd, the new screams going unnoticed.

He grabbed the man under the shoulders and dragged him behind a kiosk, quickly searching him for comms.

Nothing but a cellphone.

He returned it to the man's pocket then activated his own comm.

"Control, Zero-One. I've taken one down, Seventh Avenue entrance, behind the kiosk on the left side. He's got a phone on him with a thumb scanner. Send in a retrieval team to get it and his body, or just take his thumb if necessary. We need to know what's on that phone."

"Roger that Zero-One, retrieval team proceeding now."

Dawson spotted the women's bathroom and headed for it, rounding the corner cautiously, finding dozens inside, cowering in fear. A woman screamed when she spotted the blood on him, slapping her hands over her mouth.

"I'm with the police." He glanced back out the entrance, spotting no hostiles, the crowds thinning however, the chaos the terrorists probably wanted to create in the streets, accomplished.

So they'd probably start securing things shortly.

He turned to the civilians. "Everyone out, now. Just go straight down the stairs and outside and follow the instructions of the police officers."

Nobody moved.

He pulled his gun, pointing it upward at shoulder level. "Now!"

Someone stepped forward, just a tentative step, but it was all the impetus those pressed against the far side of the room needed.

They bailed.

Fast.

And none too quietly.

Dawson watched as the last of them cleared the steps and breathed a sigh of relief just as gunfire rang out down the corridor, a body dropping into view. A cop rounded the corner, firing blindly behind him, most shots uselessly hitting the ceiling.

Dawson grabbed him, the startled man's expression turning to panic.

"FBI! Stop shooting and help get these people out!"

The terrified officer nodded, his expression quickly calming as his training took over, his momentary panic pushed aside. Dawson left him tending the few remaining civilians, heading toward the gunfire.

"Zero-One, I'm coming up on your six," whispered Niner's voice in his comm. He glanced back to see the operator rushing up behind him as more gunfire erupted farther around the bend. Dawson advanced, weapon in front, Niner at his side as the thinned out crowds continued to rush past, eyes wide, cheeks stained with tears, more than the occasional yelp emitted at the sight of the two men in plain clothes advancing toward them.

"Two o'clock."

Dawson squeezed his trigger, twice.

The man dropped, the suppressor keeping the sounds to a minimum, the chaos around them taking care of the rest. An army corporal in uniform skidded to a halt, grabbing the dead man's weapon.

"US Special Forces. Drop the weapon!"

The corporal lowered the weapon, slowly raising his hands as he turned toward Dawson and Niner who quickly closed the gap. He slapped his Shoulder Sleeve Insignia. "US Army Ranger. How can I help?"

Dawson turned his attention down the hall. "Disable that weapon and get your ass outside. Right now I don't want anyone with a gun who shouldn't have one."

"Yes, sir!" The corporal dropped to the floor, quickly unloading the weapon and removing the bolt before disappearing from sight as Dawson and Niner continued forward.

The PA system beeped, the alarm that had been sounding halted.

Here it comes.

Center Court, Madison Square Garden, New York City

Nazari raised the mike to his mouth, slowly turning as he surveyed the thousands upon thousands of hostages now under his control. It was an incredible sight, and from all reports, their plan had gone off almost perfectly. The security office was under their control, the entrances into the arena were secure, and they had lost no men that he knew of.

His only regret was that they hadn't been able to reach the floor in time to secure the teams, America loving their celebrities. Yet as he scanned the expensive seats ringing the floor, he knew there were more than enough still here, the Hollywood types and business tycoons loving their basketball.

He spit on their hallowed ground.

"American infidels!" The murmuring, whimpering crowd, fell silent. "You are now all prisoners of the Islamic State. Any who attempt to escape will be shot. Any who attempt to resist, will be shot."

Somebody sprinted for an exit, a burst of automatic weapons fire bringing him down, his body shuddering for a moment before collapsing on the stairs.

Still.

Nazari pointed at the now dead coward. "He did not listen." More gunfire erupted behind him and he casually turned to see one of his men standing over another body. "Neither did he." Nazari surveyed the crowd. "How many more of you are willing to die? All we ask is that you obey us." He sucked in a slow breath. "I want everyone seated, now!"

The crowd slowly sat themselves down, too many hovering over their seats, ready to try and make a break for it.

He needed order.

He needed control.

And he'd have it, even if he had to kill half of them to get it.

As he took in the crowd he spotted something he couldn't tolerate, his mind racing as to what to do. He stopped his slow spin, spotting one section in the bottom level nearly empty. He pointed. "I want everyone in this section to move over to the section to your left." Nobody moved. "Now!"

Wendy couldn't control her shaking, her entire body trembling with fear as she held her terrified kids tightly. She yelped as the man pointing at them shouted. The others around her rose, but she couldn't move. The soldier who had helped her earlier reached over, getting a grip under her arm and raising her to her feet.

"Just walk toward me."

His voice was calm, comforting, though she could see the fear in his eyes. In all their eyes. She shuffled forward, everyone in the next section moving down, filling any empty seats.

"Sit here," said the young man and she nodded, dropping into a seat without thinking, her son in the seat next to her, her daughter in her lap, whimpering though saying nothing, the poor thing still in shock at what she had seen. The soldier took the seat between them and the aisle.

"Now I want all soldiers in the audience to stand up."

The man beside her was about to rise but she reached over and grabbed his shirtsleeve, shaking her head. He patted her hand and smiled. "It's okay."

"If you all do not stand up, I begin shooting children!"

Soldiers around the arena began to rise, their proudly worn uniforms not the camouflage they needed today.

What are they going to do to them?

Parker grabbed Wilson, yanking him back into his seat. "He doesn't know we're soldiers so just sit the hell down. From here we might still be able to help, from there, there's no way in hell."

Wilson nodded and they watched as their comrades were directed to the emptied section, it quickly filling with dozens of America's finest. Wilson's eyes widened. "Jesus, what the hell is that?"

Parker turned to see what Wilson was looking at, frowning as several men pushed a large crate out onto the floor, it clear from the effort involved it was heavy. They stopped at center court then someone with a crowbar pried off the top then the sides, revealing a massive bomb.

Parker cursed as he took it in. There were large bricks of C4 or some type of plastic explosives, along with what appeared to be jars of nails and ball bearings, the intent of this weapon clear.

Carnage.

He turned to the others, his voice low. "I don't think it matters whether they know we're Navy or not."

"Why?"

"It looks like they're going to kill us all."

Kane stepped back from the door, one of the hostiles approaching. He glanced back at the dozen souls huddled in the bathroom with him. "Now stay calm and do as you're told, okay?"

Everyone nodded, he already having convinced them he was an undercover cop. The gun had done the real convincing. He had managed to get inside the stadium no problem and had ducked in here to wait for the crowds to thin out. He was about to send everyone out but had spotted one of the men from his cell outside, watching the crowds rush by, occasionally shooting one of them, as if for sport.

And now he was heading this way, perhaps to use the bathroom, perhaps to kill those he assumed might be inside.

Kane stepped back, merging into the group as the hostile rounded the corner and raised his weapon.

"Everyone out, now!" He jerked his gun toward the door, the barrel aimed away from the civilians for just a moment.

It was all Kane needed.

He stepped forward, putting two in the skull, the man dropping in a heap, his brains splattered across the wall tile. Kane grabbed the man's weapon and turned to the group.

"Any military?"

A man stepped forward. "I was a Marine."

Kane smiled, tossing him the weapon. "Once a Marine, always a Marine."

"Ooh Rah!"

"Keep this room secure. Challenge is 'tornado', password is 'liberty'. Got it?"

"Tornado, liberty. Got it."

"Good luck."

Kane opened the door, peering out into the deserted hall.

Now to not get yourself shot.

Nazari watched the section now filled with uniforms, a row of his men lined up in front of them, weapons pointed at the scum. "You are all infidel cowards who have been killing Muslims all over the world for decades, answerable to no one for your war crimes. The Islamic State, under the authority of Allah himself, has sentenced you all to death!"

Cries, screams and a few shouts erupted from the crowd.

But nothing from the stoic faces glaring back at him.

Except one.

He rose, clasping his hands behind his back, his uniform Navy. "If I die today, I die knowing that every last one of you terrorist pieces of shit will die too!"

Nazari raised his weapon and shot the man in the chest, his crisp white uniform soiled with crimson as the pig fell back into his seat.

"If you shoot them, you shoot me too!"

Nazari turned to see an old man standing in the next section. "I fought for my country long before you were born, and I stand with these soldiers. You want to kill American soldiers, you kill us all!"

More men started to rise throughout the arena, most old, some young, hundreds taking to their feet, then woman and children, the entire venue now on their feet, the infidel's anthem breaking out.

How touching.

"Fire!"

Wendy screamed as everyone dropped, the inspirational moment brought to a swift halt as the brave men and women in uniform were slaughtered only feet away, the gunfire loud and sustained, the terrorists only stopping to reload as they rained hundreds of bullets down on the helpless soldiers.

It took only a minute, maybe two, time no longer making any sense to her, some in her section shot as they rushed to help, others held back by desperate wives and children, everyone helpless.

The final shots echoed through the arena as the gunmen reached the last row, and Wendy closed her eyes, unable to look as the blood poured down the seats and to the court below. She held her kids tight, her hands covering their eyes, as they both cried into her shirt.

She opened her eyes, the sacrifice these poor souls had made demanding she at least pay them that respect.

And saw the soldier who had helped them staring back at her, the spark in his eyes gone.

She turned her attention to the terrorist below, and for the first time in her life, prayed to God to actually kill someone.

Dawson held up a fist, Niner coming to a halt beside him as he peered around the corner, the security control center in sight. "Zero-Seven, Zero-One. Are you in position, over?"

"Affirmative, Zero-One, in position," replied Atlas, he and Spock on the opposite side of the center.

"We're going to assume there's no friendlies inside, but we can't be certain. We'll enter both sides simultaneously. Shoot anything you wouldn't invite home for dinner." He leaned out a little farther from his vantage point then jerked back. "I've got two hostiles on the one-two corner. Zero-Seven, is your side clear?"

"Affirmative. No hostiles in sight, over."

"Understood. Clearing a path, standby."

Dawson stepped out, putting two rounds in the first man, Niner in the second, their suppressors doing the job, there no sign of any reaction in the closed center. Dawson took up a position at the door, Niner placing a charge.

"Zero-One ready."

"Zero-Seven ready."

"Execute in three… two… one… Execute!"

Niner detonated the charge, the door blown inward as Dawson tossed a flash-bang inside, stepping back and checking their six. The blast was deafening, his Sonic Defenders cushioning the blow. Those inside weren't so lucky. He stepped into the security control center, weapon raised, eliminating the targets in his zone, Niner behind him, Atlas and Spock approaching from the other side.

It took seconds.

And he was right.

There were no friendlies.

He activated his comm. "Control, Zero-One. Target secure. Tell us what you need to give you eyes."

"Tornado!"

Dawson turned. "Liberty!" He smiled as Kane stepped into the room, handshakes and backslaps exchanged with the others. "Glad to see you made it inside."

"Touch and go for a few minutes, but I'm here." Kane nodded at the security displays, Niner quickly jacking Langley in so they could begin scanning the feeds to identify their targets.

"That's the guy I think you said was your cell commander," said Niner, pointing at a man standing in the center of the arena with a megaphone. "Looks like he's large and in charge."

Kane nodded. "That's Nazari all right."

Dawson motioned toward the screen showing the court. "According to Langley, of the eight taken down, three were heading here right from the get go, so my guess is those all had cell commanders. There were twelve, they're down three, so it's a one in nine shot he's the man."

"Unless they had someone here already," said Niner.

"Could be, but he's certainly acting like he's in charge." Kane crossed his arms, pinching his chin. "If he doesn't know where the bomb is, he'll know who does."

"Umm, I think I found it."

Dawson turned to see Atlas pointing at a screen showing center court, a massive object covering the logo. His chest tightened as his pulse quickened.

"Jesus," muttered Spock. "Look at the size of that thing!"

Dawson leaned in closer, something not making sense. "Wait a minute. Can we get a closer look at that?" Niner slid over, taking control, the image quickly zooming in on the object. "Better." He pointed. "Looks like C4, but what are these?"

They all leaned in.

"Jars?"

Dawson stood up straight, air blasting from his lips. "Filled with shrapnel. Probably nails and ball bearings."

Atlas scratched behind his ear. "That doesn't make any sense."

"Why not?" asked Spock. "It's a bomb, they want to cause the most casualties, this is a cheap, effective way. Pretty standard."

Kane shook his head. "He's right, it doesn't make any sense. They've got a shitload of radioactive material for a dirty bomb. The whole idea is to detonate it and contaminate, that way your victims suffer and eventually die." He turned to Dawson. "Better call it in."

Dawson frowned then activated his comm. "Control, Zero-One, come in, over."

"Zero-One, Control, go ahead."

"Control, I don't think this is the bomb we're looking for."

Operations Center 3, CIA Headquarters, Langley, Virginia

Morrison turned to Leroux. "Did he just say what I think he said?"

Leroux pressed the headset against his ear. "Zero-One, please repeat your last transmission."

"I don't think this is it. Are there any vehicles unaccounted for?"

Leroux looked back at his team, everyone shaking their head. "Negative, Zero-One. All were either taken down or made it into the stadium." He turned to Therrien. "Get me the best possible view of that device."

Therrien's fingers flew over the keyboard and they were soon scrutinizing several views of the massive bomb at center court. Leroux stepped closer to the screen, his expert eyes examining every detail. C4, jars of shrapnel, wires connecting everything. It was a standard bomb, much more massive than they were used to dealing with, though if the terrorists intended to kill everyone there, they would need a weapon this large. In fact, the design was impressive, it shaped in such a way that it appeared it would cover most of the seating area when it detonated.

Leroux sighed, his eyes closing for a moment as he realized what the Delta operators had figured out minutes ago.

He turned to Morrison. "Sir, I think he's right."

"Why?"

Leroux pointed at the screen. "Why have a bomb this big, designed to kill, when you're supposed to have a dirty bomb, designed to contaminate and kill over time."

Morrison stared at him for a moment, processing his words, then suddenly inhaled, his eyes widening. "My God, you're right!"

Leroux stared at the screens showing the stadium being surrounded, all of their attention focused on this one, massive target.

"Sir, we've got another target." He shook his head. "And we have no idea where the hell it is."

John F. Kennedy International Airport, New York City

"I need to use the bathroom."

The guard, for lack of a better word, nodded and Amira rose, the man opening the door and pointing. "Third door on the right. I'll watch the kids for you."

Amira smiled. "Thank you." She walked down the hall, it a bustle of activity she assumed related to those from her homeland that had clearly arrived, though she had heard nothing about anyone else being shot other than the man who had assaulted her. The expressions on everyone's faces were ones she was familiar with.

Fear.

Anger.

She walked by one room, the door open, a television blaring loudly, a crowd standing around it.

"—saying nothing at this time, however it is clear there is a significant police operation underway at Madison Square Garden. Social media reports suggest a major hostage taking—"

She stepped into the bathroom, sighing, it clear to her that whatever the murderers of her husband had planned was underway, and there was nothing she could do to stop it, despite everything she had been through.

She was just thankful to have escaped.

Especially after what they had wanted her to do.

She made quick use of the toilet, not wanting to leave her children alone for long, unsure of whether the man watching them spoke Arabic, her children's English minimal. She stood, her eyes closed, saying a silent prayer to Allah to take care of her children, no matter what might happen to her in the coming days. Her thoughts became clouded with the news report she had overheard. If there was a major terrorist attack, then that suggested more than a few of the people these Americans had feared were in their country.

Her eyes opened wide.

And at least one that knew her face had made it here. Had he been able to phone ahead and let those already here know what flight she was arriving on, and when?

She unlocked the door and pulled it open.

And gasped, stepping back, her legs hitting the toilet.

She dropped onto the seat.

"I'm so happy to see you made it," said the man standing there, a sickly smile on his face. The nametag on his custodial uniform said Marwan, but his Arabic was native to her region. He was no American. At least not born here.

"Wh-who are you?"

He tapped the nametag. "I was told you were an English teacher. Surely you can read?"

"Wh-what do you want?"

His smile broadened. "I'm here to make sure you fulfill your end of the agreement."

A lump formed in her throat as her hands pressed against the sides of the stall. "You already killed my husband and my children are safe. What more do you think you can do to me?"

The man shook his head, his smile still in place. "You truly do think you escaped, don't you?"

She felt her face drain of blood, a chill rush through her body. "What do you mean?"

"You were followed the entire time. We let you go. A genuine refugee, a woman fleeing with her children, would be trusted. Do you remember why we killed your husband?"

Her jaw dropped slightly as she thought back to those events. Nazari had told her she was to take her children to Europe where she would carry out an assignment, then she would be free of any obligation she had to them. She could think of no obligation she might actually have beyond them letting her live and continue teaching, and had said so. She had then added she would not leave her husband under any circumstances.

So they had killed him, she had assumed as punishment.

"I see you do remember. Your husband was an obstacle, we removed him. You fled, and you were helped along the way. How do you think you got through borders and onto buses and trains when so many others didn't? You were helped along, crowds held back, room made, bribes paid, messages delivered to ensure you continued to run, continued to flee your homeland."

Her shoulders slumped as she tried to think back on everything that had happened. She had always managed to get aboard the trains and the buses, though she had just assumed it was because they were prioritizing women and children when they could, yet when she thought about it, these transports were always jam packed with men, and her and Jodee's families were quite often the only people not young and male.

Her jaw dropped. "Please, please tell me that Sami and Jodee weren't involved."

Marwan smiled. "You never wondered why a desperate family would risk their own lives to help you? Paying bribes to guards, your passage on a boat? Sami was working for us all along."

"Why? Why would he help you?"

"For the same reason you will help us now. We held his family. His sisters, his brothers, his parents. You were found the same night you escaped. You were followed, then the second family was sent to help you."

She shook her head. "No, *I* found *them*. I'm the one who approached them."

"Yes, that is what you were meant to think. They were near you almost the entire time, keeping within sight, and they were to come to you if you didn't come to them. It turns out you sought the closest family's help. And from that point on, you were under our control. The bribes were paid and you were funneled quickly to Germany." The corner of his lip curled slightly. "We never thought you'd go so far as to name one of us. That was a wonderful betrayal on your part. Our intent was to activate you in Germany, but for you to actually gain access to the United States with the help of the Americans?" He shook his head, his smile spreading. "Allah is truly on our side."

Tears filled her eyes as she replayed everything that had happened over the past weeks, and as fantastic as it sounded, it suddenly made sense. This family had taken her in when they didn't need to, they had paid her way when it was necessary, they had always managed to get on the same vehicles as her, Sami always in the lead. Had he been paying people to have them move? Threatening them with who he was working with?

She looked at the man standing over her. "There's nothing you can do to me now. Kill me if you must."

The man stepped back, his smile persistent. "You seem to forget your rather extensive family back home."

She felt faint.

"We have your mother and father in custody, as well as your three brothers and two sisters. Their lives are now in your hands."

Her head dropped into her hands as she felt all hope leave her. All she had been through, the horror and humiliation, the terror of fleeing, the relief and joy of reaching safety.

It had all been orchestrated. If the planes hadn't bombed them, they would have forced her to go anyway under the same threat. Instead, they had let her go, watching her the entire time, helping her on her way, the perfect agent.

One who didn't know she was one.

She stared up at him, her eyes burning, her heart pounding.

"What do you want from me?"

"To finish what you started over a year ago."

Security Control Center, Maddison Square Garden, New York City

"How many does that make?"

Niner totaled the tally marks on the notepad. "Twenty-one dead."

Kane's head bobbed in approval. "A good start, and judging by their reaction in the arena, they have no idea yet." Things were still in a state of flux, the terrorists continuing to consolidate their position. It appeared clear to him that their objective had been to create mayhem in the streets to delay any law enforcement response by flushing those not in the arena out of the building.

They had certainly accomplished that.

What they hadn't anticipated was the fact the Delta teams would be on the scene so quickly, allowing them to gain access before things were secured.

But they'd figure it out soon enough, so they had to capitalize on their ignorance, there still at least eighty on camera.

"Move in the FBI SWAT teams," ordered Dawson, a man he trusted. With him running the show, Kane actually thought they might have a chance here. He was used to working alone, yet this was too big for one man.

Eighty-to-one only worked in a Rambo movie.

Niner called in the order and several of the external cameras showed FBI vehicles racing toward the entrances then stopping, heavily armed teams pouring out to secure the perimeter.

"So many guns," muttered Atlas.

Dawson nodded. "This is going to be ugly." He pointed at a screen showing a shot of the massacred soldiers. "But I want every single last one of these assholes dead."

A rage burned in Kane's stomach as he looked at the image and checked his weapon. "No prisoners."

Operations Center 3, CIA Headquarters, Langley, Virginia

"Sir, I've got something you're gonna want to see."

Leroux walked over to Therrien's station. "What is it?"

He pointed at the screen. "That woman that Miss Morrison brought back? The refugee with the two daughters?"

"What about her?"

"I've been running her face through the system and I just got a hit."

"What is it?"

"She's a black widow, sir!"

Leroux's eyebrows popped, his eyes wide as he watched the footage Therrien redirected to the large displays, showing a woman in flowing black robes, standing with other men and women, but behind a microphone, spewing hatred.

In perfect English.

"The file says she's been a mouthpiece for ISIL for at least a year," said Therrien. "Can she be trusted?"

Leroux's head was shaking slowly as he listened to her condemning allied air raids, condemning the killing of innocent women and children, and calling for all those loyal to Allah to strike back at the infidel, wherever they may be.

And we brought her here.

"Get me Agent White, now!"

John F. Kennedy International Airport, New York City

Sherrie sprinted down the hallway toward the room where the Syrian refugee woman and her children were being held. She had been checking in on Alexis Morrison, the Director having asked for an assessment of her condition that didn't begin with "Da-ad! I'm okay!". But Alexis *was* okay. She had taken a good wallop to the head yet she was conscious and alert, the medical staff at the airport merely recommending monitoring for a concussion.

In fact, she had just been discharged when Sherrie got the call.

She threw open the door, the startled guard jumping to his feet, the children staring up from their coloring, their eyes wide, their mouths agape.

And no Amira.

"Where is she?"

"Bathroom."

"How long ago?"

The guard shrugged. "Not sure. Ten minutes maybe?"

"And that didn't make you suspicious?"

Another shrug. "She's a woman. Don't you take longer?"

Sherrie pointed at his radio. "Lock this place down! Now! We need to find her!" Sherrie stepped back into the hallway to see Alexis Morrison walking toward her, her head bandaged.

"What's going on?"

Sherrie pointed toward the exit sign at the end of the hall. "Get your ass out of this building as fast as you can!"

Alexis just stared at her, a stunned expression on her face.

Sherrie grabbed her by the arm, hauling her toward the exit. "Move! If anything happens to you, your father will kill me."

Alexis peered through the door where Amira's family was. "What about the kids?"

Sherrie stopped, glancing into the room.

They're just kids!

"Take them." She pointed at the guard. "You make sure they all get out of the building and off airport property, understood?"

He nodded. "Yes, ma'am."

Amira stood, her arms out to her side, one of dozens if not hundreds sent out among the millions fleeing. Only she hadn't realized it. She was a devout Muslim and she did support the ultimate goal of ISIL—the establishment of a global caliphate—though she didn't condone their methods. Identified when they captured her town as someone who could speak English perfectly, they ultimately forced her to be their mouthpiece, spouting their hatred for consumption worldwide.

At first it was difficult, almost sickening, though they had treated her and her family reasonably well. And that was the way it was in the Caliphate. If you were of use, then you were left alone. But with so many converts and true Muslims coming to fight for the Caliphate, many from the United States, England and Canada, who already spoke English and quite often had a white face, the need for her skillset had diminished.

So they had found a new purpose for her.

And she had refused.

And they killed her husband for it.

"We lost you in Austria of course," continued Marwan, the man apparently enjoying sharing information on how helpless she truly had been all along. "This was disappointing, but the possibility had always been there. In fact, you were expected to die on the boat ride, so many do."

She said nothing as Marwan continued to work, images of that harrowing journey flashing before her eyes.

"When Mahmoud spotted you on the plane, it was blessed news. I was to deliver Allah's justice, my job here having been set up over a year ago in anticipation for something like this. The weapon arrived yesterday by ship and I was able to easily get it inside the airport with other supplies." He tapped a wooden leg. "Very easily."

She glanced down, her eyes seeing nothing, unable to focus on anything.

"It's too bad Mahmoud died. He didn't know what the true mission was. I assume he feared you might tell the authorities something that might stop us. He should have just let you get off the plane. I was there, in the jetway, waiting to intercept you, but his actions unfortunately messed up our plan. But Allah is merciful, and Mahmoud paid the price, and He gave us a second chance. *Me* a second chance." He tapped his security pass. "I simply followed you then waited. I knew it would only be a matter of time for things to settle down."

She drew a breath, holding it for a moment. "Why me? If you were going to do it anyway, why do you still need me?"

"Because it is Allah's will."

"I-I don't understand."

"You weren't meant to be here, yet here you are. You are a symbol. A symbol of their arrogance. A woman whose family was saved by the infidels, whose faith is so strong she would still kill them by the thousands. *That* is a powerful message that will make the infidels realize how strongly we *all* believe in our cause." He shook his head, plugging in what appeared to be the last loose wire of a terrifying looking device. "I can't wait to watch the reaction over the coming days."

She examined the contraption strapped to her chest then closed her eyes, picturing her family. She had no choice. With their lives on the line, she would be forced to fulfill the mission she had refused weeks ago.

Her husband had died for nothing.

Tears filled her eyes and she thought of her children. They would be safe and that was her only concern the entire time. Her husband was gone, but their children would survive. She would sacrifice herself for them, the family of martyrs honored.

Will they remember their mommy?

A tear rolled down her cheek as Marwan stood up in front of her. "You understand how it works?" he asked, pressing the trigger into her hand.

She nodded. "I let go of the button and it detonates."

"Yes. It's called a dead man's switch. You remember what you're supposed to say?"

Tears flowed. "I remember."

"Good. Feel free to embellish, you were always good at that." He fixed a robe over her shoulders, covering the weapon. "When you are finished, I will make sure your family is released and rewarded for your sacrifice. The shame of your husband's cowardice will be forgiven." He suddenly grabbed her by the shoulders, his eyes wide and bright, a smile on his face. "Be not afraid! You are serving Allah and His will, and today you further the cause of Islam, and for that, you are guaranteed eternity in paradise!"

She forced a smile, a single bob of the head all she could manage, then wiped the tears from her face.

"Ready?"

"Y-yes."

Marwan pulled open the door and she stepped out of the utility room and into the mass of travelers oblivious to the danger she represented.

An alarm sounded.

Sherrie pushed open the door and stepped into the public area of the terminal, an alarm blaring. She cursed, having assumed that her orders to search for Amira would have been followed a little less publicly. She activated her comm. "This is Agent White. What's that alarm?"

"It's the radiological alarm. The system's detected something radioactive, off the scales!"

She could hear the panic in the man's voice and feel it in her own stomach. This was their greatest fear—the Cesium reaching home soil, and now here she was, perhaps only yards away from what would probably be a slow, painful death. "Where's the alarm?"

"Multiple triggers. It appears to be on the move. It's in Terminal Five."

"Okay, evacuate that area, but if you ID the bomber, don't interfere, just stay out of their way. The longer they hold off triggering the device, the more people we can evacuate."

"Understood." There was a pause. "Umm, you're sure this isn't a drill?" The voice lowered. "The supervisor here says it's probably just Homeland testing us."

Sherrie closed her eyes for a moment, stupidity universal. "Tell them that Agent White of the CIA is confirming that this is not a drill. If they still don't believe you, have them contact Langley. You need to evacuate this airport immediately, otherwise thousands could die!" She looked about, trying to gain her bearings as hundreds if not thousands rushed about in all directions, panic setting in as guards seemed to be simply moving them along in no particular direction. She spotted a sign. "Where did you say the weapon was?"

"Terminal Five."

"Jesus, that's where I am!"

"Wait, another detector just went off. They're heading north."

She scanned the crowds, searching for someone not in a panic, someone moving with a deliberate purpose, someone moving against the flow. But there were too many. She cursed the entire situation. If they had only had the time to properly screen all the refugees, this woman's face would have eventually shown up, but they had believed her sob story and expedited her to safety.

Yet it had all been bullshit.

According to what Langley had told her, she was their mouthpiece, perhaps a zealot, perhaps coerced, but either way, she was working for the enemy, a Tokyo Rose of her time.

And now she was loose in one of the busiest airports in the world, with tens of thousands of people that could be contaminated when she detonated the weapon.

Though that wouldn't be the biggest effect.

From her briefing on Cesium-137, she knew that it contaminated anything it touched, and if they detonated a Cesium laced weapon inside the airport, it would be radioactive for decades, the half-life thirty years. The only way to get the airport back up and running would be to tear the entire thing down and cart it away.

Hundreds or even thousands might die, but the impact on the nation would last for years. The shuttering of JFK would cause a massive disruption to the business of the nation, and would be another reminder of its vulnerability, just as the open pit of Ground Zero had been for so many years until construction had finally erased the scarred landscape, replacing it instead with a memorial to the fallen and a 1776-foot-tall testament to the American spirit.

A detonation here would be equally devastating.

The corner of her mouth turned up with the start of a smile.

There she is.

She pushed her way through the crowd, closing the distance.

Not on my watch, bitch.

Courtside, Madison Square Garden, New York City

The crowds had settled after the shooting of the uniformed infidels, and Nazari redeployed most of the men on the floor to the entrances surrounding them. An assault would be coming, of that he had no doubt, and all they needed to do was delay that for a split second, time enough for the triggering of the bomb that stood behind him.

Then thousands would die.

All on live television.

He glanced at the broadcast booth, two of his men holding those inside at gunpoint so they could continue coverage of the events. He had to admit he wasn't sure if the networks were actually still broadcasting, though they were definitely receiving the feed, and eventually, knowing the infidel, his thirst for blood drenched entertainment would lead to its release so the masses could enjoy the titillating thrill of someone else's misery.

He had no concerns about anything being revealed to law enforcement outside. They knew he was here, and it was already too late. His mission wasn't to survive, his mission was to make demands, then when those demands weren't fulfilled, because they wouldn't be, to kill hostages, then eventually detonate the bomb should an assault begin.

He looked over at one of his men who spoke perfect English, reading their extensive list of demands into one of the television cameras, its red light on though the cameraman who had operated it earlier lay dead beside it. The world would receive their message. Perhaps not right away, though it would be his first demand when he spoke to someone, otherwise he would begin killing.

And there was no way the authorities wouldn't let the video feeds out when he shot one of his thousands of available hostages, then another for each minute they weren't broadcast.

It was one of the many advantages of having so many at his disposal.

He pulled out his phone, looking at his second-in-command, Mohammad Bata. "Time to talk." He dialed the preprogrammed number for the FBI then frowned.

No signal.

He turned to Bata. "Check your phone."

The man examined his display then shook his head. "No signal."

Nazari cursed. "They're jamming us." He raised the microphone. "Prepare for an assault!" He stepped toward the camera, pushing his man aside, holding up his phone so the world outside could see it. "You jam our phones? You don't want to talk?" He motioned for his man to work the camera then walked over to the front row of hostages and put a gun to a woman's head. "You want to see what happens when you mess with me?" He squeezed the trigger, the woman's head flinging backward, blood and brain matter spraying all over the legs of the man behind her.

The audience erupted in panicked screams as Nazari headed back toward the camera. "In sixty seconds I shoot another, then another!"

Kane pointed at one of the monitors. "Something's up."

"Zero-One, Control, come in."

Dawson activated his comm, Kane listening in with his own. "Go ahead, Control."

"They're demanding we stop blocking their cellphones or they're going to kill more hostages."

"Roger that. Disable the jammers, we're good to go on this end. Them talking isn't going to affect things."

"Roger that, disabling jammers. Out."

Dawson turned to Kane. "Now that we know the radiological weapon is at JFK, do we need these people alive?"

Kane shook his head, worried about Sherrie, they having just received word she had spotted the black widow, Amira Basara, an apparent operative of the men they now watched on camera. He had to think she wasn't doing what she was doing willingly, had to think that as a mother she couldn't do such a thing, yet too often he had seen mothers sending their children out to kill with a kiss and a hug.

The brainwashing went deep.

"No, but my concern is this guy." He pointed at a man sitting beside the bomb. "It looks like he's holding a detonator."

"Another dead man's switch?"

Kane nodded. "That's what I'm thinking. They're all prepared to die, and they plan on taking thousands with them."

Dawson looked at Niner. "Casualty estimate?"

Niner shrugged. "If it were a flat field with ten thousand people standing on it, I'd say in the hundreds. But this is an arena, designed specifically to give everyone a great view of the floor, and that weapon has been shaped to send everything outward and upward at all angles." He sighed. "They've designed this to hit essentially everything at every level. If it works, thousands of casualties for sure."

"So how the hell do we stop it from going off?" asked Spock.

Kane pulled the comm out of his ear. "I need to get in there."

Dawson turned to him. "And just how do you expect to do that?"

Kane grinned. "I've got an idea."

Nazari aimed his weapon at the next person in the stands, his phone held up as he watched the service indicator and the time. It ticked over to the next minute.

"Time's up!"

He was about to squeeze the trigger when the display changed, "Sprint" appearing in the upper left. He lowered the weapon, staring at the terrified man. "It looks like your government values your life."

He stepped away from the sobs and whimpers of the cowardly infidels, dialing his phone again.

This time it rang.

An automated message began and he cursed. One of the worst things the infidels had invented were automated attendants. Why human beings couldn't answer was beyond him.

He tapped zero repeatedly then held the phone to his ear, a human answering.

"My name is Tarek Nazari. I am the man holding ten thousand people hostage at Madison Square Garden. Put me through to whoever is in charge."

There was a pause.

"One moment please."

John F. Kennedy International Airport, New York City

Amira followed the signs, heading for the area of the airport she had been instructed to go to, an area she imagined chosen to inflict the most damage. Apparently the blast would shatter windows and spread the contamination across the entire airport including the other terminals.

It truly was the work of Shaytan.

As she neared her final destination, her heart slammed against her ribcage and tears threatened to escape as she realized she had only moments left on this earth and she'd never see her children again.

It would soon be over.

All of it.

The suffering, the fear, the heartache.

Over.

She watched the thousands of people rushing past her, guards now working in an organized, coordinated effort, moving everyone in the same direction, flagging down anyone running, trying to keep things as orderly and as calm as possible.

She understood the terror in their eyes.

She had felt it.

Felt it every time her homeland had been bombed.

She could understand the anger.

She had felt it.

Felt it every time she had read of her brothers and sisters around the world being killed while they stood up for their rights as Muslims.

And she understood her purpose.

She was following their demands to save her family.

As the infidels would follow the demands of those back in her homeland to save themselves from any further attacks.

If she succeeded here today, if she fulfilled that responsibility thrust upon her against her will, she could not only save her family, but stop the killing everywhere. If the Americans were to leave the Middle East alone, then the killing would stop there, and with the Americans gone, there would be no need for her people to continue attacking them.

She was saving lives by taking lives.

Yet she knew deep down the killing wouldn't stop. Despite what the propagandists would have the world believe, far more Muslims were killed by other Muslims than any other group, infidels a distant second. There was no greater enemy to a Muslim than another Muslim. Her family had learned that the hard way.

But there was one important fact that couldn't be ignored in all this.

It was one thing for a Muslim to kill one of his own.

A totally other thing for an infidel to do so.

And the Americans insisted on continuing to kill Muslims, no matter who was in charge, and that was a sin answerable to Allah.

If she quoted her scripture, she could almost convince herself that what she was about to do was the right thing. She would die, yes, but she would die in service to Allah. Her afterlife would be eternal joy, and her children would be safe.

She froze.

They would be safe, wouldn't they?

She glanced back at where she had come from, not sure of what to do.

They're only safe if they leave.

She knew how those from her homeland would handle this situation. They would bring her children out here to die with her, hoping she would change her mind.

The Americans are good people.

She resumed her journey, taking a deep breath. The Americans were good people; they would never use children in such a fashion. She was certain they would have already been evacuated with the others, and it had been several minutes since the alarms had started.

They're safe.

The Americans are good people.

Courtside, Madison Square Garden, New York City

Nazari shook his head, wagging a finger at the camera now trained on him. "Now remember, Simon, we have eyes everywhere. One phone call and I will know whether or not you are lying to me."

"Tarek, I assure you the order has been given to turn the live broadcasts back on, but it takes time. We can't order a network what to air, they have to agree to it."

"Tell them that if they don't, another hostage will die, one for each minute they don't broadcast." He paused, eyeing the NBA TV logo on the side of the camera. "Oh, and tell them I want the feed made available to *all* the networks."

There was a pause. "I'll let them know. Is there anything else?"

Nazari's stomach grumbled. "Do you have any idea how many people we have here?"

"You would have a better idea than I would of that. A lot, I'm sure."

Nazari looked around him. "That would be an understatement, but I wasn't asking for a count. These people are hungry and will need food. What do you Americans like to eat?"

"Ahh, pizza?"

"How many does one of those feed? Five?" He glanced over his shoulder. "You better send two thousand large pizzas, and don't forget the drinks. These people are thirsty after all their crying."

He ended the call before "Simon", his assigned FBI hostage negotiator, could reply. It was a ridiculous demand, but a fun one. He was more concerned with getting their broadcast restored so the world could hear their demands and see the consequences of their government's stalling tactics.

And he couldn't wait to see how they managed to actually acquire and deliver two thousand pizzas.

His stomach rumbled again. He was almost ashamed to admit he had acquired a taste for foreign cuisine during his time in England. In fact, he had learned to love many different types of food, and found himself at times craving a good pizza, hamburger or fish and chips. But he had been forced to deny himself those simple pleasures in order to fight for a cause he believed in so deeply.

Though it didn't mean he couldn't enjoy some pizza if it were actually to arrive.

"Sir, we still can't reach them."

He turned toward Mohammad Bata. "Still?"

Bata nodded. "I started trying as soon as the jamming stopped but can't get through. It might be nothing since every second attempt I make says the circuits are full, but it might be something. Should I send someone?"

Nazari turned away from the camera before it could catch his frown. He eyed the bomb, the volunteer manning the dead man's switch a rather simple man, eager to die for the cause.

He was using the switch to scratch his back.

"Hey! Be careful with that thing or you'll blow us all up!"

The man blanched, his head bobbing as he returned the switch to his lap, now gripped tightly in both hands.

Imbecile.

Though a useful one, too dumb to be afraid to die.

He'll let go when he needs to.

Besides being blown up prematurely, his concern was the security room. They hadn't been able to establish communications with them since the

FBI had jammed the cellphone signals. It hadn't mattered at the time, it obvious the center no longer served the infidels a purpose once he had secured the arena. If they didn't have advance warning of an assault, so be it. The bomb would be triggered, they'd all die, and he'd enjoy his just rewards.

Though it did concern him that men under his command couldn't be reached. He turned to Bata. "And the others that haven't reported in? How many?"

He almost appeared scared to say anything. "Fifteen."

Nazari shook his head.

Fifteen! Plus the six in the center!

He hid his dismay and worry. For over twenty to be dead, either the initial defense by the onsite security had been better than anticipated, or the FBI had already infiltrated the building.

Impossible!

They would have had to gain access almost immediately, and he just couldn't see the Americans getting their act together so quickly. In Iraq, when dealing with a military command structure? Sure. But here, on American soil?

Never.

He turned to Bata. "Forget them. If they're dead, then they died serving Allah and will be but the first."

"Halt!"

Nazari spun toward the sound, watching as two of his men disappeared into the shadows cast by one of the exits.

What now?

Kane walked toward one of the gates into the arena, Niner having picked the closest one that showed two guards on the monitor. His arms were out to his side, his gun, issued at the warehouse, left in the security control center, his body armor still in place, under his shirt. This was a Hail Mary attempt to gain access, it too risky to start an all-out assault when there was a hostile sitting on a dead man's switch with enough explosives to tear apart most of the hostages sitting around it.

"Allahu Akbar, friends, may I enter?"

"Halt!" shouted somebody, two men emerging from the shadows, their guns raised. "Who are you?" demanded the man in the lead, his Beretta held high, pointed directly at Kane's face.

"I'm one of you!" he replied, trying to keep his face as friendly as possible. Staying calm was easy, he was trained for this and could disarm the man in a heartbeat.

Then stop said heartbeat with two shots to the chest.

"Prove it." The man didn't look convinced, and Kane didn't blame him, though who the man thought he might be other than one of them, he didn't know.

Perhaps the poor bastard in the FBI who had pulled the short straw.

"I'm with Tarek Nazari. He was my cell commander in Al-Raqqah. Surely you know him!"

The two men exchanged glances, it clear they did.

"Where have you been?" asked the other, his weapon lowering slightly, now aimed uncomfortably close to Kane's favorite body part.

"We were hit on the way here. I'm American so I was able to bail from the vehicle and just blend in with the crowd." He wiped the smile from his face, lowering his head. "The others weren't so lucky." He shook his head. "They're all dead. Murdered by the American scum."

The second man spat on the floor. "Pigs."

"How did you get past the security outside?" asked the other, apparently still skeptical.

Kane laughed. "Easy! It's a madhouse out there! There's thousands of people running everywhere. I pretty much walked in."

"How do we know you're telling the truth?"

Kane shrugged. "Ask Tarek, he'll vouch for me. We've been through hell and back together, from Syria to Turkey, Greece to Germany then here. We even flew into JFK together earlier today." Still not convinced. He snapped his fingers. "Were you at the warehouse today? Where the commander gave his speech and sent half of us out to various cities to kill the infidels slowly, the other half here?"

The man's head slowly bobbed, his weapon lowering. "There's no way you could know that." He laughed. "I'm sorry, brother, I had to be sure. They'd shoot me if I just let you in, you being an American."

"Is it that obvious?"

A smile spread across the man's face. "You need a better beard."

Kane laughed, running his fingers over his couple of days of stubble. "They wanted me to look as American as I could."

The man slapped him on the back, gently pushing him through the entrance. "Come, my brother, I'll take you to the commander."

"Commander?"

"Yes, Commander Nazari is in charge," explained the man as they entered the bright arena. Kane took everything in with a trained eye, noting the positions of the hostiles, the bomb, the cameras, the hostages.

And the bodies.

The pit of rage burned hot as he continued down the steps, already spotting Nazari. There were two dozen men on the floor, with almost sixty at the entrances, all matching what Niner and the guys had already observed.

The good news was that there were no surprises here that he could see, though there was always the possibility there were sleepers hidden in the audience.

It was a chance they'd have to take.

"Tarek!" he called, raising his hand and waving at Nazari, a broad smile on his face. Nazari stared at him, a puzzled expression on his face. "It's so good to see you! I was afraid maybe they got you."

Nazari pointed at him. "Bring him to me!"

Huh. Not happy to see me.

Lee Fang Residence, Philadelphia, Pennsylvania

Lee Fang sat on her couch, legs curled up under her, a bowl of popcorn on her lap, a shaker of ranch flavoring gripped in one hand, a bottle of Diet Pepsi in the other. It was the most riveting thing she had ever seen, China never broadcasting anything that might terrify its populace.

But not in America.

She frankly couldn't believe the Americans were allowing the broadcast. It was now on almost every channel, commentators who seemed to be experts on everything giving their opinions, explaining what was going on and who was involved, and what might happen next.

And now there were breaking news reports that something was happening at JFK in New York.

It was exciting.

It was terrifying.

And it didn't affect her.

Yet it did.

Perhaps she truly was starting to think of this as her home, as her country, and terrorists attacking it and murdering its citizens pissed her off. She shoveled another handful of popcorn into her mouth, though not before shaking some more flavoring on the kernels in her hand. She licked her palm clean, not at all missing the episode of Castle she had been watching before the interruption.

The soldier in her wanted to head to New York and kick some ass, but the woman who lived in this apartment under an assumed identity, with no power to do anything, was forced to content herself with running scenarios in her head on how she would assault the facility.

Her jaw dropped and she leaned forward suddenly, her popcorn falling onto the floor.

"Is that—?"

She grabbed her remote and hit pause, freezing the frame on the image showing a man walking down the stairs, flanked by two others.

"Dylan!"

And suddenly she was invested in the outcome like tens of thousands of others out there watching tonight.

All with loved ones in the stadium.

She grabbed a throw pillow and hugged it close to her chest, resting her chin on it.

Loved ones?

She closed her eyes, picturing the handsome American that had saved her life and who was her only friend in the world.

And wished she were there by his side, ready to do battle against their enemies.

Courtside, Madison Square Garden, New York City

Nazari couldn't believe his eyes.

The American!

He didn't know how to react. He had never expected to see him again, though the possibility had at least presented itself when the alert message had gone out ordering everyone to report here. But when no one from his vehicle had arrived, he had just assumed they had been captured.

And in all honesty, he had simply assumed this American had betrayed those loyal men in his vehicle, he always having his suspicions about him.

Yet here he was.

As bold as brass, a smile on his face, waving as he came down the steps.

"Bring him to me!" he ordered, not about to give this convert the benefit of the doubt, not without a damned good explanation as to how he had managed to get here when the stadium was surrounded by hundreds of police.

They had been betrayed, that much everyone knew, the leadership taken down. There was no way anyone could have known where they were at that moment, unless somehow they were tracked. And if tracked, then it had to have been from the warehouse.

And his money was on one of the converts.

The only convert he had direct contact with was this man who called himself Bryce Clearwater, yet he couldn't be sure.

Why would he be here if he weren't loyal?

His teeth clenched.

To betray you again, you fool!

Several of his men rushed up the steps, weapons aimed at the new arrival, and the American raised his hands, his eyes wide with shock. "Hey man, what's this all about? You know me! We've been to hell and back together! If I wasn't on the level, why would I come here?"

He ignored the man's arguments as he watched his men search the convert, finding only a cellphone that looked much like the one issued at the warehouse to all of them. He was led down to the floor, flanked by two of his men, each with a grip on one arm.

"Where's your gun?" asked Nazari as he was handed the cellphone.

"I ditched it when I escaped. I didn't want to risk being stopped and searched."

"How did you escape?"

"Easy." The man bent over, his arm still held tight, and wiped his cheeks. "I'm a white American, above suspicion. I just jumped out of the vehicle when they hit it and blended into the crowd. In the confusion it was pretty easy." He laughed. "You've gotta love New York City, there's always a crowd."

Nazari frowned, still not sure whether to believe the man, but his story was plausible. It was the exact reason American and European converts had been used, because they blended in with the populace and were more likely to be believed.

And if he were here to cause trouble, why would he come unarmed?

Yet one thing still troubled him. It was approaching half an hour since the assault began.

"How did you get in here?"

The American huffed. "Easy. Just snuck in, sprinted for the entrance. They're still getting organized out there and some of the spectators are still escaping a few at a time." He smiled. "I guess it was Allah's will."

"Indeed." Nazari still wasn't sure, but this American was a distraction he didn't have time for. "Fine, stay here."

The men let go of their grip and the American slapped Nazari on the back. "Thanks, man. Umm, can I have a gun?"

"No!"

John F. Kennedy International Airport, New York City

Sherrie kept to the sides, out of the direct flow of the fleeing masses, an eye always on Amira as the woman continued toward wherever it was she was going. An evacuation alarm with calm, prerecorded announcements was now playing and security was efficiently emptying the airport. The update over her comm was that all flights had been diverted and everything else grounded, the authorities not willing to risk there being a second device on one of the planes waiting to take off.

If they blew up an airplane using a Cesium based weapon over the city, it would be catastrophic.

She was having flashbacks of 9/11, too young at the time really to understand what had happened, only knowing that her parents had seemed scared and angry.

But mostly scared.

And a child seeing the ones meant to protect her, scared, was a life altering moment.

They suddenly became human.

They were no longer perfect.

It had changed her.

Then when she had lost them in a car accident, it was one of the most vivid memories that remained when she closed her eyes and thought of them.

Fear.

And it gave her something to insert into the made up memory of the moments before they died, how they must have looked at each other when they knew there was nothing they could do, when they knew it was the end.

Focus!

She shoved the memories aside the moment she felt tears form. She had a mission, and that was less than fifty yards ahead of her. Her primary objective was to save lives, merely delaying things accomplishing this. Her secondary was to try and prevent the explosion and therefore protect the infrastructure.

At the moment, she couldn't care less about the building she walked through. On 9/11 everyone would have happily sacrificed the buildings if it meant saving the thousands trapped inside, and today was no different.

She had to delay, but there was no point intervening while Amira was still moving. As long as she kept moving, as long as no one interfered, she wouldn't detonate, and every second that continued gave these people rushing past another second to get to safety.

As she continued forward, keeping her distance, her thoughts turned to her boyfriend, and she wondered how he would cope if she were to die here today. They always knew it was a possibility, her job a dangerous one, and it often troubled her as their relationship progressed and she saw how he continued to fall deeper in love with her every day.

It would destroy him.

If he were to die, it would devastate her, though she was strong enough to eventually move on with her life. Chris wasn't strong, but he was stronger than he thought he was. She feared he would never be able to move forward, never be able to put his heart out there again to find a new love.

Maybe Sonya Tong will get her chance.

A flash of uncharacteristic jealousy flushed her cheeks.

Focus!

She glared at the woman through her sunglasses, the woman so many had tried to help, to get her and her children to safety, who was now going to repay those acts of kindness by detonating herself and killing possibly thousands.

Who does such a thing?

She had never been able to understand the mindset of the terrorist. She was convinced, as were many at Langley, that most were mentally disturbed. When many estimates put mental illness of some type as high as twenty percent of the population, it was easy to see how there could be a steady supply for the cause.

But she wasn't willing to so easily accept mental illness as the only reason. If that were the sole reason, then why was it almost exclusively Muslims doing it? Weren't there just as many Christians and Atheists afflicted with the same mental illnesses? Why weren't they committing mass murders every day in the name of some cause?

Did she think those who did such things were weak?

Absolutely.

Yet was weakness a mental illness? Not in her mind, that was simply a character flaw that most people shared. It wasn't that there was something wrong with them, it was simply that their lives hadn't prepared them for the types of challenges they might one day face.

If someone told her she'd have to detonate a bomb that could kill thousands just to save the ones she loved, she hoped she would have the strength to tell those demanding it to go screw themselves. The ones she loved would never want to survive at the expense of innocent lives, and if they did, then they were people she wouldn't want anything to do with anyway.

Would she do everything she could to try and save them? Absolutely. Would that involve killing? Again, absolutely. Killing of those responsible. Not an airport or a market or a border crossing filled with innocent people.

Whatever Amira's excuse was for doing what she was doing, Sherrie didn't care.

The woman intended mass murder.

And either she dies, or we both die.

Operations Center 3, CIA Headquarters, Langley, Virginia

Leroux stood, arms across his chest, the fingers of his right hand drumming on his left elbow in a repeated ring-middle-index pattern. Unnoticed. His attentions were split between security camera footage of his best friend, Dylan Kane, walking into the belly of the beast, and equally disturbing footage of his girlfriend, Sherrie White, pursuing the black widow that had tipped them off to the massive terrorist threat, and was now betraying them.

He felt guilty, more by the minute, as his mind played the odds game. *If one were to fail, which one would he prefer?* He loved Sherrie, yet he loved Kane as well, in a different way. Both were agents, both volunteered to be there, both were important to him. He had known Kane longer, but Sherrie was the first and only love of his life.

And he kept choosing her.

And it made him sick.

To be praying to God for Sherrie to live if only one could, had his mouth filling with bile, his stomach churning and his entire being ashamed of what he was hoping for.

So he had to do everything he could to make sure both survived.

Otherwise he was going to hell for his thoughts.

And that thought unfortunately gave him a new bargaining chip with God.

Let them both survive and take me.

"Are you okay?"

Leroux shot a startled glance at Morrison, then nodded. "Yeah. Just thinking."

Morrison stepped over to his side, his voice low. "Your mission is Kane, not White. She's on her own, and that's fine. Her situation demands it. She needs to delay, then hopefully distract enough to get her hand on that trigger. She's good, a fine agent." He motioned toward Kane, now on the floor of the court. "He's the *best.* I'm not worried about him for a second. And neither should you. He's got the best backup in the world just outside those gates, and all he needs is a split second to get his hands on that device. And that's your job. The moment he does, you need to order the teams in."

Leroux nodded, sucking in a deep breath and gluing his eyes to the screen showing Dylan now standing alone, only yards from the device. "Yes, sir."

Morrison stepped away, checking his phone and Leroux stole a glance at his girlfriend. His boss was right, she was good, but she was also new. If *any* other agent had been available, they'd be there instead of her. She hadn't even earned the label Special Agent yet, though he had no doubt she soon would.

Yet she was the only one available, the only one there at the time of the crisis. It was she sent to Frankfurt, a familiar face for Kane, she on his flight, she left behind to help coordinate things with Amira and her family, and to watch over Morrison's daughter.

I wonder what he's *thinking.*

He turned to Morrison. "Any word from Alexis?"

The man frowned, the worried father replacing the firm boss.

"I haven't been able to reach her."

John F. Kennedy International Airport, New York City

Almost there.

Amira glanced at the signs overhead, really not certain of whether she actually was, though she figured she must be, she having walked for almost fifteen minutes now.

Or was it longer?

For all she knew it could be shorter.

Her mind was awash with images of her life, her husband, his death, their plight, her children. Time was a concept lost to her with the knowledge that what she had left wasn't hers, it taken from her by those who held her family captive, those who had forever changed their lives.

And knowing she must die to save them, it left her wondering about death itself, and what followed. Paradise awaited those who had devoted themselves to Islam and died in the service of Allah. What she was about to do was certainly in His service, but would she get the credit the sacrifice merited if it were executed against her will, if she didn't fully embrace the cause for which she was about to die.

Did she have to believe what she was doing was right?

If I die, will Jannah await me, or eternal damnation?

If she detonated the bomb strapped to her chest unwillingly, it was murder, though if she did it willingly, embracing the twisted reasoning behind it, then it couldn't possibly be murder. Could it? The motivation was to stop the bombings in her homeland. That would save lives, Muslim lives. Was it her fault those behind this were murderers? And were they? She had listened to Imam after Imam throughout her life telling her the infidels were dirty, filthy, pigs, heathens, stupid, corrupt, vile and any other adjective one could think of to describe someone in a negative fashion.

And they had quite often called for their forced conversion or death.

And these were supposed to be good men, men of God, telling her these things from the moment she could understand the words spoken by those around her.

Not all of them delivered the same message, though their implied meanings all suggested the same thing. Muslims were better than anyone else, and Allah wanted everyone to be Muslim.

If that were so, then would killing non-Muslims here today really matter? Would it affect her reward for her sacrifice?

It can't.

But only if she believed in what she was doing. If she didn't believe, then she couldn't use the killing of the infidels as an excuse to forgive what she was about to do.

She slowed, closing her eyes slightly, thinking about everything. If the American infidels hadn't gone into Iraq, then ISIL wouldn't have been able to take over territory there. If the Americans hadn't encouraged the Arab Spring, then the civil war in Syria would have never started. If these events hadn't happened, then ISIL would never have existed.

Her home would still be there.

Her school.

Her students.

Her husband.

All would be alive if it weren't for the creation of ISIL, and ISIL wouldn't have been created if these infidels surrounding her had demanded their government leave the Middle East alone.

She opened her eyes and smiled.

She was where she needed to be.

And she was at peace with what she was about to do.

She looked around for a security camera, not finding anything, instead noticing some black orbs that seemed out of place.

That must be them.

It didn't matter. She had no doubt she was on camera, and if these weren't them, Allah would forgive her. She removed the robe covering the bomb and tossed it to the side. A woman nearby screamed and bolted, there almost no one here anymore, a few of those who remained stopping to pull out their cellphones and record her as they backed away.

Run you fools!

She shook her head.

They deserve to die if they think getting a video on the Internet is worth their lives.

She glanced down at the bomb strapped to her chest. It was heavy, three large canisters strapped to her, each about a half a meter long, filled with some sort of powdered suspension, it unlike any bomb she had ever seen or imagined. There were gray sticks between each one, they more like the explosives she was expecting, and a series of wires connecting everything, several bundled together by black tape, leading to the detonator she had squeezed tightly in her hand.

A detonator she had been told would trigger the bomb the moment she opened her hand.

The moment she finished her speech, a speech that would go down in history, a history forever altered by her actions here today.

She sucked in a deep breath.

And stared at the nearest orb.

"What I do today, I do for Allah and his children! For too long America has killed the peaceful followers of the one true faith, and today I am the instrument of Allah's judgement. Today America will pay for all the innocent women and children it has killed. Though I die here today, I am but the first of many! If you want us to stop, then *you* will stop. Stop bombing our homes, stop supplying weapons, stop supporting dictators. Let us be free! Free to live our lives without interference from *you*!"

She gasped in a few breaths, the words flowing easily, she going beyond what she had been told to say, her chest swelling with confidence as she listened to the words coming from within her, from a place she never realized was there.

And suddenly she knew why she had been one of their mouthpieces.

It wasn't just because she spoke English, it was because she was *good* at it. They had told her what she needed to convey, though she had decided what needed to be *said*. She had embellished the messages, delivered them with the gusto they demanded, but she had also felt it inside, just not realizing it until this moment. She had never needed to be so good at her job—she could have just delivered their words, yet she hadn't.

And as she felt the fervor swell inside her, she realized it was a familiar feeling.

She had felt it every time she delivered a speech for consumption around the world, to inspire the true believers and strike fear into those who didn't.

She was Muslim.

She was a believer.

And what she was doing was right.

"Should you not stop your attacks, your interference, we will kill you in your homes and in your streets, like you have killed us in our homes and in our streets. For we have arrived, and there is no way you will rid yourselves of us now!"

She raised the trigger, closing her eyes.

Adnan, I'm coming!

"Amira, wait!"

She froze, opening her eyes as she instantly recognized the voice.

Alexis Morrison.

Sherrie cursed, ducking in behind a counter as her boss' daughter inserted herself into the situation. She was less than thirty feet away from Amira and had been about to make her move as soon as the woman had closed her eyes when Alexis had arrived.

What the hell is she doing here?

The place was almost empty, there only a few people now with their cellphones out, members of a generation raised to believe they were invulnerable, glorifying those who managed to capture exciting situations on video, especially if it meant putting their own lives at risk.

She thought sometimes that these morons honestly believed they couldn't be killed, that because they were turning what was happening in real life into a film, that they couldn't be hurt, just like the actors in a movie couldn't be.

Are they truly that disconnected from the real world?

Having dealt with many of these people, some even friends of hers, she was afraid the answer was probably 'yes'. If they survived, they were 'brave' for having risked their lives to document something that needed to be documented. If they didn't, they were 'victims' of the person carrying out the dastardly deed. No mention would be made of the fact they could have left the area long ago and survived.

She wanted to start firing her weapon so they might actually flee to safety.

More likely they'd just turn their cameras on her.

Alexis was less than twenty feet from Amira, the terrorist—for that's what she was now classified as—turning to face the woman. Sherrie was just out of Amira's line of sight, but even a slight turn of her head would give away her position if she showed herself.

Alexis shouldn't be there, and she was certain the woman's father was freaking out right now, yet if she could somehow coordinate with her, she might just be able to get a hand on that detonator and save them all.

But it meant using her boss' daughter.

If anything happens to her, he'll kill you.

She sighed.

If anything happens to her, we're all dead anyway.

She activated her comm.

"Control, is she miked?"

"Negative."

Shit.

Courtside, Madison Square Garden, New York City

Kane stood, a slight smile on his face, his eyes wider than normal, mimicking the look of fervor fueled excitement all around him. He forced himself to look away from the bloodbath only feet from him, knowing it would only anger him so much his emotions might betray him.

Instead, he occupied himself with watching the crowd for any sudden movements.

Or so it would appear to Nazari and the others.

In fact, his attention was on the triggerman holding the dead man's switch, the way he was leaning on the bomb suggesting he was far too stupid to be trusted with such a responsibility, Kane having the distinct impression this man had no concerns in the world as to what might happen should he drop the device held a little too loosely in his hand.

Yet it didn't surprise him.

These men were all prepared to die.

Every last one of them.

The brainwashing was impressive in radical Islam, especially among the men. From birth they were conditioned to believe that dying in the cause of Islam would grant them entry into paradise, with access to 72 vestal virgins for eternity.

And then they sexually repressed them.

It left a massive population of young horny men with no outlet.

In Western societies you had the same massive segment of the population suffering from the same affliction, but they had outlets. Women they could actually see, girls their own age in short-shorts and tube tops, Internet pornography, and teenage sex.

These poor bastards had none of that. Most barely knew what a woman actually looked like, most had never had sex, and most probably got stiff from a hot desert wind.

ISIL had taken thousands of women and children prisoner, and the men who distinguished themselves on the battlefield were given the opportunity to buy them, to do with as they pleased.

To satisfy their carnal needs.

Whether they were born there, or converts coming in from around the Western world to have their fun then leave.

For many it was the first sex they had ever had, and for those blinded by lust and ideology, it was an intoxicating brew difficult to resist.

Yet there weren't enough women to go around, which left most alone with their unfulfilled desires.

It was no wonder they were willing to die.

They had little if anything to live for.

Was that Western society's fault? Was it the infidels' fault?

No. It was their own for letting the radicals take over, slowly, bit by bit, until it was too late. And now they didn't want to fight to get it back, either out of fear, out of apathy, or out of mutual hatred. In Mosul nearly thirty thousand American trained and equipped Iraqi troops fled in the face of less than one thousand ISIL troops.

Why?

Were they scared?

Absolutely, the ISIL treatment of captured Iraqi soldiers brutal.

But there was another reason.

They were mostly Sunni, led by a Shiite government.

And ISIL was Sunni.

They didn't flee just out of fear, they left because they hated Shiites more than they loved their freedom.

Why was it that the Muslim world took in almost no refugees? They had the money from their oil riches, yet they did nothing to help their fellow Muslims. What was it that left countries like Saudi Arabia, Kuwait and Qatar to take in zero refugees, but the Western, Christian nations of the world to criticize themselves for not taking enough?

It reminded him of the Indian Ocean Tsunami that had killed 230,000. Western countries had contributed billions upon billions in aid, sending their militaries and civilian organizations in to help.

While the rich Muslim countries did little to nothing.

At least not until somebody noticed.

Then the assistance was token at best.

These men gathered around him blamed the infidels for their problems, yet it was their own fault for rejecting progress, rejecting science, rejecting compassion. Muslim societies of the past embraced science and culture. Today they rejected it and destroyed it, bulldozing entire archeological sites.

The Doc must want to get in there and do some killing himself.

He smiled, genuinely, as he thought of Professor James Acton, the man who had counselled him after 9/11, who had encouraged him to follow his heart, a heart that had led him into the military, and eventually, into the CIA.

Maybe I'll drop in and say hi.

His smiled broadened.

Maybe I'll bring Fang.

Nazari turned his back to him and Kane scratched behind his ear.

The gunfire began immediately, suppressed pops echoing throughout the arena. Kane didn't wait to see the reaction of those around him. He strode quickly toward the triggerman and grabbed his hand, clamping down hard.

Leaving thousands of lives literally in his hands.

"Execute! Execute! Execute!"

Dawson squeezed the trigger twice, his man dropping in a heap, Niner's beside him as they rounded the corner, the assault on, triggered by Langley witnessing Kane give them the signal.

A scratch behind the ear.

Everything hinged on the operator getting his hands on the trigger and keeping them there until they could reach him. He had no weapons beyond his body and mind.

Everyone around him had automatic weapons.

He took the left, Niner the right, as they surged down the steps, saying nothing, merely picking their targets and firing, watching their arcs so multiple bullets weren't wasted on the same targets. The two other Bravo Teams were entering along with a dozen FBI SWAT teams, the coordinated assault going well for the first few seconds.

But only because no one had time to react yet.

He spotted Kane wrestling with the triggerman and raised his weapon to take out someone who had also taken notice.

A civilian leapt up in front of him.

Then hundreds were on their feet.

Then thousands.

Blocking almost all their shots.

"Get down!"

Wendy screamed as people rushed in every direction, climbing over bodies as more were added to the mix, the terrorists opening fire on the crowd. The words of the young soldier echoed in her mind.

Don't give them any reason to single you out.

She grabbed her children and pulled them to the floor, draping her body over them as the panic continued around them. She peered through the feet and could see men racing down the steps toward the floor, their boots suggesting police or military.

And she realized that they were about to be saved.

If they could just survive the next few minutes.

Dawson sprinted down the steps, shoving the civilians out of his way, unable to get a shot off, the hostiles having no such problems. Though the gunfire was heavy and widespread, a lot of it seemed directed at the entrances in the mistaken belief that more were coming and they were actually providing suppression fire.

They weren't.

And their wasted bullets meant lives saved.

He spotted Kane in a struggle for all their lives, and pushed harder, a single bullet in the triggerman all that was needed to end this thing.

A bullet that had to be delivered carefully.

Or the bomb could detonate, regardless of how tight a grip Kane might have on his opponent's hand.

Parker heard the popping sounds and knew immediately what they were. His eyes had been on the new arrival, a piece of shit traitor, the man clearly American. How anyone could betray their country was beyond him, and he would take great pleasure in killing him should he get the chance.

Then the man did something surprising.

Shocking.

He leapt for the man holding the bomb's trigger.

He glanced over his shoulder to see security teams rushing down the steps and toward the court, holding weapons like they knew what they were doing.

This was it.

He was only rows from the floor and kept his ass in his seat as the teams advanced, taking out targets around the arena, the end of this ordeal almost in sight.

Then everyone got on their feet.

Blocking the shots.

"Stay down!" he shouted, grabbing at those around him and yanking them back into their seats.

But it was too late.

The momentum had been lost.

The terrorists, protected by the standing crowd, opened fire on their human shields, dozens dropping as random, sustained gunfire drowned out the disciplined shots of the professionals.

Parker looked at the American, struggling for the trigger, wondering why someone didn't just shoot the man. "It's a dead man's switch!"

"What?"

He pointed at the struggle. "He's got a dead man's switch. If either of them let go, we're done for. We've gotta help."

Wilson nodded, elbowing their friends as Parker climbed over the few seats in front of him, bursting onto the floor, his friends just behind him. One of the terrorists spun toward him, his weapon belching lead. Parker dropped to his knees, sliding on the smooth floor, avoiding the shots and giving him a chance to reach up and twist the weapon from the man's hands. They grappled for the gun, Parker sweeping the man's feet out from under him as the arena filled with screams and gunfire, chaos reining.

Wilson jumped into the fray, yanking the man away, leaving Parker with the gun. He pumped two rounds into the man then spun, firing on the hostiles nearest him then tossing the weapon to Wilson. Parker rushed toward the struggling American, the triggerman having the advantage of not caring if he lost his grip, raining blow after blow on the man who seemed to take each punch in stride, landing his own, the terrorist's face a bloody mess, the American seemingly unscathed.

He's good.

He made eye contact with the man who then looked past him, his eyes widening slightly as he shouted a warning.

"Look out!"

Kane's grip was firm for the moment, but how long that would last he had no idea. The man was continually trying to yank his hand away, yet Kane held on, knowing that should he fail, even for a moment, the man would be able to loosen his grip and drop the trigger, killing them all instantly.

Blow after blow landed, most on his arm as he blocked many of them, delivering his own counterpunches and the occasional headbutt. His opponent was weakening, his nose broken, blood streaming down his face, Kane's forehead having done some damage, but the bastard kept fighting. It was as if he had only one thought, the slightly dazed expression Kane had noticed before he had even triggered the assault suggesting this man wasn't completely there.

And now he was too stubborn to just give up.

A civilian bolted onto the floor, struggling with one of the hostiles for his weapon, another coming to his aid, the terrorist shot, then a couple more before the first man tossed the weapon to the second. Two more civilians picked up weapons from the fallen, opening another front, but putting themselves at risk of being mistaken for the enemy.

The first man charged toward him, their eyes meeting. It was exactly what he would need, a second pair of hands to pull this asshole away from the trigger.

"Look out!" he yelled, spotting Nazari raising his weapon.

Nazari wasn't sure if he was the first to react, but he was certainly one of the first.

He opened fire on the crowd.

And it immediately had the desired effect.

Thousands jumped to their feet to flee, and he continued to fire bursts of gunfire at them, he not concerned in the least whether he killed any of them, he merely needing to give the triggerman time to react.

Time seemed to slow as his weapon continued to fire, round after round tearing into the flesh of the infidels, and he began to say his prayers, preparing himself to leave this life and begin the next. A sense of peace washed over him, filling him with an almost joyous rapture as the life he had meant to lead was almost over. He had been led astray years ago by the temptations of the infidel's world, but he had been brought back to the path, and today his actions would help strike a blow so powerful, the ramifications would be felt for eternity as he helped bring about the prophecies.

For should the Americans not heed their demands, and instead seek revenge, they would land troops in Syria to fight his brothers, and one of their rally points would be Turkey.

Fulfilling the prophecy that indicated the beginning of the end-times.

"The Hour of Resurrection will not come until the Romans land in Al-A'maq or in Dabiq."

He smiled as he reloaded.

Allah will surely grant me entrance to paradise.

He turned to see why the bomb hadn't detonated and found the American fighting for the trigger.

I knew it!

Rage filled his peaceful heart as all of his suspicions were proven. He glanced to see at least half his men down and cursed the infidels. Yet none of that mattered as long as the weapon detonated. He raised his weapon, spotting a civilian running to help, and squeezed the trigger.

Something slammed into Parker's back and he hit the ground, an incredible pain racing through his body, his breath knocked out of him as he realized what had just happened.

He had been shot.

"Parker!"

Wilson was at his side almost immediately, as were the others, guns firing at the hostiles, they providing the only cover he had.

Yet none of it mattered.

He was going to die.

But the rest didn't have to.

He pointed at the American.

"Help…him…"

His world faded, the last sounds he would ever hear, gunfire and terror.

And his friends' sneakers squeaking on the floor as they followed his last order.

Kane felt his rage build as the man dropped to the ground, immediately surrounded by what he assumed were his friends, but he had no time even to say a silent prayer for the man's soul, a man he didn't know, a man who had rushed into the danger rather than away from it.

He'd have made a good soldier.

The triggerman suddenly spun and he felt his grip about to break.

This has to end!

He grabbed the man by the back of the neck and pulled him closer, planting a kiss on him that had his opponent freeze in homophobic horror.

Kane headbutted him, dropping him to his knees, then tore the trigger from the man's hand. A knee to the nose had his opponent on the floor then Kane stomped his heel on the man's head, hard, crushing his skull in one blow.

He dropped to a crouch, surveying the scene around him, gripping the trigger tightly, watching for anyone who might take a potshot at him. He spotted Nazari raise his weapon then his body jerk as he took two rounds to the chest, collapsing to the ground in a heap. Kane looked to see where the shots had come from and spotted Dawson and Niner, still engaging the dwindling terrorists.

Stay alive, boys!

Something moved out of the corner of his eye and he turned, his jaw dropping as Nazari rose, his weapon swinging toward him.

"BD!"

Dawson laughed aloud as he squeezed the trigger, having caught sight of Kane's victory in the hand-to-hand match, it a brilliant move that he had used himself on more than one occasion. Islamists were so homophobic it was actually a tactical disadvantage at times. As he took out another hostile he heard Kane yell.

"BD!"

He spun, as did Niner, and spotted the wounded Nazari on his knees, his weapon aimed at the bomb. Dawson took quick aim and fired, emptying his mag into the man, Niner's weapon belching fury beside him as Atlas and

Spock poured on additional firepower, approaching from the opposite direction.

Nazari was a bloody pulp by the time it was done.

And then the guns were silent.

Dawson headed for Kane, tossing him a roll of duct tape, the operator easily catching it and immediately taping the trigger closed.

"You okay?"

Kane nodded, clearly exhausted, collapsing in a heap on the floor. He nodded toward his opponent. "Tough bastard."

Niner stepped over. "So, I've gotta know."

"What?"

"Was he a good kisser?"

"You saw that?"

"Oh buddy, you don't know the half of it." He pointed at the television camera. "The whole damned planet saw that."

Kane closed his eyes. "Shit. Not sure if my reputation can survive that."

Dawson decided to save the man. "Don't worry, we shut down the feeds the moment the assault started. Your sexual preferences are still your secret."

Kane opened his mouth then stopped, apparently not sure of what to say.

Somebody clapped nearby.

Then another.

Niner pulled Kane to his feet and they turned to see thousands staring at them from every direction, the entire crowd beginning to clap, the claps breaking into a roar of cheers that sent goosebumps racing throughout Dawson's body. It was something he could honestly say he had never experienced before.

And he prayed to God he never did again.

The price was simply too high.

John F. Kennedy International Airport, New York City

What the hell am I doing?

Alexis had no clue what had possessed her to follow Amira when she overheard one of the security officers reporting where the woman appeared to be heading. The children were safe, but she felt compelled to save this woman. She had seen firsthand the terror on her face, had heard her story, had helped her get her family to safety.

She felt she knew the woman.

And the woman she knew would never be doing this willingly.

So she might be able to help. If she could just make contact with her, find out what hold it was these horrible human beings had on her, she might be able to get her dad to help.

And all these innocent people could be saved.

Including Amira, a victim if there ever was one.

Yet when she had spotted her standing with her eyes closed, the bomb revealed for the world to see, her words delivered with such passion, she began to have second thoughts. What she had just heard wasn't coerced. There was no fear there, no reluctance.

It was fervor.

Religious fervor.

She had heard it before, and she recognized it for what it was.

She had just never heard it delivered by someone holding the trigger to a bomb, a bomb she understood might be radioactive.

Her intention was to stop this woman by convincing her they could deal with any threat made against her.

But now she wasn't so sure.

If this woman truly believed in what she was doing, then there were no threats against her. Or if there were, they didn't matter.

She clearly believed in what she had just said, there was no faking that passion.

What am I doing here?

She glanced at one of the security cameras, realizing at that moment her father was probably watching her.

Asking the same question.

Amira raised a hand into the air, a hand that appeared to be holding a trigger.

"Amira, wait!"

"What the hell is she doing there?"

Leroux shook his head, recognizing the desperation in his boss' voice. It was a desperation he had shared on more than one occasion, and was feeling it now as he watched the love of his life hide behind a counter that would provide zero protection against the blast about to occur. "I don't know, sir, our last report had her evacuating with the children." He turned to Sonya. "Find out what happened." Sonya nodded, activating her comm, though it didn't matter. It didn't matter who was to blame for letting a civilian get this far, and there probably was no one to blame.

The orderly evacuation relied on people behaving as expected, that they'd either want to escape, or they'd hunker down and hide.

It didn't count on a friendly walking deeper into the situation.

But now they faced it. His girlfriend and his boss' daughter, about to die.

Unless together they could come up with a plan.

A plan they had no way to communicate to each other.

Alexis spotted a woman behind a counter nearby, just out of the corner of her eye. She seemed to be watching them, and for a moment Alexis was ready to dismiss her as merely a traveler hiding in panic from the woman with the bomb strapped to her chest.

Yet there was something familiar about this woman.

Something unafraid in the way she was watching.

Could she be law enforcement?

If she was, she wasn't wearing a uniform.

Undercover?

Now that was a possibility. A definite possibility. Few of her dad's people wore uniforms. Actually, she wasn't sure if any of them did. And sometimes the best security were those who just blended in with the crowd, and if there was one thing JFK had a lot of, it was crowds.

What do I do?

If the woman was just a civilian, then she had to give her a chance to escape, so she couldn't let Amira see her.

And if she were law enforcement, then she had to give the woman a chance to act.

What would Dad do?

She had to think like a spy. It was because of her father that she was here. She felt it was almost a family duty to help people. He helped them by killing those who would kill Americans, she tried to help those in need, the victims of the chaos he fought.

And today, for some reason, she had felt compelled to come back the moment she knew the children were safe.

That's it!

"Amira, why are you doing this?"

The woman stared at her, genuine dismay on her face, as if she hadn't expected anyone she knew to see her commit the horrendous crime she was about to. "No, you shouldn't be here. Go now, before it's too late!"

She was clearly concerned, which made no sense considering she was willing to kill thousands. Perhaps it was easier to kill a thousand strangers than just one person you had a connection with, one who had saved your life and that of your children.

The woman behind the counter poked her head out and suddenly Alexis knew why she seemed familiar.

She works for Dad!

She stepped slowly to the side, trying to make it look as casual as possible, forcing Amira to turn to keep facing her, putting her back to the agent.

Sherrie!

"Amira, what about your children? You fought so hard to save them, why would you want them to die now?"

Amira's eyes widened, her jaw dropped, and the trigger lowered, if only slightly. "You mean they're still here?"

Alexis felt sick to her stomach as she nodded, lying to the woman. But it could save them all if she thought her own children might die.

"But why? Why didn't you evacuate them?"

Alexis lowered her gaze, staring at the floor, as if in shame. "I made a mistake. I thought they'd be safer staying where they were." She motioned toward the bomb. "But that's no ordinary bomb, is it? I heard someone say it was some sort of nuclear device."

Amira shook her head. "I know nothing of these things. I just know that it will cause pain and suffering on an untold scale."

"Then why are you doing this? You're a good woman, Amira. I know that. Only a good woman would go through everything you did to save her children, only a good woman would have told me about the terrorists that were in your midst. Why are you doing this? What hold do they have over you?"

"My family."

"But your children are safe."

Amira shook her head. "Not my children. My parents and brothers and sisters. They have them back in Syria, and if I do this, they will all be safe."

Alexis continued the lie. "But your children won't be. Is killing them worth saving the others?" Her stomach churned, knowing it was a horrible question to ask.

The woman emerged from behind the counter, walking quickly toward Amira. Alexis resisted the urge to glance in her direction.

Amira's shoulders slumped. "I don't know what to do." She looked up at her. "Go! You go, get my children, and get them out of here."

Alexis shook her head. "I can't do that."

Amira closed her eyes.

"Then they die serving Allah."

Sherrie surged forward, reaching up with her left hand and squeezing it around Amira's trigger hand, the other shoving her Glock in the back of the woman's head and squeezing the trigger.

Alexis screamed as Amira's body crumpled to the floor, Sherrie still gripping the trigger. She didn't risk removing the woman's hand from the device, instead deciding to leave it to the experts.

She activated her comm. "Target is down, bomb is secure, send in the bomb squad, now!"

"Roger that, bomb squad on their way."

She recognized Chris' voice and closed her eyes, thanking God she had survived this, more for his sake than hers. She loved that man, and when she got home tonight she looked forward to forgetting what had happened today, at least for a little while.

Boots hammering on the floor rapidly approached, the bomb squad apparently trailing them at a distance.

Alexis had dropped to her knees, her face in her hands as she continued to sob, staring at the pool of blood rapidly expanding toward her.

"Are you okay?"

Alexis looked up, shaking out a nod, the sobs continuing as the bomb squad came into sight. Suddenly she rose and walked toward the body, taking a knee, then doing something Sherrie wasn't expecting.

She reached over and brushed some hair that had come loose from Amira's chador, tucking it back out of sight. Then she looked at Sherrie.

"Did you have to kill her?"

Sherrie regarded her for a moment then looked away, saying nothing. She knew the woman didn't mean it, was looking for someone to blame for the entire situation. She knew she had done the right thing.

And knowing it would haunt her for years to come.

Landing Pad Alpha, CIA Headquarters, Langley, Virginia

Leroux held his arms open wide as Sherrie ran into them. He hugged her tight, tears burning his eyes as he struggled to keep control, the scene repeated as Morrison embraced his daughter Alexis. The chopper that had brought them lifted off, and those gathered, those in the know, began to clap, showing their respect for these two brave women who had risked everything to save the lives of strangers.

Though they had succeeded, and only the terrorist had died, it was a bitter day for America. The death toll at the stadium was approaching two hundred, the wounded at least that, but the bomb had been disarmed, the terrorists killed.

The bomb strapped to Amira had contained the missing three canisters of Cesium-137, it now confirmed that it had all been recovered, the risk to the country neutralized from that perspective, though they had no way of knowing how many others may be here already, or still on their way, the largest human migration since World War Two continuing, despite the events of today.

For most of those people were innocent victims, desperate to save themselves and their families.

And helping them felt like the right thing to do.

After all, it was the Christian way.

Leroux loosened his grip on Sherrie, gazing into her eyes, then kissed her. Hard.

"What were you thinking?"

Leroux broke the kiss, looking over at Morrison and his daughter, the chopper now gone, conversations possible.

"I can't believe you did that!"

"She's a brave woman," said Sherrie, wrapping an arm around Leroux's back and resting her head on his shoulder.

Morrison brushed his thumb over his daughter's cheek, smiling down at her. "She's a stupid woman."

"She takes after her father."

Zing!

Morrison glanced over at Sherrie. "Are you saying I'm stupid?"

Sherrie wasn't as familiar with Morrison to recognize the bemused smile on his face, so she quickly backpedaled. "Umm, I'm going with the brave part."

"Uh huh."

Morrison patted Leroux on the shoulder and shook Sherrie's hand. "Thank you for saving my daughter's life."

Sherrie nodded. "I think she saved mine, sir."

Morrison smiled then turned away, his arm over his daughter's shoulders as those gathered broke away to give them privacy. Leroux led Sherrie back inside the building then into an empty meeting room. He turned toward her.

"You okay?"

She nodded. "Yup, no problem."

Then she began to shake, first her hands, then her lips, finally her entire body.

And she collapsed into his arms, weeping uncontrollably. It was so unlike her that he at first wasn't sure how to react. He held her, holding her head against his chest as he gently stroked her hair. "It's going to be okay," he whispered. She said nothing, leaving him to his own thoughts, tears silently flowing down his cheeks as he worried this woman he loved so much was turning into yet another broken soul like his best friend, the horrors seen and committed on the job too much for any human to take.

Lee Fang Residence, Philadelphia, Pennsylvania

Kane knocked on the door, three quick raps, flowers in one hand, a bottle of wine in the other, not sure what kind of reception he might receive. He could have called first, but he wanted to surprise Fang, and he also had a slight worry that she might have said no if given the choice.

After all, it had been weeks since they had seen each other, many weeks, and feelings could change in that amount of time. If anything, he was sure his had strengthened. Strengthened to what, he wasn't sure. He just knew he couldn't stop thinking about this woman, and the thought of her had kept him going during the horrendous events he had experienced since he last saw her.

But she might have moved on.

Time to think could go both ways.

She may have decided in that time that this wasn't the type of relationship she was interested in, one where he would disappear at a moment's notice, go for weeks or months without any form of contact, then just appear on the doorstep, expecting everything to be normal.

He stared at the flowers and wine.

Too much.

He turned to hide them around the corner when the door was yanked open and a little bundle of Asian goodness leapt into his arms, wrapping hers around his neck, burying her head on his shoulder as her legs locked around his waist.

Maybe not.

"You're okay!"

She sounded surprised.

He walked them both inside, she still imitating a pretzel, and kicked the door closed. "Why wouldn't I be?"

She let him go, dropping to her feet, staring up at him. "You've been gone for over a month with no contact. Then I see you on television, walking into the middle of a hostage situation, then the coverage stops and all I hear on the news is that hundreds are dead." Her chin dropped to her chest. "I've been worried about you."

Kane felt his heart thump hard, her words everything he had wanted to hear, her reaction telling him everything he needed to know. She was happy to see him, she wasn't mad, and she cared enough to worry. She grabbed his hand and led him to the couch, taking the flowers with a smile.

"For me?"

"Who else?" he said, grinning as he put the bottle of wine on the table. She rushed into the kitchen, putting the flowers in a vase, humming her little lullaby about a girl and her forbidden love, and Kane felt a warmth sweep through him he had never felt before. She returned, placing the flowers in the middle of the table before sitting down beside him.

"So you were worried about me?"

"Of course. Can't a friend worry about another friend?"

His smile broadened, and he moved aside some stray hairs with his finger. "Friend?"

She blushed, her eyes darting down for a moment, then looking back up at him, wide and earnest. "Good friend?"

He leaned in and she closed her eyes.

"The best."

THE END

ACKNOWLEDGEMENTS

This book is dedicated to a real life hero, an actual Delta operator who recently lost his life. You can read this man's amazing story here:

http://www.nytimes.com/2015/10/24/us/joshua-wheeler-killed-in-isis-raid.html?_r=1

When I look at his photo, I almost picture Red. When I read about his joking around and his mischievous side, I think of Niner. When I read about how he had to tell his wife he was going on a training mission, I think of them all.

Master Sergeant Joshua L. Wheeler was a true hero who charged into the fray, the result—over seventy lives saved. The sacrifice he made, along with that of his family and Unit, is appreciated.

A lot of violent, horrible things are said and done in this book, with various characters' perspectives representing many of those in real life. As stated at the beginning, many of the events described in this book actually did happen, from bombings of towns, burning of innocents, overflowing refugee camps, Christians singled out and thrown overboard, an Austrian woman hauled out of her car and assaulted, refugees refusing food with a Red Cross symbol, young men getting off buses and hiding their faces with their hands, and more.

The numbers involved in this crisis are staggering, and history has shown how a sudden influx of those who share nothing in common with the culture of the area they move into can overwhelm what was once there.

And ultimately destroy it, often unintentionally.

With a recent survey of refugees completed by the Doha, Qatar based Arab Centre for Research and Public Policy Studies, showing 31% support for ISIL, 41% holding an unfavorable view of Jews, and 97% of gays, perhaps it is wise to exercise caution.

It's something for all of us to think about.

And now for more fun things. The Jag Jab, as many have come to call them, is based on a true story. I owned convertibles for almost a decade, never having the roof leak in the carwash, but every time, the Jag would leak, to the point where we had a small Tupperware bowl with us that we would hold up against the edge of the window and roof, following the track of the spray to catch the water.

My daughter thought it was great fun.

I mentioned it to the dealer when I was in for the umpteenth time with who knows what new problem, and they said that was normal. I expressed my doubts. They insisted. My reply:

"It may be normal for Jaguars, but it's not normal for convertibles."

Surprisingly, they weren't sure what to say to that.

Interestingly, my next convertible, purchased after dumping that albatross, didn't leak.

And the Tupperware bowl was retired.

As usual there are people to thank. Brent Richards for weapons and tactics help, Ian Kennedy for tactics, equipment and explosives, Greg "Chief" Michael for military terminology, and my father for his research. And of course, my wife, daughter, family, and friends.

To those who have not already done so, please visit my website at www.jrobertkennedy.com then sign up for the Insider's Club to be notified of new book releases. Your email address will never be shared or sold and you'll only receive the occasional email from me as I don't have time to spam you!

Thank you once again for reading.

ABOUT THE AUTHOR

USA Today bestselling author J. Robert Kennedy has written over twenty international bestsellers including the smash hit James Acton Thrillers series, the first installment of which, The Protocol, has been on the bestsellers list since its release, including a three month run at number one. In addition to the other novels from this series including The Templar's Relic, a USA Today and Barnes & Noble #1 overall bestseller, he writes the bestselling Special Agent Dylan Kane Thrillers, Delta Force Unleashed Thrillers and Detective Shakespeare Mysteries. Robert lives with his wife and daughter and writes full-time.

Visit Robert's website at www.jrobertkennedy.com for the latest news and contact information, and to join the Insider's Club to be notified when new books are released.

Available James Acton Thrillers

The Protocol (Book #1)

For two thousand years the Triarii have protected us, influencing history from the crusades to the discovery of America. Descendent from the Roman Empire, they pervade every level of society, and are now in a race with our own government to retrieve an ancient artifact thought to have been lost forever.

Brass Monkey (Book #2)

A nuclear missile, lost during the Cold War, is now in play--the most public spy swap in history, with a gorgeous agent the center of international attention, triggers the end-game of a corrupt Soviet Colonel's twenty five year plan. Pursued across the globe by the Russian authorities, including a brutal Spetsnaz unit, those involved will stop at nothing to deliver their weapon, and ensure their payday, regardless of the terrifying consequences.

Broken Dove (Book #3)

With the Triarii in control of the Roman Catholic Church, an organization founded by Saint Peter himself takes action, murdering one of the new Pope's operatives. Detective Chaney, called in by the Pope to investigate, disappears, and, to the horror of the Papal staff sent to inform His Holiness, they find him missing too, the only clue a secret chest, presented to each new pope on the eve of their election, since the beginning of the Church.

The Templar's Relic (Book #4)

The Vault must be sealed, but a construction accident leads to a miraculous discovery--an ancient tomb containing four Templar Knights, long forgotten, on the grounds of the Vatican. Not knowing who they can trust, the Vatican requests Professors James Acton and Laura Palmer examine the find, but what they discover, a precious Islamic relic, lost during the Crusades, triggers a set of events that shake the entire world, pitting the two greatest religions against each other. At risk is nothing less than the Vatican itself, and the rock upon which it was built.

Flags of Sin (Book #5)

Archaeology Professor James Acton simply wants to get away from everything, and relax. A trip to China seems just the answer, and he and his fiancée, Professor Laura Palmer, are soon on a flight to Beijing. But while boarding, they bump into an old friend, Delta Force Command Sergeant Major Burt Dawson, who surreptitiously delivers a message that they must meet the next day, for Dawson knows something they don't. China is about to erupt into chaos.

The Arab Fall (Book #6)

An accidental find by a friend of Professor James Acton may lead to the greatest archaeological discovery since the tomb of King Tutankhamen, perhaps even greater. And when news of it spreads, it reaches the ears of a group hell-bent on the destruction of all idols and icons, their mere existence considered blasphemous to Islam.

The Circle of Eight (Book #7)

The Bravo Team is targeted by a madman after one of their own intervenes in a rape. Little do they know this internationally well-respected banker is also a senior member of an organization long thought extinct, whose stated goals for a reshaped world are not only terrifying, but with today's globalization, totally achievable.

The Venice Code (Book #8)

A former President's son is kidnapped in a brazen attack on the streets of Potomac by the very ancient organization that murdered his father, convinced he knows the location of an item stolen from them by the late president.

A close friend awakes from a coma with a message for archeology Professor James Acton from the same organization, sending him along with his fiancée Professor Laura Palmer on a quest to find an object only rumored to exist, while trying desperately to keep one step ahead of a foe hell-bent on possessing it.

Pompeii's Ghosts (Book #9)

Two thousand years ago Roman Emperor Vespasian tries to preserve an empire by hiding a massive treasure in the quiet town of Pompeii should someone challenge his throne. Unbeknownst to him nature is about to unleash its wrath upon the Empire during which the best and worst of Rome's citizens will be revealed during a time when duty and honor were more than words, they were ideals worth dying for.

Amazon Burning (Book #10)

Days from any form of modern civilization, archeology Professor James Acton awakes to gunshots. Finding his wife missing, taken by a member of one of the uncontacted tribes, he and his friend INTERPOL Special Agent Hugh Reading try desperately to find her in the dark of the jungle, but quickly realize there is no hope without help. And with help three days away, he knows the longer they wait, the farther away she'll be.

The Riddle (Book #11)

Russia accuses the United States of assassinating their Prime Minister in Hanoi, naming Delta Force member Sergeant Carl "Niner" Sung as the assassin. Professors James Acton and Laura Palmer, witnesses to the murder, know the truth, and as the Russians and Vietnamese attempt to use the situation to their advantage on the international stage, the husband and wife duo attempt to find proof that their friend is innocent.

Blood Relics (Book #12)

A DYING MAN. A DESPERATE SON.
ONLY A MIRACLE CAN SAVE THEM BOTH.

Professor Laura Palmer is shot and kidnapped in front of her husband, archeology Professor James Acton, as they try to prevent the theft of the world's Blood Relics, ancient artifacts thought to contain the blood of Christ, a madman determined to possess them all at any cost.

Sins of the Titanic (Book #13)

THE ASSEMBLY IS ETERNAL.
AND THEY'LL STOP AT NOTHING TO KEEP IT THAT WAY.

When Professor James Acton is contacted about a painting thought to have been lost with the sinking of the Titanic, he is inadvertently drawn into a century old conspiracy an ancient organization known as The Assembly will stop at nothing to keep secret.

Saint Peter's Soldiers (Book #14)

A MISSING DA VINCI.
A TERRIFYING GENETIC BREAKTHROUGH.
A PAST AND FUTURE ABOUT TO COLLIDE!

In World War Two a fabled da Vinci drawing is hidden from the Nazis, those involved fearing Hitler may attempt to steal it for its purported magical powers. It isn't returned for over fifty years.

And today, archeology Professor James Acton and his wife are about to be dragged into the terrible truth of what happened so many years ago, for the truth is never what it seems, and the history we thought was fact, is all lies.

Available Special Agent Dylan Kane Thrillers

Rogue Operator (Book #1)

Three top secret research scientists are presumed dead in a boating accident, but the kidnapping of their families the same day raises questions the FBI and local police can't answer, leaving them waiting for a ransom demand that will never come. Central Intelligence Agency Analyst Chris Leroux stumbles upon the story, and finds a phone conversation that was never supposed to happen but is told to leave it to the FBI. But he can't let it go. For he knows something the FBI doesn't. One of the scientists is alive.

Containment Failure (Book #2)

New Orleans has been quarantined, an unknown virus sweeping the city, killing one hundred percent of those infected. The Centers for Disease Control, desperate to find a cure, is approached by BioDyne Pharma who reveal a former employee has turned a cutting edge medical treatment capable of targeting specific genetic sequences into a weapon, and released it. The stakes have never been higher as Kane battles to save not only his friends and the country he loves, but all of mankind.

Cold Warriors (Book #3)

While in Chechnya CIA Special Agent Dylan Kane stumbles upon a meeting between a known Chechen drug lord and a retired General once responsible for the entire Soviet nuclear arsenal. Money is exchanged for a data stick and the resulting transmission begins a race across the globe to discover just what was sold, the only clue a reference to a top secret Soviet weapon called Crimson Rush.

Death to America (Book #4)

America is in crisis. Dozens of terrorist attacks have killed or injured thousands, and worse, every single attack appears to have been committed by an American citizen in the name of Islam.

A stolen experimental F-35 Lightning II is discovered by CIA Special Agent Dylan Kane in China, delivered by an American soldier reported dead years ago in exchange for a chilling promise.

And Chris Leroux is forced to watch as his girlfriend, Sherrie White, is tortured on camera, under orders to not interfere, her continued suffering providing intel too valuable to sacrifice.

Black Widow (Book #5)

USA Today bestselling author J. Robert Kennedy serves up another heart-pounding thriller in Black Widow. After corrupt Russian agents sell deadly radioactive Cesium to Chechen terrorists, CIA Special Agent Dylan Kane is sent to infiltrate the ISIL terror cell suspected of purchasing it.

Then all contact is lost.

Available Delta Force Unleashed Thrillers

Payback (Book #1)

The daughter of the Vice President is kidnapped from an Ebola clinic, triggering an all-out effort to retrieve her by America's elite Delta Force just hours after a senior government official from Sierra Leone is assassinated in a horrific terrorist attack while visiting the United States. As she battles impossible odds and struggles to prove her worth to her captors who have promised she will die, she's forced to make unthinkable decisions to not only try to save her own life, but those dying from one of the most vicious diseases known to mankind, all in the hopes an unleashed Delta Force can save her before her captors enact their horrific plan on an unsuspecting United States.

Infidels (Book #2)

When the elite Delta Force's Bravo Team is inserted into Yemen to rescue a kidnapped Saudi prince, they find more than they bargained for—a crate containing the Black Stone, stolen from Mecca the day before. Requesting instructions on how to proceed, they find themselves cut off and disavowed, left to survive with nothing but each other to rely upon.

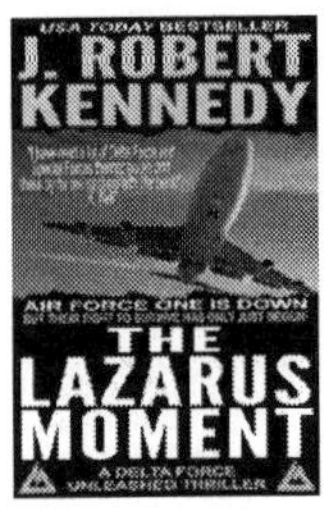

The Lazarus Moment (Book #3)

AIR FORCE ONE IS DOWN

BUT THEIR FIGHT TO SURVIVE HAS ONLY JUST BEGUN!

When Air Force One crashes in the jungles of Africa, it is up to America's elite Delta Force to save the survivors not only from rebels hell-bent on capturing the President, but Mother Nature herself.

Available Detective Shakespeare Mysteries

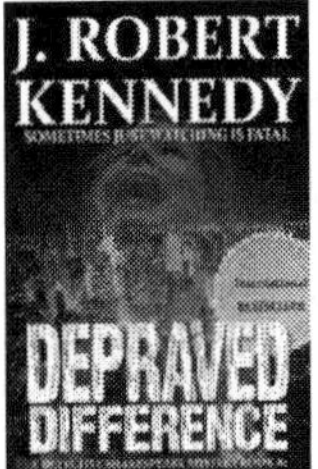

Depraved Difference (Book #1)

SOMETIMES JUST WATCHING IS FATAL

When a young woman is brutally assaulted by two men on the subway, her cries for help fall on the deaf ears of onlookers too terrified to get involved, her misery ended with the crushing stomp of a steel-toed boot. A cellphone video of her vicious murder, callously released on the Internet, its popularity a testament to today's depraved society, serves as a trigger, pulled a year later, for a killer.

Tick Tock (Book #2)

SOMETIMES HELL IS OTHER PEOPLE

Crime Scene tech Frank Brata digs deep and finds the courage to ask his colleague, Sarah, out for coffee after work. Their good time turns into a nightmare when Frank wakes up the next morning covered in blood, with no recollection of what happened, and Sarah's body floating in the tub.

The Redeemer (Book #3)

SOMETIMES LIFE GIVES MURDER A SECOND CHANCE

It was the case that destroyed Detective Justin Shakespeare's career, beginning a downward spiral of self-loathing and self-destruction lasting half a decade. And today things are only going to get worse. The Widow Rapist is free on a technicality, and it is up to Detective Shakespeare and his partner Amber Trace to find the evidence, five years cold, to put him back in prison before he strikes again.

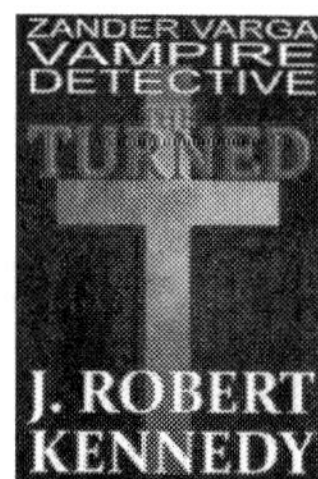

The Turned: Zander Varga, Vampire Detective, Book #1

Zander has relived his wife's death at the hands of vampires every day for almost three hundred years, his perfect memory a curse of becoming one of The Turned—infecting him their final heinous act after her murder.

Nineteen year-old Sydney Winter knows Zander's secret, a secret preserved by the women in her family for four generations. But with her mother in a coma, she's thrust into the frontlines, ahead of her time, to fight side-by-side with Zander.

Made in the USA
Middletown, DE
27 March 2016